I0554320

TONY BENSON

AN ACCIDENT OF BIRTH

Published in 2013 by Tony Benson

Copyright © Tony Benson

All rights reserved. No part of this publication may be
reproduced or transmitted in any form or by any means,
electronic or mechanical, including photocopying,
recording, or by any information storage and retrieval
system without the written permission of the author,
except short excerpts for review purposes.

This book is a work of fiction. Names, characters,
places, and incidents either are products of the author's
imagination or are used fictitiously. Any resemblance
to actual persons, living or dead, events, or locales is
entirely coincidental.

Cover Design by jdsmith-design.com

01L130726

ISBN: 978-0-9576527-0-5

Dedicated with love to
Margo Benson

Acknowledgements

I owe a huge debt of gratitude to my lovely wife, Margo Benson, for her wise advice, kind support, tireless feedback and endless patience. I would like to say a special thanks to my editor Sher A. Hart, to Jip McTavish for his expert advice on firearms and their use, and to cover designer Jane Dixon-Smith. Thank you to all those who have generously helped with valuable feedback on the manuscript – Wendy Toole, Mary Pax, Misha Gericke, Gary Baker, Hazel Scott, Anita Carter, Elizabeth Haynes, Rachel Burren and Jip McTavish.

All of you have played a big part in helping me to make this book what it is, and I couldn't have done it without you.

1

Two security guards fell to the ground as the last shots shattered the night air. Craig smiled. Nobody would stop him now. The *Atelier* Marlborough, resembling a fortress behind high walls, was quiet, its guards either dead or hiding.

Two of his men held the girl. Her bare feet twisted in the damp dirt shaded from the pale moonlight by the overhanging branches of a dense tree. She hung her head, dazed, shivering in her nightclothes. Craig indicated with hand signals for his men to pull back. They turned towards the woodland so they would be far away before the peacekeepers arrived. The whole raid had lasted three and a half minutes.

Ten minutes later, Craig stood under the harsh strip lights in a small, bare room at the rendezvous point, watching the last of his men crowd in. In front of him, a young man held up his chin as though determined not to appear afraid. Craig looked at him, then at the girl still held by two of his men. Her damp hair and torn nightclothes gave her an air of forlorn dejection.

This time he would enjoy a bonus. Not only would he get his usual high fee for freeing the girl from the atelier, but he would have the pleasure of finishing some important business. He turned back to the young man, who spoke.

"Thank you, Baron." He hesitated. "I'll take Alice and we'll get going then. All the money's in your account."

Craig's eyes hardened. "You haven't been honest with me, Brandon."

"What?" Brandon's eyes widened. "All the money's there – look." With a shaking hand he tapped at the com-pak on his wrist. "I'll show you."

Craig scowled. "You're an idiot. Of course the money's there or she wouldn't be here." He indicated the cowering girl. "I'm talking about your little business enterprises."

Brandon trembled "But, Baron –"

"When you try to set up your connections to change ID chips and help people disappear, do you think that doesn't get back to me? Do you?" Brandon squirmed. "When you sell black market items for people who want to bolt from ateliers, do you think I don't hear about it?" Brandon's mouth dropped open. "Did you think I would just stand here while you set up in competition with me?" Brandon tried to step backwards, but two of Craig's men were close behind him.

Craig studied him for a moment. Brandon's mouth hung open, perspiration on his forehead betraying his fear, but that wasn't enough. Craig shouted in his face. "This is *my* turf!"

Brandon lifted his chin in a gesture of defiance, so Craig turned to the men who held the girl. "Dispose of her. Make sure it sends a message to anyone else who might try to set up on my turf."

Brandon cried out and tried to move towards the girl, but Craig's men restrained him.

"Please, Baron! Leave her alone. This is between you and me. It's not Alice's fault. I just wanted to keep her safe, not set up –"

Craig leaned in and punched him in the kidneys. The men were already on their way out of the door with the girl. Craig watched Brandon struggle and cry in pain, then turned on his heel and walked to the door.

"Kill him."

2

Francesca turned the pages of the aged, fragile book, reading the verses she knew so well. Ballads, stories passed down through generations by word of mouth until the old scholars and collectors finally committed them to paper. Mid-sentence, the words of a newscast drew her attention to the large Axis screen on the wall facing her sofa.

"Police investigating last month's attack on the Atelier Marlborough and the subsequent discovery of the dismembered body of the escaped breeding *queen*, Alice Draper, this morning raided a house in Midfield. We go now to the scene."

The scene cut to a reporter standing outside the house. "Police discovered records here of five people whose ID chips had been surgically swapped in a sophisticated, illegal identity change scheme. Using information discovered on the premises, the Police Intelligence Corps raided a house in Devon where they found Kelly Walton, the queen who was abducted from the Atelier Cavendish last year, together with five family members"

Francesca's heart raced. Kelly Walton! Francesca had a vision of armed *pekays* stepping over the bodies of Kelly and her family. The book dropped onto her lap.

Kelly had been kept in the Atelier Cavendish as a breeding queen for seven years when Francesca first arrived. She mentored

Francesca in those difficult early days, and they became close friends. Francesca leaned forward. *Please let Kelly be alive.*

The camera went back to the news anchor. "More after this commercial break."

Kelly had helped Francesca to find her way around the facilities offered by the atelier and adjust to the regime and routine. In Kelly, Francesca discovered a kind hearted person, loved by all who knew her and visited frequently by her family and friends from outside.

Francesca stroked the book with trembling fingers, remembering the ill-fated plan. After dinner one evening, together in Francesca's room, Kelly confided that her family had made plans to set her free. They talked for hours about the risks of escape and life on the outside as a bolter. Kelly assured Francesca that her family had thought of everything, and the plan was well funded. The break-out took place in the depths of night, and from what Francesca saw in the news reports at the time, was successful.

The news came back on and after a summary the reader continued. "Earlier today, the Police Intelligence Corps led a team of armed police peacekeepers to a holiday home in Devon where Kelly Walton and five members of her family were arrested."

Francesca stared, open-mouthed. Kelly was alive, but under pekay arrest. She would be returned to the atelier and kept under permanent lock-down.

"As a result of an escape attempt during the trip back to the police headquarters, the five members of Miss Walton's family were killed. Kelly Walton alone survived." The newscast showed four heavily armed pekays marching a dispirited and broken Kelly into the police headquarters.

Francesca sobbed as she switched off the Axis. She hadn't expected to see Kelly again after the escape, but she never anticipated this. Nobody deserved such a fate. Was freedom a hopeless dream? It would be now for Kelly.

Francesca brushed her tears from the tooled leather spine of the ancient book. She looked around the beautiful room. Her home. Her prison. The high ceilings, plush carpeting, and walls decorated in a delicate shade of peach were no compensation for the oppression of captivity. The soft furnishings, in contrasting terracotta, consisted of a large, billowing sofa and armchair. Both would swallow a person in their folds. They did nothing to make up for the complete lack of windows.

A faint chime sounded, and the door opened. Hannah, slim with brown hair and a little shorter than Francesca, came in carrying fresh towels. She smiled and sang the words, "You have a visitor."

"Dom?" Francesca's heart quickened. "I'd better get ready." Wiping her eyes, she studied her reflection for a moment in the glass front of the bookshelf, then touched her forehead. "A worry line, and I don't turn twenty-one until next year!"

Hannah put a hand on Francesca's shoulder. "Look on the bright side." She lifted a lock of Francesca's long brown hair. "Not a strand of premature grey like some of the others."

Francesca sighed. When they'd brought her here at sixteen, she thought Dom would show up one day, her hero, and spring her free. It was too much to expect, though. To break out of such a secure environment and stay free was an unachievable fantasy. She turned to Hannah. "Four years I've been separated from Dom! It seems more like forty." In all that time, neither of them had come up with a workable escape plan.

Hannah gave her a hug. "I'll take you to him. I think he's got a few little gifts for you."

She followed Hannah out, and when they came to the elegant visitors' lounge, Hannah left. Francesca took a deep breath and tried to put Kelly from her mind.

Dom sat at the table, facing the door. At nearly twenty-four years old, he still had the youthful look she always admired. His dark, curly hair, neatly trimmed, framed his expectant expression. "Hi, Hon." His hazel eyes lit up.

"Hello, Dom." They gave each other a peck on the cheek, and she sat on the opposite side of the table. Dom glanced at the camera in the corner of the room while he pulled little packages, wrapped in gift paper with ribbons, from his bag. He put them on the table and she felt his appreciative gaze.

Dom kept his voice low, almost a whisper. "Hannah's a real darling. She knows what's in this one. The scanner picked it up straight away, but she didn't miss a heartbeat. She just let it through without saying anything."

Francesca opened the top of the package and saw a bottle of blackcurrant vodka. Maybe that would help her forget Kelly's fate. She put it back on the table without taking the bottle out. "Thanks, Dom."

Next she opened an envelope and took out a piece of paper. Dom had sketched a portrait of her parents, charcoal on paper. She gasped. "Darling, it's wonderful. Thank you so much." Dom had a knack of finding his way into the very soul of whatever he drew, bringing it out on the paper. She stared at it for a few moments. "I'll put this up on the wall in my suite."

She opened the other gifts – perfume, a small, silver rabbit to go with the other curiosities on her charm bracelet, and books. Books! Every new book offered a glorious few hours of escape from this controlled, institutionalised life. She read everything she laid her hands on. As she took the wrapper off the last one, her lips trembled and her eyes filled with tears. Dom jumped up to put his arm around her.

"I'm sorry," said Francesca. "The presents are lovely. I just feel like they're time fillers. Ways to pass the time until they force me to have another baby I can't keep. Then eventually, after more babies than I can count, I'll just give up and die. It all seems so hopeless."

Dom opened his mouth to speak, but Francesca wasn't finished. "I'm glad you'll never really know what it's like to go through nine months carrying a child, and when it's born, when your hormones are raging, when all you want is to hold your baby, nurse it…they take the child away. There and then. They give us drugs that are supposed to fix how we feel, fix the hormones, but nothing can take away the gut-wrenching loss. What they're doing here…" She looked boldly at the camera. "It's inhuman."

Dom glanced at the camera again. "It won't be like that anymore. Honestly, soon," he leaned closer and whispered, "I'm getting you out."

The smile on his lips didn't reassure her. "We've talked about this over and again for four years and two babies. Look at me!" She realised she'd raised her voice, so she checked herself. She didn't want a member of staff to come in and stand guard while they talked.

Normally when they had heated words, Dom would look down sheepishly, but now his eyes sparkled. "Trust me, it's different this time."

Different. She gazed into his eyes – those beautiful eyes. She'd loved him since they first met when she was six years old and he was nearly ten. When she reached fifteen, he'd tried so hard to convince her to use a black market fertility test kit. He even bought it for her. It cost a small fortune, and she could have discovered whether she had the misfortune to be one of the rare *fertiles*.

Why had she refused to use it? Partly because she didn't believe she would be fertile. After all, how many people were? Almost none. Few enough to make them a precious resource to a society that had become increasingly barren over twenty generations. A society that imprisoned its fertiles, forcing them to breed artificially inseminated babies for adoption by the infertile majority.

What a fool she'd been. Now she saw it clearly. Fear had stood in the way of her only route to freedom. To run away, become a bolter, and live in exile would have been far better than this. Four years of captivity passed with nothing better to look forward to than a lifetime of having babies she would never see. Always waiting for Dom to deliver on the promise he'd made when she was sixteen.

Now it would be different?

"What's changed?" She lowered her voice. "Surely if it was possible, we'd have done it years ago? I'll just end up like Kelly. Surely you've seen today's news." Seeing the pain in his eyes, she felt guilty. "I'm sorry."

"I know that's what you think, but I really can do this. The thing is I've been saving, and I have quite a lot put aside. I'm seeing someone tomorrow who will help. I can afford the deposit, and I can pay the rest in instalments. These people are professionals. They will help."

The only people who would agree to do that were the underground bosses. "Dom, don't go to those people. They're not *professionals*. They're criminals."

He smiled. "Trust me, Fru, I know what I'm doing, and maybe it's not who you think. They help people like us all the time. It's what they do. They have a really good track record. They always succeed."

Francesca sighed and made herself smile. She wanted to believe him because the alternative of giving up hope was unbearable. It wouldn't be cheap, of course. Everyone knew that some crime barons made a profession of helping bolters – for the right price. "Maybe. But we've spent years trying to plan this, then realising our ideas won't work. I suppose it doesn't seem likely anymore."

Dom leaned forward. "That's only because we didn't have a good plan. We do now. This will work. Honestly."

She wished she could share his optimism and hoped he was right. "If it really does work, imagine what the future holds. Just think, my next insemination is due any time now."

As long as the insemination was carried out before the escape, she would bring up the next baby with Dom. At least she could bear them a child, even though his infertility meant he couldn't father it himself. She would live with Dom somewhere they weren't known and take on a new identity."

His eyes widened. "Yes, of course."

She whispered, "I'll need surgery to change my ID chip. That'll be expensive. Will you have enough?"

Dom looked more relaxed. "It's part of the package. They'll do that for both of us. You see, I've thought of everything."

Francesca frowned. "Listen, I'm sorry about earlier. After what happened to Kelly the whole prospect is terrifying." She sighed. "It seems like I'll never have a life of my own. My friend Liang, she's a queen too. She says I should be grateful because I never need to worry about money, and I live in absolute luxury. Why would I want more? She thinks I'm daft wishing I wasn't here. Most of us don't think that way, but sometimes I wonder. Maybe Liang's right."

"Fru, wanting control of your own life isn't daft."

"No. But if I was on permanent lock-down I'd have even less control than now. All the same, I wouldn't mind giving up this luxury if I could have my life back and be with you."

His eyes shone. "I'll do whatever it takes." He leaned forward and whispered, "We'll get a little house in some town a long way away. Nobody will recognise either of us. We'll be left alone."

How wonderful that sounded. If she allowed herself too much hope, though, she'd only be disappointed if this didn't work. "When will I see you again?"

"I need to get some stuff sorted out and see a few people. Then I'll have some more news. Hopefully I'll come again in a few days."

She smiled. "Wow, this is nice. I get to see more of you when you're scheming." She put her hand on his arm. "Please be careful."

"I will. This is too important to mess up."

Francesca pulled a small envelope from a pocket in her blouse and handed it to Dom.

"I made this for you."

Dom took the envelope and opened it, taking out a

hand-drawn card. The picture on the front depicted trees and grass with two people sitting under a tree in a loving embrace. Dom opened the card and read the words, "For my Dom, because I love you."

They stood and hugged. Francesca, stifling her misgivings, melted into his arms, losing herself in their parting kiss. Their embrace lingered, so much warmer than their earlier greeting.

Walking back to her room, Francesca noticed a crowd of staff members gathered near the entrance foyer. She stopped to watch, straining to see what had attracted their attention. The foyer doors slid open and two pekays came in. One stood at each side of the door, their guns held ready. Four more armed pekays brought Kelly, at a brisk march, into the building and towards the door to the lock-down wing. From there, she would never return.

3

Dominic left his apartment and headed down the communal stairs to meet his taxi. He told the driver his destination and climbed into the clean smelling but worn back seat.

He had Martin to thank for his planned rendezvous. Dominic taught maths and physics as a substitute teacher. His friend Martin taught maths at Midfield secondary school where Dominic frequently worked. Two weeks ago Martin had taken him aside in the teachers' common room and said they needed to speak.

They knew each other well, so Dominic was not surprised when Martin came straight to the point. "Dom, I know you want to get your girlfriend out of the atelier. I know someone who can help, but we can't talk about it here."

They agreed to meet the next day in the park near the leisure centre. Dominic smiled when they met at a park bench like in the old spy stories. "Should I pretend not to know you?" he asked.

Martin turned to him. "Don't be dopey. We work together."

They laughed, and then Martin became serious. "I have a friend who can help you get your girlfriend out. It's a business he runs – if you see what I mean."

"You mean it's illegal?"

Martin sighed. "Dom, if you want to get her out, you can't do it legally. My friend's name is Craig Drake. He has all the contacts and he's very professional. He'll get her out."

Dominic thought for a moment. "Drake? Isn't that the guy who sponsors the Midfield Guardian Agency? Good homes for cute babies?"

"Yeah. He's very involved. They see to it that every child from the Atelier Cavendish is placed in a suitable home. Craig Drake takes a personal interest in every case, you know. He does other stuff too. He's on the Midfield Council Advisory Committee."

Dominic grinned. "Civic rewards for a do-gooder?"

"I'm not sure about rewards. From what I hear, the advisory committee members work pretty hard. He's quite prominent in local politics. Owns an entertainment arcade."

Dominic asked more questions, looking for reassurance that Drake was trustworthy. Martin told him stories of the kind things Drake did for his customers.

"What about the girl who escaped from the Atelier Marlborough?" asked Dominic. "The one they found chopped up on Chessington Common. Was that anything to do with Drake?"

"Oh, God no," said Martin. "Somebody's put the word out that it was, but Craig Drake has enemies. People like him always do."

"Oh?"

"Well, think about it. He's helping people like you, so he hardly makes friends in the police and the government. He covers his tracks well, but they suspect he's involved, and they want to put him out of business."

"So they tell lies about him?"

"Either them or his business rivals. Somebody wants him blamed for the murder, but it wasn't him. No, he doesn't make that kind of mess, he does a good job." Martin gave details of three different queen escapes Drake had orchestrated.

Dominic nodded. "I remember the news reports."

"Every one a happy customer of Craig Drake," Martin assured him. He glanced around as though afraid they might be overheard. "Last year Drake got one of my relatives out of an atelier up north." His eyes lit up. "Obviously I can't say who, but we paid Drake and he did everything else." He stood. "Come on, let's walk."

They walked away from the lake, avoiding the few people who were there.

"Drake got her out," said Martin. "Sorted out a new identity and took her safely a long way away to make a new home. He took care of everything without fuss. Even offered to follow up with any help if we needed it."

Dominic took a deep breath of the late summer air, fresh and alive with the scent of newly mown grass. "So that was a year ago, and there have been no undesirable repercussions since?"

"Right. The escape was flawless. We can even visit. We use a special, secure arrangement to communicate our meeting plans."

Dominic turned to Martin. "Impressive. So, what's he like? Drake."

Martin put his hand on Dominic's arm, and they stopped. His eyes displayed an intensity Dominic had rarely seen. "He's the kind of guy who'll get your girlfriend out of the atelier. That's what he's like." He turned and walked on. "Don't talk about this to anyone. Okay? Not even your friends."

Dominic frowned. "I'll be careful. Fru's future is at stake."

Martin gave him a contact number. "Wait a day. Drake will be expecting your call."

After the meeting, Dominic researched all of the escapes Martin had told him about. Each was well executed and successful. Interestingly, he found no rumours connecting Craig Drake to any of them.

Dominic considered the pros and cons. The media reports seemed to back up Martin's claims. They had plenty to say about Drake, praising his work for the Guardian Agency and portraying him as the kind of philanthropic politician every community would love to have.

Dominic decided to see Drake and called for an appointment. A couple of days passed, during which Drake's men checked him out. He suspected that they followed him, but he didn't care. He had nothing to hide, and they had to protect themselves from the authorities.

What Dominic cared about more were the stories about people Drake had helped. Bolters who were in trouble, people who wanted to test their fertility before the government did, people who had done so and wanted to bolt. Craig Drake was a legend in the bolter underworld.

Rumours about his underworld activities and a few articles portraying Drake in a bad light were sure to be attempts to discredit him by business or political rivals. Martin's explanation made sense – nobody would chop up someone they were rescuing and make a macabre public spectacle of the remains. It would be naïve to believe such stories.

Now, on his way to meet the man himself, Dominic found the anticipation invigorating. He'd made a bold decision. A move that would lead to Fru's freedom and bring them together forever.

While the taxi navigated the roads of Midfield, he watched from the window. He loved Midfield. At this time of morning the wide streets were busy. But the low buildings mingled with open green spaces lent a feeling of tranquillity in contrast with the crowded pavements. Busy people.

How many of them were bolters?

Probably not many. After all, most fertiles were in ateliers around the country. It took careful planning and good connections to get someone out, and he would have both with the arrangement he was about to make. He needed to get her out with one attempt, or he would face the consequences. It would be much harder or impossible a second time. Besides, Fru had been losing faith in him and now he'd made a promise.

He wouldn't risk squandering her trust again.

He took a photo of Fru from his wallet and kissed it. Taken shortly before she was sent to the atelier, it showed a beautiful, vibrant young girl, glowing with love. Her long, straight brown hair framed high cheekbones, large brown eyes, and her beautiful smile. Her slim figure emphasised her curves.

He kissed the photo again, recalling the touch of her lips just four years ago – before that fateful day. They'd kissed many times since, but that day was the last time they'd been together with no intrusive cameras or watchful staff.

He put the photo back into his wallet and safely in his pocket. At the edge of town, the houses and businesses were scarce. The taxi driver pulled over to let him out.

He'd seen this place before but never stopped. The shabby, garish, fairy-tale building had a brightly coloured, fake portcullis at the main door and towers with pointed roofs and balustrade balconies. On each side of the main entrance, Gothic windows punctuated the façade sporting a grimy mix of ageing, mismatched styles and once vibrant colours.

A huge placard across the top of the portcullis spelled out the words *Drake's House of Fun*.

He walked up the path to the portcullis. His pulse quickened as two men stepped out of the shadows to block his path. They were heavily built minders dressed in expensive black suits, tight over their muscles. One looked like a giant with a thick neck, blunt nose and shaved head. The other had a deeply pock-scarred face and a crew cut. Neither spoke. They just stared at him.

He tried to look confident. "Er. I'm Dominic Fadden." He cleared his throat. "I have an appointment with Mr Drake." He breathed deeply.

They led the way into a small windowless room to the left of the entrance, and one of them closed the door behind him. Against the wall, a long table held several devices including an identity chip reader and others that carried out functions he couldn't guess. Dominic put shaking hands in his pockets and forced himself to look them in the eye.

"Over here."

Dominic went where he was told, and the giant waved a scanner over him. "The com-pak." He held out his hand.

Dominic entered his security code to release the clasp and took off his com-pak. It shut down when he moved it away from his wrist, losing proximity to his identity chip. He handed it to the giant who put it in his jacket pocket.

The one with the pock-scarred face pointed to the identity chip reader on the table, so Dominic went and placed his wrist close to it. The device lit up, showing his name and identity number. The two men inspected the information carefully.

"Wait here," the giant said. They left the room, locking the door. Dominic flexed his hands. He had to get over this shaking or Drake would think him weak.

He looked at his naked wrist where the com-pak should be. Maybe people in their business routinely took com-paks from their visitors, but he didn't like it. However, it was an understandable precaution. Without it he couldn't record the discussion or transmit it somewhere else.

He thought through what he would say. Drake and his men knew why he had come because he'd told them when he called. He'd been careful not to name anyone or say which atelier even though the com-pak channel was encrypted.

Fidgeting, he eyed a small black metal box on the table with a display and several knobs and switches. He was just about to press a switch when the door opened and the giant returned, glaring at him. He came and stood in front of Dominic, his face too close, smelling of tobacco smoke and expensive cologne. He spoke slowly, as if to a child. "You will address him as Baron."

Dominic shied away, resenting the fact that these clumsy attempts to intimidate him were working. If he wanted to help Fru, he needed the strength to deal with these people.

"Come on." The man walked out, leaving the door open.

Dominic followed him through the corridor into a large hall. He had to hurry to keep up. The hall was poorly lit, shadowy, with machines standing everywhere. Each was either a game of skill or chance. People milled around, some using the machines. Most of them were young men, between about sixteen and twenty-five, looking as shabby as the House of Fun itself. Music played over loudspeakers with a relentless, tuneless beat, adding to the cacophony produced by dozens of machines. Each made a different dramatic and exciting sound to accompany a win or loss.

The man led Dominic to a bare, black door at the rear of the hall where two more minders stood. Once through the door, his guide led Dominic via a warren of corridors to a double door with an armed guard. His guide knocked and waited. Getting no reply, he opened the door and motioned Dominic through. Inside the room, his guide pointed to a surveillance camera, then another, and left.

Alone, Dominic stood in a large office with dark wood panelled walls. A desk, polished mahogany with a leather top, was positioned to face the entrance door. Two burgundy leather upholstered wing chairs faced the desk.

A door at the back of the office opened, and a man walked in. He appeared to be about thirty-five years old with dark, shoulder length hair. His tough, weathered face had an olive skinned, Mediterranean look complementing his muscular build. He was handsome with expensive clothes that had obviously been tailored for him.

Dominic shifted backwards, faced with the power of the man's imperious bearing as he walked to the desk and sat behind it.

Craig Drake bridged his fingers and looked at Dominic for the first time. His sharp eyes showed no trace of friendliness. "Sit down, Mr. Fadden." His voice was gentle but commanding with a hint of threat. Dominic sat facing him and waited.

"Mr. Fadden, I understand you wish to spring Miss Napier from the Atelier Cavendish."

Miss Napier! How did he know? The atelier was an easy guess, but Fru's name was not.

"I…" He let out a heavy breath. "Yes."

The Baron pushed a small piece of paper across the table. "That's the payment schedule. I'll take the deposit now."

That was it? No more discussion? Dominic picked up the paper to find that the total was higher than he expected. He had to say something, maybe negotiate. "Er, Mr. Baron, sir, that's a lot of money." His face was hot. He bit his tongue at his own awkward words.

The Baron regarded him for a moment without speaking, then tapped his com-pak. The door opened and the guard brought in Dominic's com-pak.

"The deposit, Mr. Fadden." Once more, gentle, commanding and slightly threatening.

Dominic took his com-pak and strapped it to his wrist. With a sick feeling in his stomach, he tapped in his security code and made the money transfer. When he'd finished, the guard held out his hand for the com-pak.

The Baron rose and left the room without speaking. Dominic half raised his hand, unsure whether to shake hands or wave goodbye, but the Baron was already gone. Following the guards back to the portcullis, he still felt the hot blood-rush in his face. The giant returned his com-pak, and he felt the guards' eyes on his back as he left.

The journey back to his apartment passed in a blur. Should he have done more to negotiate the price? Maybe. But these people were scary. Nonetheless, they had an air of power about them. Calm, capable power. If anyone could get Fru out, it was the Baron.

4

12 noon

Craig Drake slammed his hand on the desk, and the two men in front of him stood completely still. He kept his voice quiet. Menacing.

"Business down twenty-four percent since your stupid little game with…" He looked down at his fingernails for a moment, then back at the two men. "You disgust me. Leave body parts on someone's doorstep by all means." He curled his lip into a smile. "That would be a warning." The smile evaporated. "But on the common! That's just a big advertisement on the headline news saying, 'I'm a complete callous bastard.'" He paused, then studied them with exaggerated concern. "Do you think that's what I am? A callous bastard?"

Gurt and Mog shook their heads. "No, Baron."

"No." He gazed slowly around the room. "This is nice, isn't it?" Then he looked back to the two men. "Nice suits. Expensive. Do you know why you're able to live and work in this comfort?"

He watched them struggle with whether it would be better to say yes or no. "I'll tell you why. It's because you do good things that make my business prosper. Not stupid things that harm me."

"Baron –"

"Yes?" Craig cut Gurt off, daring him to speak.

The giant man's bulldog face contorted for a moment, then slumped. "Yes, Baron."

Gurt was shaking. Weakness! Weak people were no use in this organisation. He opened a desk drawer and took out a handgun, lifting it to point at Gurt.

Gurt opened his mouth, and his lips trembled. Craig pulled the trigger, and the hammer clicked home, but nothing happened. The only sound was liquid running onto the floor by Gurt's foot.

Craig looked on in disgust as Gurt closed his eyes as though praying.

"Mog," He put the gun back in the desk drawer. "Use as many men as it takes. I need people in pubs, clubs and everywhere else talking about what a great job I do for my clients. Got it?"

"Yes, Baron."

"And Mog…" Craig got up, ready to go.

"Yes, Baron?"

"If that" – he pointed to the puddle by Gurt's foot – "still smells bad when I come back, you know what will happen, don't you?"

Mog's pock-scarred face broke into a smile. "It'll smell of lavender and roses, Baron."

Outside the room, Craig smiled. There was a time when he would have killed Gurt for his show of weakness, but now he knew better. Gurt's skills with weapons were the best on the team and his connections in the arms trade would make most barons salivate. He just needed to develop some backbone. Craig had the perfect job for that.

The simpering little Fadden creep who came wanting his Miss Napier out of the Cavendish would do nicely. Fadden himself wasn't important, but when the Napier girl successfully freed from the atelier, Craig would mount a nice PR campaign, and soon he'd have new clients lining up outside.

Gurt would lead the attack on the atelier.

Craig crossed the corridor and pushed open a door. Inside the room, a young blonde woman quickly stood and greeted him. "Come here, Trish." She swayed closer and his eyes roamed her body. He pulled her head to his and gave her a long, deep kiss. Afterwards, she took a step back and raised her shirt.

Craig shook his head. "No time. Be here after dinner. I may want you then."

"Yes, Baron." She smiled.

Craig walked back to his suite and let himself in. Dahlia was already there. She was slim with long black hair and dark eyes. She worked on his PR team, but she knew the key code to his suite and handled many of his delicate business connections. She was far too intelligent to allow Craig to take advantage, but he knew it suited her to be here. She was using him as much as he was her, but he trusted her with the most intimate knowledge of his business.

She stood as he entered, without turning off the Axis she'd been watching. Craig went over and gave her a lingering kiss, his hand caressing her bottom.

He gazed deep into her eyes. "Lunch?"

She smiled. "All ready. Can I get you some wine with it?"

"No thanks. I'll have some juice, though."

He watched her pour tropical fruit juice into a glass, taking in the graceful way she moved, the way her hair fell on her shoulders, enjoying the sway of her hips as she came back to him with the glass.

The food was in warming trays next to the table, so Craig led her to her chair and held it out for her to sit. He then served beef stroganoff and rice onto both plates before sitting to face her.

"Bon appetite," he said.

She echoed the words back to him with a broad smile, raising her glass and touching his with it.

"I need you to do something for me," said Craig. "Gurt and Mog are spreading the good word about my business, and I want you to monitor the results and let me know. Use anyone you want."

She smiled. "No problem."

Craig glanced at the Axis, his attention drawn by a documentary on genetic disorders in fertility.

"Over the last twenty generations each generation of men has been statistically less fertile than the last. Metzner's Disease is a result of lost information. With each generation, more men have been born with key genetic information missing from their Y Chromosome – the information that enables the development of healthy sperm. Metzner's Disease is a particular form of Y chromosome infertility."

Dahlia laughed, eyeing Craig's physique with a smile. "You seem to have evaded any sort of defect."

Craig raised an eyebrow. "Yes, I have."

The narrator continued. "Eventually the numbers of infertile men rose to the point that women expected a fertility test before they would get involved in a serious relationship with a man. People panicked. Funding was thrown at the research teams, and fertility research became an industry."

Dahlia smiled. "An industry which needs entrepreneurs like you."

Craig scowled. "There's only room around here for one entrepreneur like me."

"Carrick Syndrome, also a genetic disease for which there is no cure, prevents the development of ovarian follicles in women. Unlike Metzner's Disease, Carrick Syndrome hit the world suddenly. In some continents it took longer to set in than others, but within three generations most women were infertile. It is caused by toxins in the air, food, and water. About forty years ago, most governments set up programmes of changes to industrial and agricultural processes."

Forty years ago. Craig's father would remember that if he was still alive.

"They began treatments to clean the air, the water, and the

soil where food was grown. The most difficult part was the eradication of certain new plant and life forms that had resulted from genetic modification. Their objective was to detoxify the world. But the benefits have barely begun to show."

Dahlia busied herself with her meal. As they ate, Craig pondered. He stared across the room at the large, framed photograph of his father hanging over the fireplace. His father's voice echoed in his mind. "You have to be decisive, boy. Life doesn't favour the weak." He was right, of course. Such a strong, passionate man, his life needlessly wasted, far too young.

Guilt swept over Craig, and he turned back to his food. Dahlia would be kind if she saw his emotions, but he wouldn't show them. Hadn't been able to since he was a fifteen year-old boy. Since he'd let his father down so terribly. Watched him die when he didn't see the pekays arrive, didn't warn him to abandon the raid.

Everything became horribly complicated then. The police interviewed his mother, but he went into hiding. His mother knew little of what had happened, and however hard the police tried, they were unable to pin her husband's crime on her. Craig stayed out of sight. He couldn't risk being seen. Not after what he'd done.

In the agony of guilt and shame, he tried to carry on. He needed to participate in society but could never again use his real name, so he did it the hard way. He found out how to fake an ID, remove the old chip, and implant a new one. Rather than spending money he didn't have, he learned to do it all by wheeling and dealing.

About to turn sixteen, he figured he should check whether he was a *fertile*. He discovered the worst. He made his new ID for a seventeen year old, ensuring he'd never be tested by the state – and in doing so he became a bolter.

Out of the disaster came a rebirth. As Craig Drake, he found a new vocation. He made seemingly impossible things happen, keeping his true activities under the radar while presenting a respectable public persona. His gift for subterfuge surprised him, but he grasped it as his father's legacy.

He found Dahlia's eyes on him, a concerned frown on her face. He reached his hand across the table and laid it on hers, and the frown turned into a smile.

He brought his thoughts back to business. An idea was forming, but it would take some planning, some action. He would have to see to it that the Napier girl was suitably prepared for what he had in mind. This time, he would depart from his usual method and make a personal visit.

There shouldn't be any problems getting her out, but he'd need to make sure Fadden didn't get in the way. There would be no second chance to boost his reputation with this one. He tapped his com-pak.

"Mog?"

"Baron?"

"I want some photos of Trish with the Fadden creep. I don't care how creative you have to be, but make them compromising. Show him with Trish at her most depraved. Get Baz to help you. One more thing. Watch Fadden. Don't let him become a nuisance."

"Yes, Baron."

5

8 pm

On his way to the pub, Dominic relived his visit to the House of Fun. He thought of different ways he should have handled the encounter. He pictured the Baron handing the paper across his desk.

That's the payment schedule. I'll take the deposit now.

You have the numbers wrong, Mr. Baron. Correct the figures and I'll pay the deposit.

Well, Mr. Fadden, it seems you're right. Here, the corrected figures.

His heart raced as, too late, adrenaline rushed through his body. Why was he able to fight the shadows now, but not come up with the goods when it mattered? Damn!

The old Share and Coulter was nearly deserted. Most people preferred the nearby King's Arms, but Dominic liked the pub despite the cranky landlord. The irregular shaped public bar had dark nooks and crannies holding secluded tables.

A door labelled *Snug Room* led into a small room at the back. It was rarely used by other customers, with only one table that seated about eight people. Dominic and his friends almost always used the Snug Room as their unspoken meeting place.

Spotting his friends through the Snug Room door, Dominic

made his way over, carrying a pint of beer.

"Dom, my old chum, how the hell are you?"

Did they really want to know? "Fine. Well, not that fine, but okay. Fact is I've had a difficult day."

Four of his friends sat around the table. Brett, dressed in well-worn camouflage combats, his sandy hair in a military style crew cut at odds with his soft features, asked, "What's up, Dom?"

Dominic sat down. "It's Fru. I should be used to it by now, but I can't just sit back and wait while she's in that place."

"I've got the answer. We'll storm the Cavendish, burn the opposition, and get her to safety. The rest is up to you, of course." Brett winked.

"Christ, Brett! All you think about is when you'll next get your guns out. I can't do it that way."

"Lighten up, man. You know they'd be just as quick to shoot you. You have to stick it to them before they stick it to you." He grinned and the others laughed.

Dominic got to the point. "Anyone here know Craig Drake?"

"What, Baron Drake?" Asked Al, his penetrating, dark eyes fixed on Dominic from beneath his lank, black hair.

"Yeah." Dominic sighed. "Martin, a friend from work, put me in touch with him. He's a tough git, but he'll be able to do it. I know he will." His friends' faces were incredulous. "It just wasn't much fun talking to him."

Across the table, Gerald pushed his thick, fair hair away from his glasses and exchanged nervous glances with Brett. "So do you want to tell us what you've done?"

"Done?" Dominic shrugged. "I've paid a deposit to Drake to spring Fru from the Cavendish."

Four pairs of eyes stared at him while Brett glanced at the door. A moment of silence hung over them.

"Christ, Dom!"

"Bloody hell!"

"Come on, Dom," said Gerald. "He's a complete bastard."

Al leaned forward. "You've done the right thing. He'll get her out."

"Sounds like a good idea to me," said Tim. "He's like a Rottweiler. You want him on your side."

Dominic was buoyed by Al and Tim's support even if the others didn't agree. He spoke quietly.

"She's been in there for four years and I've let her down. I've made more plans to get her out than I can count. None of them would have worked. The security there is too tight, and the staff, well, they love to help with a bit of mischief, but an escape? It's not going to happen."

"Why are you so sure of that? Have you tried?" asked Gerald.

"You're kidding. The authorities would be knocking on my door in five minutes."

"I think that depends on who you ask."

"Maybe."

A cold, damp cloth wrapped itself around Dominic's stomach, squeezing. Some of his friends were encouraging him with the plans he'd already dismissed, alarmed at the one he'd chosen.

They didn't understand. He no longer believed he could do it himself, and the idea of going to Baron Drake felt much more positive. In fact, from what Dominic had seen, unlikely to fail.

"I don't see the problem," said Tim. "You've asked Drake to do it. I bet he's perfectly capable. I'm with you all the way."

Gerald spoke. "Have you forgotten what happened at the Atelier Marlborough? The queen who was abducted? I heard that Drake got her out."

Brett laughed. "Oh, yeah. Then they found bits of her all over Chessington Common." He bounced in his seat. "That was really cool." Looking at Dominic's face, he stopped bouncing and added, "Well, no, not cool, but... Well, you know what I mean."

"Hardly surprising, really," said Gerald.

Dominic looked from Brett to Gerald. "Do you really believe that gossip? Those stories are just put around by business rivals and enemies. Probably the government too. They want us frightened of stepping out of line, that's all."

"Dom's right," said Al. "It's government propaganda. If they weren't so oppressive, we wouldn't need people like Baron Drake. They help us keep our dignity, our freedom."

Gerald spoke again. "I don't know about that. Earlier this year up North, a bolter was careless about his identity. The police were ready to take him in, so he went to a baron for help."

"And the baron was a bolter too, right? Didn't want the competition?"

"Exactly. So the man paid him a lot of money to help him disappear, and soon afterwards he was found floating in the sewer. Nasty." Gerald turned to Al. "Did he keep his dignity?"

"You don't know the facts of it, though," said Al. "You assume it was someone like Drake who did that, yet all you know is what the media told you. They have an agenda, and trust me, your best interests aren't on it. I wouldn't be surprised if the pekays dumped that girl on Chessington Common just to discredit whoever sprang her."

"I don't know about that," said Gerald. "But there's not much doubt about yesterday's news, is there? The Walton girl. Her family murdered by pekays. I shudder to think what will happen to her now."

Dominic wasn't ready to go home and be alone, but he needed a couple of minutes without the horror stories. He took his glass to the bar and waited to be served.

What if they were right? If they were, he'd made a terrible mistake. He'd been so sure he was doing the right thing. But now, he was having serious doubts.

He wondered what his father would say. They'd always been close. Particularly since the divorce from his mother after she went to Hong Kong with a wealthy banker. His father, Dr. Alex

Fadden, was a successful genetic scientist and had since re-married. As the barman handed him a pint glass, Dominic wondered whether he should talk to them about this. He trusted them completely, but surely they would think him foolish to take such a risk.

He went back to the Snug Room with his pint. He sat down, rummaging in his pocket, and pulled out a piece of paper. He unfolded it and put it on the table. Earlier, he'd done a charcoal sketch showing Craig Drake, strong and victorious, his biceps bulging and displaying a wide, white toothed grin. He stood over a cowering woman who, while recognisable as Mildred Knatchbull, the principal of the Cavendish, was depicted as a witch.

His friends rewarded him with laughter.

"Look, this is all very funny," said Gerald, "but Drake's dangerous. I don't like it."

"What can we do to help?" Tim's brow wrinkled in a frown.

"I don't know. I'm not sure there's much I can do but wait for Drake to finish the job. I'm not going to cross him."

Brett touched his glass against Dominic's. "There's one way out of this. We have to get her out before he does. You've lost the money, but you don't want to risk losing her too." Dominic stared at him. "We'll go in fully armed and grab her first. My mates at the Combat Society would love to help. Christ, just show 'em the door, and she'll be out of there quicker than you can fart."

"Brett, just give it a rest with the murder and mayhem, will you? If I was willing to do that, I'd have done it long ago, and I'd have come to you to do it. I know the people who work at the atelier, and they're just nice people who have a job to do. Death and mutilation isn't going to come into it."

"Let me know when you change your mind." Brett grinned.

"What amazes me is you really mean it. You're serious, aren't you? If I said to go ahead with it, you'd gather a small army of your weird friends and storm the place with more guns than a troop of pekays. You're one of my best friends, Brett, but you're crazy. Completely crazy."

Brett levelled his gaze at Dominic, then nodded. "Yes. Yes, I think that's right." He burst out laughing and slapped Dominic on the back. "Me and my weird friends are ready whenever you are."

"There is another way, you know." Gerald said. "Just climb under a rock somewhere and shut your eyes until it's all over."

Dominic sighed. "Thanks, Gerald. I can always rely on you."

"Man, I'm going to see what I can find out about Drake. I don't trust him," said Brett.

Gerald put down his beer. "I have a friend who's got connections in the police. I mean high up. Not the grunts with guns, I mean in the Intels."

Dominic stared at him. He'd always thought of the Police Intelligence Corps, the Intels, as an unreachable, scary elite. "Oh?"

"I'll see what they can find. There must be reams of stuff there, and whatever they know about him can only help."

"Okay. Find out what you can."

The conversation around the table gradually took on a lighter tone. Dominic watched them, listening to their humour without noticing it. He wanted to be alone. He drank the last of his beer and left. There was no rock to hide under, and he had to make sure he was able to pay the Baron's fee.

Outside, putting his folded sketch back in his pocket, he walked towards home. Work as a substitute teacher was not reliable – several days a week at best. Whatever else he did, he couldn't back out of paying the Baron. Drake would kill him. Maybe he should get a second job.

He walked the last few yards to his apartment building and climbed the stairs to his door. A symbol had been carved into his doorpost while he was out. He didn't recognise the design, but it looked like a gang sign.

It was neat, precise, obviously cut with a sharp blade. What on Earth was it? It must have something to do with the Baron. But why?

Dominic locked himself indoors and checked the windows, finding no sign that anyone had been in the apartment. The wall of bookshelves in his living room didn't look any different, and neither did the untidy bedroom and kitchen or the clutter on the wooden dining table. But his entire home was filled with a sense of someone else's presence.

He sat on his sofa and switched on the large Axis display on the wall. He entered his security code and displayed the public site of the Midfield Advertiser. Creating a new advertisement, he offered his services for extra tutoring of school children.

Then he turned to the news channel and caught an item part way through. It showed a large crowd gathered around a speaker who stood on a platform under a banner labelled *Nationalist Party*. Two other people flanked the speaker. They all wore grey uniforms with matching grey, peaked caps, and an armband displaying a red five-pointed star. The man in the centre spoke with passion, his voice amplified.

"We are losing our identity. With every child born in an atelier, our heritage is polluted by more foreign blood. Foreign fertiles are kept in the same ateliers as our own people, and they are interbred with no consideration for ethnic purity." The crowd shifted. Some jeered and some cheered. "They try to suppress our voice, but we *will* be heard." A cheer from the crowd. "They can ridicule us. They can arrest us, but they cannot silence our voice. Ours is the voice of reason. Without our national identity, what do we have?" He surveyed the noisy crowd. "We must preserve the spirit of our people, our language, customs and faith. This is not just our cause, it is your cause. Join with us and help to secure your future. Help to make your nation great once more." He finished with a flourish, indicating the table where a young man in a grey uniform waited for people who, after the impassioned speech, might wish to join the Nationalist Party.

The news did nothing to lift Dominic's spirits, so he programmed the Axis to display a window on the Thames, poured a nightcap of neat Afterburner, and watched people crossing the River Thames to St. Paul's from the Axis viewpoint on the South Bank.

His eyes strayed to the front door. Although he couldn't see the mark, it was a violation. And he'd put Fru right in Drake's path. The man was dangerous. *I have to do something.*

6

Friday 27ᵗʰ August, 9 am

Francesca sat watching Sydney Harbour. The tourist boat pulled away from Circular Quay for its evening trip. She knew which way it would go, and when the boat crossed the harbour mouth she would be able to see the deck lights lift and drop as the boat was picked up on the swell. She desperately wanted to go there herself and take the tourist boat.

She would also take the trip under the bridge and away up the river. She couldn't see where it went from her viewpoint on the Axis, but she'd seen the maps and wanted to find out firsthand. She would go to the restaurants in Darling Harbour and visit the shops and museums.

Was this all a dream? If the escape attempt failed she would have even less freedom than now. What if she was on lock-down for the rest of her life? Once past child-bearing age, the queens were offered a choice. They could move to a retirement wing of the atelier or leave and live with what was left of their family. So many queens, after spending their years in an atelier looking forward to retirement, did not survive their last childbirth. Most were so institutionalised or ill that they were not fit to leave.

The older women became either tougher or weaker as the years went by. Which would she be? Maybe she would never stand on Circular Quay and look out over the harbour.

Francesca's com-pak beeped. Liang's pretty face appeared on the small display.

"Fru, are you coming to the High Life Bar tonight?"

She wasn't in the mood for small talk but didn't want her friends to think anything was wrong. "Sure, I'll be there."

"Glad to hear it. You spend too much time with those dusty old books."

Francesca laughed. "There's no such thing as too much time with books."

When Francesca had finished talking with Liang, there came a knock on the door, so she touched the Axis controller to undo the latch. Hannah came in and shut the door. This must be a social call or she wouldn't have knocked.

She came to where Francesca was sitting. "Have you got a few minutes?"

"Of course. Is everything okay?"

"Oh yes. More than okay." She sang, as though reciting a nursery rhyme, "I have a date tonight."

"Hannah!" Francesca grinned. "Who's the lucky guy?"

"You might know of him. His name is Tim. Tim Squires. He's one of Dom's friends."

"Oh, that's wonderful. Of course I know him." She paused. "Knew him I should say. Dom is still friends with several people we both grew up with. I haven't seen Tim since I've been here, though. But I remember he was quite cute."

Hannah smiled. "He still is. He's gorgeous." They laughed.

They talked about Tim for a while. Francesca told all she could remember about him, and they talked about how to make the first date successful.

"I'd always been dating Dom," said Francesca, "but a couple of years before I came here, another one of our friends said he was in love with me. He said we were supposed to be together."

"What, he tried to come between you and Dom?"

Francesca pulled a face to show her distaste. "I know. It was a horrible thing to do. Anyway, I didn't fancy him. He was too intense. A bit slimy, too. He changed after that, though. He's still friends with Dom, but I don't think they're as close as they used to be. I never told Dom. I don't think he did, either."

"Oh dear! I never thought of you as a heartbreaker," said Hannah, grinning. "Well, I shall certainly try not to break Tim's heart."

They laughed and hugged each other. When they had exhausted the subject, Hannah said, "There's a meeting for you later this morning. I don't know what it's for, but they want to see you in the Red Room."

"Oh, probably to give me instructions for my insemination. It's due in about two weeks, so they'll be telling me what to eat and drink and probably how often to breathe. You know what they're like."

Hannah grimaced. "Anyway, I've sent the details to your com-pak."

"Thanks." Francesca braced herself, unsure how Hannah might react to her next question. "Is Kelly okay? Will I be able to see her?"

Hannah cast her eyes down. "Fru, I can't talk about Kelly. I'm not allowed to – you know that."

"Please… I just wish I knew."

Hannah checked the time, and her expression registered concern. "Got to go now. I'll see you later." She hurriedly let herself out, leaving Francesca to fret about Kelly and anticipate the meeting about her next insemination.

She had never told Dom in any detail what happened on the day of her first insemination. To do so would have meant to re-live it, and she couldn't bear to do that. When she first arrived at the atelier, just sixteen years old, they gave her a medical, and once she'd passed that, they proceeded with the ovulation tests.

When they decided the time was right, one of the staff led her to The Dungeon, as the queens called it. There, in the treatment room, they planted in her the seed of a man she would never be able to identify. Almost immediately, a sensation that her body was no longer under her control overcame her. A child would grow inside her. It would remain an uninvited stranger while she carried it, and she would never see it after the birth.

The words kept going through her mind, "I'm sixteen. I'm old enough to cope with this. I'm sixteen. I'm old enough…"

Now, nearly four years later, she was due for her third insemination. This would be the last time if she could escape while pregnant.

Francesca needed some air, so she headed for the garden. In the corridor she caught up with two other queens, also walking towards the garden, one with her hand on her rounded stomach as though to reassure herself the precious baby was still there.

The others talked excitedly about the Autumn Ball. It was less than two weeks away, and they compared notes about what they would wear and whether they had a date with one of the *lords*. They giggled, and the red-haired girl, who wasn't pregnant, complained, "It's so unfair that we're never allowed to take a lord back to our rooms."

"Better than Kelly Walton," the pregnant girl said. "She has no one to visit her now."

"Kelly should think herself lucky," said the redhead.

Francesca frowned. "Why?"

"Well," the redhead drew a long breath. "The pekays often beat bolters really badly. Sometimes they do worse. They can do anything they want, you know."

"What are you talking about? They've already killed her family. It can't get much worse than that."

"I'm not so sure," said the redhead. "They'll want to go on making her suffer." They all walked in silence for a few minutes. Then the other two began to talk about Joseph, who the red-haired girl admired. He was tall and very handsome, and because of that he was always popular with the queens.

Francesca said little. Thoughts of Kelly distracted her, and she didn't share their excitement over the lords. Particularly not Joseph. He was arrogant and became aggressive when she refused his advances. He didn't seem to hear the word no and had an infuriating habit of ignoring her answers as though she didn't know her own mind. He'd cornered her and tried to push himself onto her, often literally, too many times.

Nonetheless, the Autumn Ball would be fun. It always was. At least it would be a chance to dress up and have a good time with her friends – one last time?

The Autumn Ball was one of the rare occasions when the queens were allowed physical contact with the lords. Not intimate contact, though, as dancing was carefully monitored by the staff. A heavy price to pay for being a fertile.

Few queens missed the ball, and then only if their pregnancies were so far progressed that they weren't allowed to go. Many of them would willingly take a lord back to their suite if allowed, but if they could pick the father of their own children, the atelier administrators would not be able to maintain genetic diversity. Management planned and controlled who was mixed with whom for breeding purposes. Strict policy dictated that the queens never knew which lord was the father.

Dom could never father her baby, but she could bear a child for them to bring up. All she needed was for the escape to take place after her next insemination. Very likely, considering it was due so soon.

If only he could come to the ball.

In the corridor, the discussion moved on from Joseph. Francesca tuned out of the conversation, and when they came into the garden she walked in a different direction, wanting to be alone.

She turned onto the path across the lawns and noticed Mildred Knatchbull, the Principal of the atelier, coming the other way. Mrs. Knatchbull rarely came out in the garden and never spoke to the fertiles unless it was absolutely necessary. Her short, unstylish hair, combined with a high neckline, long sleeves, and the overall grey colour of her clothes to give the impression of an old-time puritan. The kind Francesca had seen in her history books.

She kept her eyes ahead, hoping not to attract any attention. "Ah, Miss Napier."

With a silent curse, she stopped. "Hello, Mrs. Knatchbull."

"Miss Napier, you really must make sure you take proper care of your suite."

Francesca frowned, confused. "Is there a problem, Mrs. Knatchbull?"

"Yes, there is a problem. You know perfectly well there is. The staff members spend more than twice as long in your suite than anyone else's. They have work to do, and you must not keep them from it."

Francesca flushed. "If you don't like how I keep my suite, I'd be happy to leave, Mrs. Knatchbull." She immediately regretted her words.

"Miss Napier, you are in the happy situation of having many desirable privileges. You may wish to reconsider your attitude if you expect to keep them."

She cast her eyes down. "I'm sorry, Mrs. Knatchbull. I didn't mean to be rude, and I shall do what I can to make the staff's job easy in my suite."

"Yes, you will." Mrs. Knatchbull turned and walked away.

Francesca had a miserable morning. Why had Mildred Knatchbull picked her out for a drubbing? In all her time so far at the Cavendish, it had never happened, and Hannah had always spent time with her. It was nothing new. What was going on?

When the time came, Francesca left her suite and went to the Red Room. The door was ajar when she arrived, and Ingrid, one of the atelier administrators, was waiting for her. Lounge chairs and a coffee table were arranged in the room, and a window opposite looked onto part of the garden.

The décor and the upholstery of the furniture were mostly shades of red. Deep reds, autumn reds, all elegant colours. The room gave a feeling of warmth and comfort.

"Hello, Francesca."

"Hello, Ingrid. How are you?"

"I'm fine, thank you. The reason we've called this meeting is that a special arrangement has been made for you."

The words had an ominous ring to them. "Oh?"

"Yes." Ingrid paused, blinking as if surprised. "You've been granted a *free stay*."

"What?" A free stay? A complete two-year cycle without having a baby! "Er... Okay."

"Nothing else will change, of course. Your allowance will continue and you will carry on in the same quarters. Your fitness regime will remain unaltered, and near the end of your free stay you will be interviewed again and receive instructions for the next cycle."

"Ingrid! Er...thank you!" She knew she mustn't show her disappointment – it would look suspicious – but she wanted to leave this place carrying a baby!

"I don't know who you have to thank, Francesca, but I assure you it is not me."

This was unbelievable. It was almost unheard of to get a free stay without a pressing medical reason. Adding the recovery time from the last cycle, that would make over three years without a pregnancy.

Francesca's stomach knotted. "Thank you anyway, Ingrid."

Ingrid stood up. "Take care, Francesca." She left the room.

Francesca, dazed, didn't notice the walk back to her suite. What on earth was happening? Somebody must have moved mountains to make that happen, but who?

Then she made a connection. She thought of the conversation she'd had with Dom. He was getting help, and he was paying a lot of money for it. Maybe Dom had made the request and this person, whoever he was, really had the power to do it.

Why on Earth hadn't Dom consulted her before he did that? Did he think it was better to take a child from an atelier mother than for her to carry the baby herself once she'd escaped? Had he learned nothing?

Now that she saw some chance of escape, the thought of what an atelier queen would suffer to enable her to have a child of her own was too much to bear. She would never have guessed that a free stay would seem like the worst kind of injustice.

Back in her suite, she planned her next move. If the escape was to be soon, she would need to say her goodbyes to people, but she mustn't let them know she was leaving. How could she say goodbye to someone without telling them she was going away?

Spend some time with them and do something memorable. Tell them she loved them and leave them feeling good. That's what she would do. Her friends would get a small gift, and she would spend some quality time with each of them. Would she still go to the ball? If she was still here, of course she would. After all, what better way to say goodbye to friends than to celebrate at the annual ball?

Could Dom's escape plans succeed where Kelly's had failed? It was her only hope for freedom, but if it went wrong, Dom could be killed. She willed herself to believe that the plan wouldn't fail and sat watching Sydney Harbour, tears on her face for the child she couldn't take with her to a new future with Dom.

7

Mildred Knatchbull closed the door and contemplated the stark interior of her office. No wasteful luxury here, in contrast to the the rest of the atelier. Just a simple, functional office with a tidy desk set in the middle and a row of filing cabinets together with a large cupboard along one wall. The hard chair at the desk, without upholstery, was no more comfortable than the guest chair facing it. Plain curtains blocked sunlight from the tall, double window.

She hated waste. Taxpayers worked hard, and many of them lived in difficult financial circumstances. They had a social duty to pay taxes and a right to know the money wasn't wasted providing government employees with luxuries they couldn't afford for themselves.

The queens and lords were government employees. She saw no reason why their lack of choice in their employment should be compensated with any kind of extravagance at the expense of the hard-pressed taxpayer. Government policy, however, dictated the facilities and comforts provided, and she was obliged to comply.

She crossed the room to her desk, scowling as she passed through the small ray of sunshine peeping between the curtains. The last time she'd truly felt happy was that morning twenty-three years ago today. Her husband Jack, dressed in his peacekeepers' uniform, held her close and promised he'd be back from his shift as early as possible. That night, he would take her out to dinner to celebrate their fifth wedding anniversary.

They talked about the future. Maybe it was time to adopt a baby. They would discuss it during their anniversary dinner. Their joint income was certainly enough to support a child.

She admired his physique as he walked to his car.

That afternoon, Jack's squad was called to an attempted breakout at the Atelier Caledonia in neighbouring Cradleford. Unlike the Cavendish, the Caledonia was situated in town. Inquisitive onlookers made the operation far more difficult for the peacekeepers. During a firefight, several people were killed, including one of the atelier queens and two peacekeepers. Jack never came home.

After that, life had been different. Joyless. Mildred devoted herself to her work, and as a result, built a successful career. Gaining experience in atelier management, her opinions hardened about how the queens and lords should conduct themselves. How they should be handled. Disciplined.

She learned that since not all members of society accepted their moral responsibilities, legislation and enforcement must ensure they did. It was no use enacting legislation making too many concessions to those very people whose social obligation was the most important. They, most of all, had to understand that duty was not a matter for barter. Their willingness to do the right thing was a measure of their strength of character.

She shut her eyes, trying to put out of her mind the picture of the intolerable Napier girl with her pretty face and laughing friends. Her exasperating self-satisfied attitude was hard to tolerate. The comment she made four years ago during her orientation interview was a presage of the attitude she had shown since. *It must be easy for you, not being fertile.*

Such smug indifference to the fate of the majority of women – to Mildred's own fate – coming from the mouth of a budding young fertile woman, was the height of arrogance. Four years on, the girl still needed to be tamed.

A low chime came from the door, so Mildred touched the small console on her desk to release the door catch. Ingrid came in, and at a gesture from Mildred, sat down in the hard chair facing the desk.

"I'd like to know how Ms. Napier responded during your meeting this morning."

"Quietly," said Ingrid. "I confess I expected her to be more demonstrative, more pleased. She hid how she felt. She thanked me, of course, but it was as though she didn't want to."

"Really?" Mildred gently clasped her hands together on the desk. "Did she give any indication why? Any clues?"

"Nothing. I'm pretty sure I read her expression correctly. When I gave her the news of the free stay, I believe she was shocked."

Mildred frowned. "I see. This means one of two things. Perhaps in the strange fantasy world she occupies, she romanticises the child bearing. I've seen it happen before. One might be forgiven for believing that would make our jobs easier, but don't be fooled. It's a sign of instability that eventually leads to damaging psychotic behaviour. If so, she'll need treatment."

Ingrid raised an eyebrow.

"If that's not it, though, there's only one other possible conclusion. She's up to something." Mildred paused, thinking. "Please arrange for a log of her activities, particularly any unusual behaviour, to be submitted with the daily reports."

"Certainly," said Ingrid.

When Ingrid left, Mildred sat, deep in thought. Running an atelier was demanding work. She had to balance the needs of nearly three hundred residents with those of a large staff and make sure everything went smoothly. Most of all, she had to maintain an output of more than fifty healthy babies a year. The last thing she needed was for upstart residents to make her job more difficult.

Ms. Napier was a girl with a casual sense of entitlement that was not only ugly but created more work for all the staff. Now, to make matters worse, and against Mildred's better judgement, came this bizarre free stay.

Humiliating as it was to grant the girl a free stay, Mildred had been forced to do so. And now that the Napier girl knew, it would reinforce her innate belief that she was somehow not only different from the others, but better.

That wouldn't last though. However insufferable she was, however smug, she would learn not to cross Mildred Knatchbull.

8

1:30 pm

Dominic walked through the glazed entrance into Midfield Secondary School. The uninspiring concrete building had been one of his main sources of work since he finished his teacher training. In the common room, he nodded greetings to the other teachers and sat in an unoccupied chair. He was due in class in half an hour, which left time to have a coffee and get his thoughts together. As he settled down, Martin came in.

"Hi, Martin."

Martin grunted.

He tried again. "I'm getting a coffee. Want one?"

Martin grunted again.

Dominic went to the coffee machine in the corridor and brought back two cups of coffee. He put one on the table next to Martin. "There you go."

No response. *Suit yourself.* Because Martin was so unresponsive, Dominic kept to his own thoughts while he enjoyed his coffee. On the way to class, his com-pak signalled an encrypted call from Brett.

"Hi, Brett. I'm working at the moment. Is it urgent?"

"Actually, yes. Got a minute?"

Dominic stopped in the corridor and sighed. He hated to arrive late in class. It was a recipe for a disrupted lesson.

"Man, there's something I think you should know. I just found out."

Dominic couldn't help his curiosity. "Oh?"

"You know Drake sponsors the Guardian Agency? Well, it turns out he does it in exchange for his position on the Midfield Council Advisory Committee. Appointments to the committee are made by an office in Whitehall. They handle all appointments to Quangos. One of my Combat Society buddies is a clerical worker there."

Dominic checked the time. "Brett, this is all very interesting, but –"

"The senior official in the office overrode everyone else to appoint Drake. They all thought it was a terrible idea. Anyway, my buddy overheard him in his office one day, talking to Drake on his com-pak. Drake's blackmailing him."

"Really? Are you sure?"

"I wouldn't be telling you if I wasn't sure. The problem is, he's getting paid more than he puts in as sponsorship, and some of the atelier babies disappear without trace. Presumably gone to his clients. Being on the committee helps him run his illegal operations. All this generosity, helping atelier kids. It's a con."

Dominic pressed his fingers into his forehead. "I see."

"Drake's doing some dirty stuff out there. They trust him with the Guardian Agency, and he's stealing children from under their noses."

"Okay. I get it. Listen, see what else you can find out. I've got to go. I'll talk to you later." Dominic terminated the call. His heart was pounding. How could he get Fru out of this mess – alive?

9

After two days of fretting, it finally dawned on Francesca why Mildred Knatchbull had crossed her path in the garden. Mildred knew she had a free stay and wanted to be sour about it.

That alone told Francesca something about the free stay. It wasn't willingly granted by the indomitable Mrs. Knatchbull. In fact, she hated it so much she had to come and spoil Francesca's day.

That meant whoever made the decision had some kind of power over Mildred Knatchbull. And it was only tolerable because Mildred hated it.

A message arrived telling her she should expect a visitor at 2 pm. It didn't say who, but it would be Dom keeping his promise to come back in a few days. Four days after his last visit, it seemed like ages.

This was her chance to ask who he'd paid to get her out. He must have asked them to set up the free stay, and she wanted an explanation. He must have a good reason, though she couldn't imagine what it might be.

Would Dom really go through with it? Could he honestly get her out? Keep her safe from the trigger-happy pekays? Despite her doubts, she sincerely hoped he would. She would live in peace with Dom and never see the inside of an atelier again.

What a wonderful thought.

She hummed a tune as she got ready.

On Saturday night shall be all my care
To powder my locks and curl my hair,
On Sunday morning my love will come in
When he will marry me with a gold ring.

She paused and studied herself in the mirror. Satisfied with the result, she sat and selected a photo album on the Axis screen and paged through it. The photos from her childhood were of her and Dom playing on swings or splashing in a pool, and as she went farther through them, she and Dom grew older and their demeanour together changed.

They fell in love. Instead of two children laughing, adolescents held hands. Then she was in his arms, laughing at something he said. His hair was longer and his soft features accentuated his youth. Every photo recalled a memory she savoured before going to the next.

Her com-pak beeped. Time to go. She checked the reminder to see which visiting room to attend and set off. When she arrived, the door was ajar.

Pushing the door farther open, she went in. "Hello, Darling –" She stopped short.

The severe look on the man's face softened to a friendly smile as he stood to greet her. "Well now, that's a nice greeting." He held out his hand. "My name is Craig. I'm an acquaintance of Mr. Fadden." His eyes went down to her feet and then slowly back to her face.

Her face flushed hot. Who on Earth was this handsome man being so familiar with her? "I'm sorry, I…I thought you were Dom." She sat down without taking his hand. "I don't remember

Dom mentioning anyone called Craig."

"Ah. Well, he's an acquaintance, not a friend. I'm here because he's asked me to help you."

Her heart jumped. "Oh…" This must be the person Dom talked about. Her ticket to freedom. "Well, Craig, it's nice to meet you. Can I get you any refreshment?"

"Just water, thanks." His eyes smiled as he watched her face.

While she poured two glasses of water, she stood with her back to him to gather her thoughts. What should she do now? Perhaps he would tell her there was something he wanted her to do to facilitate the escape. Within reason, she'd be pleased to do it.

She smiled, handing him his water. She tried not to make the smile too warm. After all, she didn't want to give him the wrong impression, but somehow the way he looked at her made her tingle. His eyes held so much passion. More so than she'd seen in any of the lords.

Why should she care about his eyes? This was simply a business transaction – yet he was her only real hope of a better life.

"Are you here because there's something you need me to do?" She bit her lip. They'd just met, and already she was placing herself at his disposal.

"It's not as simple as that, Francesca. You see, many things need to happen to meet your objective, and we have to make sure nothing endangers our preparations."

"Like what?"

"Like careless talk. Placing your trust in the wrong person."

"The wrong person?"

"I'll get to that, but first you have to promise me you will not talk about this to anyone."

"Of course."

"I wonder if you fully understand what I just said."

"Mr. Craig." She tried to sound as formal as possible without knowing his last name. "Your use of the English language is very clear, and so is my understanding of it."

Craig's smile broadened into a grin. "I like your pluck. I'm sure you understood my words very well." The grin was gone, but the smile was still there in the corners of those dark eyes. "But you may not have understood me to mean you can't talk to Mr. Fadden about this either."

She stared at him for a few moments. "He knows about it already. For goodness sake, he arranged all this. I've already talked to him about it."

"I know. It's okay, but you can't do so anymore. He can't be trusted."

"Look, this is going too far. I've known him since I was six years old, and I would trust him with my life. He's the most honest, kind-hearted person you could meet, and you're sitting there, after you've known him for what, a few days, telling me I can't trust him?"

"I'm sorry, Francesca." His voice was gentle. "There's no easy way to say this, so I'll just tell it straight."

Francesca frowned and watched him.

"When Mr. Fadden came to me and told me what he wanted, I took the precaution of having my people investigate him. In my position there's too much at risk. I can't be incautious. During those few days I discovered some things you might not be aware of."

"What things?"

"I'm afraid Mr. Fadden has been careless. He's been sleeping with a pekay's wife. Her husband suspects something and is having them watched. You mustn't have anything to do with him, or I can't do my job."

"Sleeping with a pekay's wife?" She laughed. "That's nonsense. Of course he's not. Not my Dom."

Craig's voice was gentle. "I don't blame you for not believing me." He tapped his com-pak. "I'm sending you some photos my people took. I'm using an encrypted message. Please be discreet with them."

Photos showing Dom with a young woman appeared on Francesca's com-pak.

Her stomach turned.

"I need to take a closer look at these. How do I know they haven't been interfered with?"

Craig sighed. "Of course. You're right to be concerned, but think about it. What possible reason would I have for lying to you? Anyway, take a closer look. Judge for yourself."

Francesca flicked through the tiny pictures on her com-pak display. *This is disgusting.* "I'll take a closer look on my Axis. I can't tell anything from looking at them like this."

"Please do. Meanwhile, are you agreed not to have any contact with him?"

"I need time to think about it." What did she see in his eyes? They didn't give much away. There was still that smile in the corners. Was it kindness or mockery? It was all very well for him to have that flattering twinkle in his eye. To come in here confident, strong and assertive. But to say things like that about Dom?

She didn't know whether to trust her instincts with him. He did seem to be just doing the job he was paid for, but she hardly knew him. Was he telling the truth? Surely Dom wouldn't be unfaithful. Then again, he had been alone for four years. Could she expect him to live like a monk?

Craig studied her for a few moments, then rose from his chair, shook her hand and left. Did he have any reason to lie?

10

10 am

Mildred watched from her office window as Craig Drake climbed into his car and sped off towards Midfield. This was the first time she'd known him to visit the atelier without seeing her.

He'd been here many times since he started his generous sponsorship of the Guardian Agency. She wasn't impressed with the slogan, *good homes for cute babies*, but that wasn't his fault. The agency, in addition to carrying out the statutory fertility tests, played a necessary part in the process of matching atelier babies with the most appropriate homes. It wasn't a simple matter to match the psychological and physical profiles of both biological parents with those of the prospective adoptive parents.

She had to admit that Craig Drake was a bit of a nuisance on the Midfield Council Advisory Committee, but he didn't do any real harm, and he was quite charming. He always remembered to ask after her and seemed to genuinely like her. She couldn't say that of many people these days. It was quite refreshing.

The first time she met Craig was the officer selection meeting of the advisory committee when she hoped to be elected as chair. It would have given her more influence over the strategy and decisions of the committee, and she was the right person for the job.

Craig was a new member of the committee, attending for

the first time. Mildred circulated among the members during the informal gathering prior to the meeting, canvassing their support for the position of chair. When she came to him, he leaned forward and kissed her hand.

Kissed her hand!

Of course, she snatched it away and glared at him, but it stirred something deep inside that she'd forgotten was there. Despite her reaction, he held her with his sparkling eyes and treated her as though she were special. She enjoyed the warmth he showed and admired the fact that he didn't stop just because she responded with a show of cold indifference.

Now, here he was, visiting the irritating, flighty Napier girl. The insolent, high-minded queen who thought the rules of the atelier were above her. What on Earth did he want with her?

Surely it wasn't anything to do with the free stay?

The free stay made her angry every time she thought of it. After the last Nationalist Party meeting, a seriously unpleasant looking giant of a man, in a black suit, approached as she walked home.

"Come with me."

Mildred had never responded well to being pushed around, particularly not by bullies. She decided the best response was no response since he obviously had the physical advantage. She turned her back on him and carried on walking.

"Mrs. Knatchbull, you'll regret it if you do that." He formed the words as though each one was a strenuous effort. "You need to talk to me."

Regret it? That might have been a physical threat, but the claim that she needed to talk to him was not, at least not directly. What he said piqued her interest, and she was not one to ignore a threat she did not understand.

She turned to face him, and he beckoned her into the shadows. Before following him, she felt in her pocket for the reassuring bulk of the stun pistol. One thing Jack had taught her, all those years ago, was to always carry one. If she used it now, even this great thug would fall instantly. Her heart quickened, thrilling in anticipation of a chance to use it. She stepped into the shadows.

"Here's what you will do."

Mildred wondered whether his slow, painfully formed words were the result of a speech defect or just a simple mind.

"Ms. Napier will have a free stay."

Mildred raised her eyebrows. "And if I don't do as you ask?"

"Your boss finds out about them." He jerked his thumb towards the other Nationalist Party committee members leaving the building.

"I see. So this is blackmail."

The man turned to leave. Mildred didn't intend to leave it at that.

"I don't know who you work for, but I have a message for your boss."

The man turned back to face her. In one swift movement, she pulled out the stun gun and fired it into his groin. A soft moan escaped his lips as he fell to the ground.

She'd enjoyed that. The satisfying sense that she'd extracted some kind of payment for what they were doing to her. Whoever *they* were. The man clearly wasn't working alone. He didn't have the intelligence for it. That meant whoever he worked for was more intelligent and probably just as much of a thug.

Would the man tell his boss what she'd done? Probably not. His boss wouldn't relish employing a thug who was so easily overpowered by a woman. No, he'd nurse his wounds and hopefully keep away from her.

She'd done as the man asked. She couldn't risk not doing so. It was difficult to give the Napier girl a free stay, but not because anyone would ask her to explain herself. She had enough autonomy in running the atelier to make such decisions. It was difficult because she hated doing something to benefit the Napier girl. Worse, it affronted her authority – her dignity. All that, however, was nothing to the problems those people would cause if they exposed her as a member of the Nationalist Party.

Whoever they were, she was now in their power. Ultimately, when she found a way, she would see to it that these thugs paid for their deeds ten times over. A hundred. What they'd done made her angry, and she would have her revenge. Meanwhile, she had to figure out why they were so interested in the Napier girl and why Craig Drake showed up to speak to her so soon after.

Was it a coincidence?

Mildred Knatchbull didn't believe in coincidences, and it was quite possible that there was some kind of link between Craig Drake's visit to the Napier girl today and the blackmail over the free stay. But what? Why would Drake want her to have a free stay? Why would he even have any interest in her?

It would make more sense if the rumours about his underworld dealings were true. As a well-practised cynic, Mildred was not easily taken in by either side of any argument. But it was obvious that a successful businessman who sponsored the Guardian Agency, and held an important post on the Midfield Council Advisory Committee, was bound to be the subject of dishonest rumours put out by those who wished to harm his interests.

No, she didn't give any credence to such rumours and considered them the irresponsible rantings of weak minded fools.

She went to her desk, and using her console, she changed the status of Francesca Napier to code yellow. The staff would be more vigilant, and the security guards would be on alert. She opened yesterday's daily reports. Somewhere in the detailed section on the Napier girl, surely there would be a clue, however cryptic.

11

1 pm

Francesca sat with Hannah, facing the Axis display, inspecting the images Craig had sent one by one. She hated having Hannah there, but she needed her opinion. Humiliation twisted her gut. Hannah gasped with each new picture, every one a vile depiction of depravity and treachery.

When they'd seen them all, Francesca's devastation was complete.

She was at the same time fascinated and appalled. Despite the knot in her gut, she couldn't tear her eyes away from the pictures. She'd never seen Dom completely naked, yet this woman had. Francesca's cheeks flushed as she stared at the pictures.

"They don't look doctored to me," said Hannah. "It certainly looks as though Craig was telling the truth, but I don't get it. It's just not like Dom. It could be a really well done fake, you know."

Francesca knew that, but she couldn't risk being wrong. It seemed that Dom had betrayed her.

She'd never had any reason to distrust Dom. He'd always been kind to her. A good person. Yet, should she hold it against him if he sought the comfort of a woman's arms when he was alone for years on end? She'd wanted him to wait for her. Was that too much to expect?

She'd held on to the dream that their first true intimacy would be together. Now that dream was lost behind these images burned into her mind. What other aspirations didn't he share? Did he really want that home, some place far away, with her? The life together they'd so often talked about.

She sent him a message, forwarding the pictures. She said, "What the hell is this?"

He replied seconds later by trying to make a voice call, but she wasn't ready to talk, so she didn't answer it. A flurry of messages followed.

"Good God, I've no idea what these are, but they're nothing to do with me. Where did they come from?"

"So, you're saying it's not true?"

He sent several messages reassuring her that the photos weren't really him. He sounded so shocked, so convincing.

She told him, "I don't know what to think. I need some time. Leave me alone for a while."

He sent a few messages after that, but when she didn't respond, they dwindled in frequency. It was better if she didn't communicate with him. Whatever the truth, she had to play safe. If Dom's actions really had led to his surveillance, she wouldn't put her whole future at risk. No, she was doing the right thing. Nothing could be allowed to jeopardise her escape.

Soon after Hannah left the room, Jen and Liang arrived, Jen heavily pregnant, and Liang wearing a maternity dress despite the barely perceptible swelling underneath. Walking into the room, Jen thrust a magazine into Francesca's hand.

"Have you seen this?"

It was a new edition of the *Atelier Life* magazine, and on the cover, below the title, were the words "Penal Ateliers, Combating Crime." The photograph showed a building with functional, drab architecture, quite unlike normal ateliers.

"Penal ateliers? What's this about?" asked Francesca.

Liang went to the sofa and sat in silence. Jen was not so reticent.

"Prison cells for fertiles who bolt. You get no comforts, no possessions of your own. You just breed. It's supposed to be a punishment."

Francesca sat down heavily. She had no idea whether either of them had plans to bolt, nor did they know of her plans. Few people would confide such a dangerous secret. Her stomach sank, and a chill settled deep inside as she imagined what her own life might be like in such a place.

She had no desire to see anyone kept in a penal atelier and she was sure most of the fertiles felt the same. Particularly anyone who harboured dreams of freedom.

"I think what scares me most," said Jen, "is it's obviously a concession to pressure from the Nationalist Party. If they had their way, we'd all be kept in those conditions. Not just bolters. They call it *austerity*."

"I don't understand," said Francesca. "What do they have against us?"

"It's not that, darlin'. They believe everyone lives for their duty to society. For them it's all about self-sacrifice. They're weird."

Liang scowled. "If the government is making concessions to them, it must be afraid. Do you realise what it would mean if the Nationalists were in government?"

"I don't like them having this kind of influence," said Jen. "But I don't think there's much chance of a majority vote."

Liang shrugged. "Maybe not. Who needs the majority vote when they can wield that kind of power?"

Francesca's thoughts were not on the Nationalist Party. Several fertiles in the Cavendish had, like Kelly Walton, bolted and been caught. They were under strict security, but otherwise treated like the rest of the fertiles. What would happen to them? Would they all be moved to these new prisons, or would they go on with a better life than more recently captured souls? So unfair.

Then there was Craig Drake. He really was rather strong and reassuring. Maybe, just maybe, he would pull it off. He would keep her safe. For a fleeting moment, she wondered what it would be like in his arms.

12

2 pm

Dominic glared at the pictures on the Axis screen. His head ached, and he couldn't think straight. Brett had arrived with a carrier bag full of beer bottles, but Dominic didn't want any. Not now, anyway.

"You old dog." Brett laughed. "Where the hell did she get these?"

"She didn't say. I asked, but she wasn't much in the mood to talk to me."

"Ha! I'm not surprised." Brett glanced across, and his broad grin deflated. "She must know these are fake. She doesn't believe all this, does she?"

"She's not sure. Can you blame her?" Dominic sighed. "Who hates me enough to do this?"

"I don't know who hates you, but I can think of someone who's a slimy bastard and quite capable of doing something like this."

Dominic jabbed his finger at the Axis control, blanking the screen.

"What do you expect me to do? Just walk into his House of Fun and say, 'I think you've made up some naughty photos of me'? He'd laugh from here to Christmas."

Brett's voice was gentle. "No. But he's shafting you. You can't just ignore it."

Dominic took a deep breath. "I'm not going to ignore it." He steeled himself. "Brett, I don't know if Drake was behind this, but I have to call him off."

Brett studied him for a few moments. "There's something you need to see. On Sunday, me and my Combat Society pals are re-enacting the Bataille Pas de Calais. I think you should come along."

"What? No. You know me. I'm not much of one for violence, even if it took place fifty years ago."

Brett laughed. "We don't use live firearms! We do it because of the lessons we can learn from history."

Dominic studied him for a moment. "Lessons learned from history? Your enthusiasm for firearms seems quite the opposite to me."

"I thought you'd be interested to learn more about the Bataille Pas de Calais," said Brett.

Dominic wasn't in the mood. "I'm sure the history is very interesting, but I'm not going. Sorry."

"Man, it's a part of history everyone should know," said Brett. "It was during the expansion of the second Roman Empire last century. The Italians had occupied France and our government worried they would come for us next.

"Queen Anne III was married to the French Duke Charles de Gramont, Duc de Gramont. She went on a diplomatic mission to the Roman occupiers to try and negotiate for peace on behalf of the French, but the Italians took her hostage and made threats." He grimaced.

"Anyway, the Roman forces said they'd invade England, threatening to kill the Queen, hoping we'd submit. But rather than wait for them to arrive on our beaches, we went to fight them in Northern France in Pas de Calais where they were massing their forces."

Dominic was interested despite his desire not to witness the exhibition of violence.

"The main fight was aerial. But without establishing a supply route through Pas de Calais, the Italians wouldn't achieve anything by aerial battle. So there it was. The Bataille Pas de Calais decided the war."

Dominic thought for a moment. "I suppose in hindsight it wasn't such a good idea for Queen Anne to go to France."

"That's what the history books say," said Brett. "There's a saying that always comes up when that battle is mentioned. *If you poke a sleeping tiger, you have to stand and fight.*" His eyes were intense. "It's a lesson we should all learn."

Dominic shrugged. "I agree it's interesting history, but I don't want to go to the enactment. And I'm not going to fight this tiger. I'm calling him off. " He composed an encrypted message. "To Baron Drake. This is to notify you that I no longer require your services. Thank you." He hit send, and immediately received the reply, *No such recipient.*

Brett frowned. "What's up?"

Dominic showed him the reply. "I'm going to see him." He stood.

Brett jumped to his feet. "Oh, man, I'm coming with you."

"No. Thanks, but I have to do this myself." He called a taxi and waited for it in the street.

When he arrived at the House of Fun, he asked the taxi driver to wait and walked towards the portcullis. A large man stepped out in front of him at the door.

"Hello. I'd like to see Baron Drake, please."

The man stood, feet apart, hands at his sides. "No."

"Er, then I'd like to make an appointment, please."

"No."

This was ridiculous. "Look, I have to see the Baron. Please will you let him know –"

The man stepped forward and grabbed his collar with one hand, tightening his fist. Dominic heard his shirt rip as he choked, his breath cut off.

"Leave." The man's cold blue eyes drilled into him.

After a few seconds, the man released his grip, and Dominic almost fell backwards, gasping for breath. He backed away, then turned and hurried back to the waiting taxi. He climbed into the back seat and the driver turned to him. "Bloody hell, mate. Are you alright? Where to next?"

"Home. Back home." *I have no choice now. I must get her out first.*

13

4 pm

Craig Drake turned the glossy page of the thick brochure. Now, that was more like it. A glorious stateroom and enough suites for guests, but more important, a high crew to passenger ratio. Sun decks, bar, gym, dining salon. Comfort and luxury. He peered at the deck and cabin layout and found suitable quarters, below the waterline, for Gurt and Mog.

Tapping his com-pak, he said, "Mog, my office. Now."

Craig sighed and tossed the brochure onto his desk. This was all very well, but before he bought this pretty yacht, he would need to strengthen his position. His business idea was taking shape. Now to put flesh on its bones. The arrangements would be easy.

The door opened and Mog came in. Craig indicated one of the leather upholstered chairs.

"I'm starting a new business venture."

Mog's scarred face showed no sign of emotion. "Yes, Baron."

"Find two adjacent rooms on the basement level and convert one to bed and living and the other to a bathroom. Nothing special, and make sure there's only one door into the suite. Brick up the other."

"Yes, Baron."

"Make the entrance door secure, and Mog –"

"Yes, Baron."

"No mirrors. A bed, a table and a chair. Will she need anything else?"

"No, Baron." Mog never asked impertinent questions, but his face betrayed his curiosity.

"Yes, *she*. Mog, we're starting a new line of business. I shall sire babies and sell them. I have my first queen identified, but she won't be here for a while. You will be ready. There will be more queens later, but for now we'll make preparations for the first."

There was a brief pause. "Yes, Baron."

"You have a problem with this?"

"No, Baron. I am, as always, in awe of your business acumen." Mog never smiled. Today he made an exception.

Craig didn't need Mog's approval but enjoyed it. He levelled his stare at Mog.

"I want the entrance to the basement obscured. I don't want the ordinary person to see it's there."

Mog's smile lingered. "Yes, Baron."

"One more thing." Craig brushed his hand over the brochure on his desk. "I still want a publicity drive when the Napier girl is free from the Cavendish. No one will know where she went."

Mog's smile widened. "Baron…"

"Yes, Mog?"

Mog guffawed. "Baron, you're a genius!"

14

Monday 30ᵗʰ August, 9 am

Dr. Alexander Fadden walked from the car park to the front doors of the Progenetics Midfield West Laboratory. He always enjoyed the short commute to work because it took him out of Midfield and into the beautiful countryside. The building's stark, angular architecture, with its darkened, mirror-glazed windows, looked out of place among the trees and greenery.

He paused before entering the building to enjoy the fresh autumn aromas, which he wouldn't smell again until he left at the end of a long day. It helped clear his head of the headache that had troubled him the last few weeks.

These were exciting times. His research team was on the verge of a major new breakthrough. Success was in the air, reminiscent of that day, four years ago, when he'd hoped for a similar success at their sister lab the other side of town, Midfield East. There he'd been working towards a solution for Carrick Syndrome, the genetic flaw preventing the development of ovarian follicles, rendering most women infertile.

Alex had worked on the research team for about eight years, heading it for the last four. During that time he fell deeply in love with one of the volunteer research subjects, Janet. They decided to marry, but for ethical reasons, he waited until her involvement in the research concluded.

He hadn't found a cure, but working alone late one night he discovered something very interesting. The age sixteen fertility test used by the Guardians of Life was fallible. One in every five million who tested infertile was actually fertile. That in itself was a huge discovery with far-reaching implications.

Government policy on fertility testing, and on who was required to spend their life in an atelier, was based on the test's infallibility. If they knew the results of this research, they would retest the entire free female population under the age of menopause. They would also change the law releasing a girl from further obligation after she failed the test once. He would be unpopular among the family and friends of anyone who retested fertile.

All of that he could live with. He was a scientist, after all. He was searching for truth, not popularity. He could even publish the work without his name on it. If he asked, Progenetics would agree to take credit for the result. But there was a much bigger problem. Janet retested fertile. He intended to marry her and spend the rest of his life with her, not condemn her to a life of servitude in an atelier.

He'd worked late into the night altering the data so his team would never realise the Guardians of Life test was fallible – that Janet was fertile. He couldn't carry on with the work after that. He didn't want to. He discussed it with Janet, and they decided she would withdraw as a research subject, and he would seek a transfer to the other lab to work on Metzner's Disease, which afflicted most males.

Entering the building, he muttered under his breath, "For the greater good," as was his recent habit on arriving at work.

His close relationship with the researchers in Midfield East had proved very useful. A serum provided by his friend Dr. Harland, prepared from fluids extracted from certain of her patients' spinal cords, had opened the door for their present advances.

Neither of them liked the price Dr. Harland's patients were

paying, but the results for their Metzner's Disease research were too important to allow such squeamishness.

Alex had told his team the serum was a by-product of Dr. Harland's research at Midfield East, and no more. They were both Progenetics labs, so Alex obtained the serum without documentation, and he'd worry about the ethics himself.

He pushed open the door to his laboratory and faced the usual bustle of activity. Assistants and technicians went about their daily routine. Claire and Ralph were already there. His senior researchers were both early starters, although Alex preferred to savour his breakfast and work later. When he first applied for a job at Progenetics, the interviewer said, "We only hire the best people." Claire and Ralph were living proof of that.

Claire looked up as Alex came in. "Hi, Alex. Big day then."

Alex wanted to be optimistic, but long experience told him the results of tests could differ from even the most confident expectations.

"Yes," he said. "Let's hope so. Are we all set for Jake's tests?"

Jake Roseberg was their voluntary test subject, an ordinary infertile male. If the procedure worked, he would be the first to become fertile. Technically, he would have to go to an atelier. But surely with a cure, there would be no need to send fertile males to ateliers. He ought to stay free.

Alex and his team couldn't make any promises about the legal status of the subject if the test was successful. They found no lawyer or government department willing to offer clarification. Volunteers had to take their chances, and Jake was one of the few who said yes. Jake's father was the smart one who had secured Progenetics' promise to pay the legal cost of his fight to stay free. Jake might not be the sharpest tool in the drawer, but he wanted to be in the news – the new stud everyone talked about.

Alex didn't approve of Jake's craving for notoriety but overlooked it for the sake of the research.

Jake was the first to receive the new treatment. Alex hoped the introduction of an engineered Y chromosome, derived from the serum supplied by Dr. Harland, would stimulate the necessary repairs to the host Y chromosome.

A cure for Metzner's Disease would consign the first half of the human fertility catastrophe to history. There might even be a Nobel Prize. As a bonus, it would renew hope that the research at Midfield East would find a cure for Carrick Syndrome, the dominant cause of female infertility.

Alex went to the drinks dispenser and was on his way back into the lab with three coffees, balanced on a book, when his com-pak beeped. "Agh. Ralph, take this, would you?"

Ralph took the precarious arrangement with two hands. Alex licked his hand where the hot coffee had spilled over the edge of the book and tapped his com-pak to answer the call.

"Dr. Fadden, I have Mr. Roseberg in reception for you."

"Excellent. Thank you. Someone will collect him shortly."

Alex beckoned Sam, one of the technicians, and asked him to collect Jake from reception. While he waited, he sipped his coffee and talked over the arrangements with Claire and Ralph.

"Claire, we'll need to apply for government approval to use an atelier queen for our testing if he proves to be fertile. Can you get onto the legal department and babysit them through the process? I don't want this to go wrong. If we're denied, it's going to be much harder to apply again."

"Okay." Claire frowned. "But don't you think we're a little premature? We've no idea if this test has worked, and we'll not know for at least twenty-four hours. Shouldn't we hold off until we know we have something to test?"

Alex sighed. "I know. You're right, of course. But I don't want to wait. If we get a positive test result, we'll go down in history as the ones who did it. But we don't have any way to know whether any other company is on the brink of the same discovery. We can make the first atelier baby from a cured male father. That's what this is all about, isn't it? The end result has to be babies, not just test papers showing great data. But if someone else got there first, we'd be forgotten."

Ralph and Claire stared at him. Maybe he'd gone too far. He was a scientist seeking the truth, seeking solutions. It wasn't dignified to become agitated about who beat whom to the result. What mattered was the research, not the people who did it.

He turned away, embarrassed at his outburst, and sipped his coffee. The door opened and a white coated technician led Jake in.

"Thank you, Sam. Hello, Jake." Alex offered his hand and Jake shook it.

"Bloody hell, mate. Can't you just get me a pass or something?" asked Jake. "It's a bleeding nightmare getting in this place."

Alex smiled. "I hope I can offer you a place in history. Maybe more. If this works, you will have a son or a daughter. Just think. But no, I can't get you a pass into this building. I'm afraid Progenetics won't let me." He cast his eyes down in an apologetic gesture of humility.

"Blimey. We'd better get on with it then."

Sam walked out. Alex led Jake to a seat and asked him to sit.

"I have just a few questions for you. I hope you don't mind."

Jake shrugged.

"Since we administered the gene therapy drug yesterday, have you had any alcohol or drugs, prescription or otherwise?"

"Come on, mate. What do you take me for? You said yesterday –"

"I know." Alex raised a pacifying hand. "I know what I said, but please understand. I have to ask these questions to satisfy the authorities who administer the clinical trials."

"Yeah, yeah. I know all about that." His face brightened. "I know about clinical trials. I saw that video you showed me. Bloody amazing, some of that stuff. Blimey." He exhaled heavily. "Did you know –"

"Jake, I know what the presentation says. I was in it, remember?"

Jake was thoughtful for a moment, then laughed. "Oh, right, yeah, you were with that bloke –"

"Right, well let's get on with this, shall we?"

Alex worked his way through the remainder of the short list of questions required for this stage of the clinical trial. Ralph and Claire watched with amused expressions.

"Now, we have to take a biopsy from one of your testes. We need you to lie on this bed and Ralph will insert a special needle. It only takes a small sample of tissue."

"Shit. You're not poking me in the balls with that thing." Jake's eyes bulged and his face reddened.

"Jake," Alex sighed heavily. He'd talked Jake through this several times already. "Don't you want to go on? We can stop the whole clinical trial for you if that's what you want."

"No, mate, just…" Jake looked around as though desperate. "Just get on with it. All right?"

Alex hoped that would be the last of the drama. He stood back while Ralph drew a curtain around the bed and, with help from one of the assistants, carried out the biopsy procedure. He took the sample and left the lab with it.

They needed to calm Jake's nerves somewhat, but he would be okay, and the rest was just a matter of staying polite and getting him out of the lab as quickly as possible. Claire was more outwardly compassionate than Alex, so he left her to gather Jake up and get him back to reception.

Ralph would set up the tests on the biopsy sample. If the results came back negative, the team's hopes would be dashed. If positive, they would test his sperm. The outcome could signal probably the greatest ever advance in genetic medicine. The world would never be the same again.

15

10 pm

Dr. Robyn Harland stood at the door to Kevin's room and watched him sleep. The patterned quilt rose gently with each breath, a barely audible wheezing sound with each exhalation. Kevin's face was turned towards her, mouth open, a little dribble running into the pillow.

Just fourteen years old, and Kevin could expect to live maybe another fifteen years. More if he was lucky. The true cruelty of Bartrev-Moskalet's Disease, however, was not in the shortened life expectancy so much as in those symptoms that undermined his quality of life, eroding what was left as his condition degenerated. Slow, inexorable, ultimately deadly.

Robyn had never wanted to get involved in the research team. Three years ago, she was happy working in Progenetics' Midfield East laboratory towards a cure for Carrick Syndrome. She had no desire to bring up a child, and the resulting, inevitable emotional detachment from the work enabled her to maintain a focus and keep pushing the research forward wherever it led.

It led in a direction she didn't expect. She established a link between Carrick Syndrome and Bartrev-Moskalet's Disease, showing they were closely related genetic disorders. She was due a promotion, and management's recognition of her discovery secured an offer of her own research team, her own funding, a lab, and a fully staffed residential facility. She would host twelve Bartrev-Moskalet's Disease patients and research to find a cure.

Even though she would have preferred to stay with the Carrick Syndrome research, this was an opportunity too good to miss. If she turned down the offer, she would be branded as a person without the necessary drive for success. Someone else would take the project, and her career would stagnate.

It turned out the so-called residential facility was more like a hospital wing than a home, and despite many long arguments, she failed to raise the funds to make it more comfortable. The promotion, it seemed, came with limited power.

The disease was instantly recognisable, and Kevin showed all the classic signs. The extra high forehead and small ears, the drawn, emaciated look of the face, and when undressed, the rest of the body. He suffered all the other usual symptoms as well, mostly related to severe learning difficulties, incontinence, and a tendency to become nervous with little cause.

None of that, though, had anything to do with personality, and that was where Kevin shone. He was a beautiful person, loving and generous, and he always responded warmly to the people around him. His tendency to nervousness was due to innate fear because he trusted people implicitly and made new friends easily. She couldn't help but grow to love him in return.

Now Robyn went to Kevin's bedside and crouched down to his level. Looking into his face, her mind formed the same words as the last time she'd done this. *For what I'm about to do, please forgive me.*

She glanced at the door, but there was no need. The care staff had finished their evening rounds and wouldn't check the rooms again for another hour. The whole residential wing was quiet, as though sleeping.

She carefully rolled Kevin over onto his front, lifting his nightshirt to expose his back. She took a syringe and a phial from her lab coat pocket and drew the dark liquid into the syringe, then injected it into the skin over Kevin's spine.

While the anaesthetic did its work, she pulled a rack of equipment near and turned each piece of equipment on. The displays all came to life, registering their settings as each established a connection to the computer facility.

Robyn dialled in Kevin's name and pulled up the system parameters to correspond with his profile. Once the displays settled, she checked everything, then took the probe from its cradle. It was connected to the equipment by a long hose containing thin tubes and fibre-optic cable. She attached a sterile needle to the business end of the probe and rested it back in its cradle.

She turned back to Kevin's bed, leaned down, and gently kissed him.

"I love you."

She knew Kevin couldn't hear, but that wasn't going to stop her saying it. She took the probe and poised it over the gap between the first and second vertebrae.

"I'm sorry, darling. I wish there was another way."

Her earlier tests had yielded groundbreaking results. The machine created a serum from cerebrospinal fluid, but once extracted, the patient's rate of degeneration increased.

That alone was good enough reason never to take the fluid again, except the serum probably held the key to a cure, or at least a way to slow or even stop the degeneration. Unfortunately, the research could only continue if she took more spinal fluid. And the patients' deterioration would accelerate until the research was successful.

Another result came as a blow to the team. When the fluid was extracted, the patients' bodies did not naturally replace it, and stimulation hadn't worked so far. Some suggested that they attempt to synthesise the serum, but Robyn knew that because of its genetic complexity, they were a long way from inventing the technology to synthesise such a product.

The team was stuck with a terrible choice. Carry on the research, but extract the serum at terrible cost to the patients, or re-direct their research to ways to stimulate the spinal cord to manufacture more fluid. The team chose the latter course and started work in earnest.

That was all very well until one day when Robyn was talking over these results with her friend, Dr. Alex Fadden, of the Midfield West laboratory. He was particularly interested in the composition of the serum and asked for a small sample to carry out some tests of his own.

Robyn had known Alex for a long time, and indeed, she'd worked with him on the Carrick Syndrome research team before he moved to the Midfield West lab. She trusted him completely and knew that if anyone could help, he could.

When he came back and told her he'd found the serum could be used to create a cure for Metzner's Disease, she was excited but shocked.

Alex couldn't further his research without more serum, but she could only give him that if she hurt her patients. Even then, the serum could never be used more widely without doing this terrible thing to most of the world's population of Bartrev-Moskalet's Disease patients.

She knew that wasn't a realistic plan, but the prize was huge. It could result in a discovery that would dwarf every other scientific achievement in living memory.

So she agreed to supply serum only on the agreement that some better way must be found. The problem was, she could only supply it by being furtive, going behind her team's backs. So here she was, late in the evening, poised with a tear in her eye and a needle over Kevin's spine.

16

Dominic hurried away from his tutoring session. Today, with no more work scheduled, he was anxious to see Fru, but first he would do a charcoal sketch for her. He would draw an impression of their new home, in that town far away, where they would be so happy after she was free. A peace offering and reminder that he loved her – and her alone.

There were few people out in Fore Street as Dominic entered his apartment building, anticipating his meeting with Fru, hoping to get her to see the truth. The atelier, outside Midfield, was not on any bus routes, so he called a taxi and arranged a pick-up for fifteen minutes' time.

He sat down to draw. The imaginary new home took on a life of its own. It was reminiscent of her childhood home, which would comfort her, but newer, brighter and bathed in sunlight. He put a house name sign at the end of the path, and on it, he wrote *Over the Moon*.

Finished, he held the sketch at arm's length and inspected it. It was sentimental, but that's how he felt, and she'd felt the same last week. He laid it on the table and sprayed it with fixer so it wouldn't smudge. He slipped it into a large envelope and put on his coat.

On his way to the atelier, he dialled the newspaper archives on his com-pak and searched for Drake. One common theme emerged. Drake was almost always portrayed as a socially minded, benevolent politician and businessman. Occasionally a news report touched on the same subjects as the rumours, but retractions and apologies always followed a few days later.

The taxi climbed uphill towards the atelier, stopping at the grand front entrance. Dominic climbed out with the envelope, anxious to see Fru's face when she opened it.

Inside the foyer, he smiled at Aaron who sat behind the reception desk. He'd known Aaron a long time, and he was always friendly. "Hi, Aaron. I'm here to see Fru. Could you let her know, please?"

Aaron avoided Dominic's eyes. "Sorry, Dominic, she can't have visitors at the moment."

"What's the problem? Surely you can tell her I'm here."

Aaron levelled his gaze at Dominic. "I'm sorry, but you'll have to leave."

"Leave? What on earth is going on? Is Fru okay?"

"I don't know anything, but you won't be allowed in."

This was ridiculous. To be turned away without even an explanation. Dominic's blood rose, but it wouldn't do to let Aaron see his irritation. Aaron was just doing as he'd been instructed and wouldn't want a scene.

"Will you at least get this to her?" Dominic put the envelope containing his sketch on the reception desk in front of Aaron, who took it and put it under the counter without a word.

Dominic went back outside where he tapped his com-pak to call Fru. The call was denied. He placed a call to Hannah and this time it was answered.

"Hannah, Dominic."

"Ah... Oh, hi, Dom. Listen, I can't talk now. I'll call you back later." She hung up.

He placed a call to Mildred Knatchbull, also quickly denied. Now he was worried. It wasn't only Fru who wouldn't take his calls, and Aaron had given him no information at all.

It was one thing if Fru wouldn't see him, but why the stonewall? Why couldn't Aaron tell Fru he was here? He would keep trying to get through to her with voice calls, and he would send her a message to contact him. Sooner or later Fru would reply. He tried to call again, but it was denied.

There was no point waiting around, so he called a taxi.

Back in his apartment, he opened a cabinet, took out a bottle of Afterburner and poured a large one. He put some drawing paper on the table, and on the first sheet, he drew the layout of the Cavendish. He showed all he could remember and made detailed sketches of the parts he knew best. Then he made a list of the staff and notes about what kind of people they were, how much of a threat they posed or how much help they might be.

Under normal circumstances, a few of the staff would be sympathetic and helpful. Of course these weren't normal circumstances. Nobody would talk to him, but he'd crack that. He needed help from the inside. He'd find a way.

Next he wrote down everything he knew about shift patterns and security guard duties. He marked the places where he needed more information.

After an hour or so, he felt as though he had made progress. He set his Axis on the news channel. As he sipped his drink, a news item caught his attention.

"The Crown Court in the town of Midfield will hear the case of Craig Drake tomorrow."

Dominic stared at the screen.

"Mr. Drake, who is notorious in Midfield for his good works as a politician, is charged on five counts of murder and extortion."

With five counts of murder, surely he'd be on remand, not free to go about his business. Why on earth would they grant bail? How did Drake manage that?

"This case has, until now, been subject to a reporting ban because of the sensitive nature of the evidence. However, when first one witness and then another were found dead in mysterious circumstances, the police stepped up their investigation.

"Since then a third witness has been found dead, and several jurors have allegedly received anonymous threatening messages. The news reporting ban was lifted late last night despite objections from Mr. Drake's lawyers."

Dominic frowned. *Three dead witnesses.* Fru was in serious danger, and it was his fault.

"We understand Mr. Drake's lawyers have today alleged that much of the key evidence against him has been manipulated and tampered with by the police Criminal Investigation Division. If proved true, this would clear the otherwise untarnished reputation of this politician. Our enquiries have revealed that several officers who were on the case are now under investigation, suspended from duty pending the outcome. This allegation comes as a major blow to the prosecution case."

"Considering the accusations of police misconduct, the witness deaths and alleged jury tampering, a not guilty verdict will be no surprise. Mr. Drake made no comment this morning when he arrived at the court building."

The news camera showed Drake glaring as a reporter thrust a microphone at him. When he saw the camera, he smiled.

"That concludes this report for World News."

Dominic turned off the Axis. Drake might be acquitted, but the court appearance made him vulnerable. He would be distracted with it while Dominic freed Fru.

17

7 pm

Alex climbed from his car with a bouquet of flowers. He was early home from work, and wanted Janet to look back on tonight as one of the most special, most memorable occasions of their wonderful life together.

He walked indoors, and Janet spotted the flowers.

"Wow. Darling, thank you." She peered at him. "Don't tell me – you've been unfaithful and you want me to forgive you."

He roared with laughter. "All you need to forgive me for is being an old fool who loves you more than the world."

She held him close for a moment as though reluctant to let go.

When she released her embrace, he went to the kitchen and took a bottle of wine from the fridge.

"Is there something I should know?" she asked.

"Maybe." He popped the cork. "Let's not rush, though. You can't hurry a good meal."

"I see. The good meal is a euphemism for you tantalising me with whatever's going on?" She appeared pensive for a moment. "I know. You've booked our holiday in Saint Lucia."

He laughed. "Like I said, you –"

"I know. You can't hurry a good meal. All right, you win, but don't keep me waiting too long. Okay?"

He kissed her again. "Don't forget Dom's coming over after dinner. He'll be here around seven thirty."

"I haven't forgotten. Why didn't you invite him for dinner?"

Alex grimaced. "My son has a busy life these days. He couldn't get here that early."

He asked about her day as they ate, keeping the conversation away from his work until she dished up desert. Putting it on the table, she asked, "So what is it? You're building up to tell me something, and you can't keep the smile from your face. Have you been promoted?"

It was time to break the news. "Actually, no. Even if they tried to promote me, I'd say no. I'm in the right job now. I don't want to end up as an administrator."

She waited, her expression an endearing combination of expectancy and impatience.

"Since we married, I've talked you into not having a black market insemination in the hope that our research might succeed. You've been so patient with me, yet sometimes I've thought I'm being unfair, that too much time is passing."

Her eyes widened. He'd broached the big subject. The one they'd talked over so many times, always with the same outcome. Government policy dictated that a married couple could only adopt one child. Never a second. Since he'd been married before and adopted Dominic during that marriage, he would not be allowed to adopt again.

If they had another child, they would need new identities, and Alex would have to leave behind his name and his career. If they chose a black market insemination, he would have no realistic chance to father a baby of his own. Their one chance for a natural baby would be if he found a cure for Metzner's Disease.

Of course, she couldn't be seen pregnant. People would have to believe they had adopted. They would have to tell everyone they were taking a year away and go somewhere where she could stay out of sight. Once the baby was born, they would get black market identities and move somewhere nobody knew them.

He saw that she was calculating, but she wouldn't want to raise her hopes.

"Well, today we got the final results from some critical tests. We've treated a volunteer with a gene therapy drug called Priapus that, put simply, should solve his infertility. We got the positive results of the 46XY gene analysis and as far as we could tell, it worked. Today we got the results back from the semen tests."

"Oh, God! You've done it?"

"He's fertile."

Janet burst into tears, and he put his arms around her. This wasn't only the greatest moment of his career, but it was the best blessing their marriage could have received. They would be able to have a baby of their own.

He knew they wouldn't get much sleep that night, but he didn't care. He'd been able to bring Janet the best possible news.

He found her gazing into her wine glass, a smile on her lips, as though enjoying a private joke.

"Care to share?" he asked.

"Oh, I was just thinking. You said you'd called the gene therapy drug Priapus. It just seems so appropriate. Inspired really."

"Well, yes. Greek god of fertility. He seemed a good choice."

"Ah." She sniggered. "I take it you know the story of Priapus."

Alex hadn't expected this. "Story? Like I said –"

"God of fertility, yes, but you knew he was infertile, right?"

"Er –"

"He was the son of Dionysus and Aphrodite. It was a kind of stop, start love affair. More stop than start, and more affair than love. Anyway, she fell pregnant, and at the end of it all, out popped Priapus."

"Well," said Alex, "doesn't seem too much like a god of fertility to me, but who am I to argue with the classicists?"

"Oh, you haven't heard the best bit. He had a massive" – she hesitated as though to choose her words carefully – "a massive thingy. You know. He was more than just well endowed. He could terrorise neighbourhoods with it. I mean, it was, you know…big." She took a long sip from her wine.

Alex was beginning to feel uneasy. Maybe Priapus wasn't such a clever name after all.

"Anyway," Janet continued, "He was ugly and had this notable deformity, so his parents abandoned him, and he was taken in by some shepherds. He had to guard their orchard for them, and every time anyone came along…" She snorted and took another sip of wine. "He would wave his great thingy at them and scare them off."

Priapus was a disastrous name.

"Well, as you can imagine," said Janet, "there weren't many apples stolen." She laughed out loud.

"I wish I hadn't chosen the name now. We'll be the laughing stock." said Alex.

"No, don't worry about that. Most people won't have any idea what the name means. Of those who do, most will think the same as you did. Trust me, anyone who knows the story will die laughing at your sense of humour. It's a great name."

She peered into his face, laughter sparkling in her eyes. After a moment, her expression turned serious.

"Darling, this news is unbelievable. If you hadn't told me yourself, I wouldn't believe it. But it's true. You've succeeded."

He hoped he'd never have to tell her of the real cost of the success. He needed to talk to Dr. Harland now. Priapus wouldn't exist without the serum she supplied, but they had to think of a way to make it legal. A way to deal with the inevitable public outcry when the true cost of its production was known.

18

8 pm

Dominic pushed his hat firmly into place and stepped from the bus into the heavy rain. He turned up his coat collar and hurried to the large Georgian terraced house. Up the front steps stood his father and Janet's ever welcoming front door.

The dinner invitation hadn't been a surprise, but he'd already agreed to a tutoring session, so he'd had to settle for drinks later. The door opened as he reached the top of the stairs.

"Hi, Dom. Come on in. You're soaked!"

"Hi, Dad, Janet." He came into the warm front hall and smelled the delicious aroma of dinner. He took off his hat and coat. His dad shook his hand and Janet gave him a hug. He followed them into the living room where his dad poured him a large glass of wine.

When they all had their glasses, Dominic's father raised his and said, "I've got some big news. It's not public knowledge yet, but I want to tell you." He glanced across at Janet, who smiled broadly. "We've found a cure for Metzner's Disease."

Dominic's heart leapt. "A cure? You mean you can make an infertile man fertile?"

His dad took a sip from his wine. "Not in every case, no. But when it's caused by Metzner's Disease, we're pretty certain now that we can cure it. We have one successful trial subject already."

Dominic sat down heavily. "Wow, Dad! Congratulations. That's amazing. But…" He struggled with the enormity of the implications. "Everything's going to change now, isn't it?"

His father frowned. "Steady on. This does nothing for infertile women, and we're probably years away from any solution to that. Carrick Syndrome is a much bigger problem. A small number of fertile men can sire plenty of babies, but nature dictates that a small number of women can only bear limited numbers of babies."

They talked about the implications, the trial and what the news meant to the world until Dominic's stomach rumbled. Janet cleared her throat. "Alex, why don't you offer Dom something to eat?"

"Oh, of course. I'll grab some snacks." He left the room.

Dominic was glad she'd suggested it. He'd had no time for dinner.

Janet smiled. "How's Fru?"

He didn't really want to answer, but he wasn't going to lie. "Things aren't going well at the moment. I haven't seen her for a few days."

"Oh? I hope it's nothing too serious. She's such a lovely girl."

Dominic's dad came back in with a tray of snacks and put it on the table in front of him.

"Thanks." He turned back to Janet. "I'm afraid it is pretty serious. Fru's refusing to see me, and it seems she has good reason. I think it's my fault."

His dad narrowed his eyes. "What's happened?"

Dominic didn't want to go into too much detail, but he gave them a summary of what had happened. His father and Janet listened in silence. He didn't mention Craig Drake's name but explained that he had hired someone to get her free. Janet winced, and his father's frown deepened. When he told them about the photographs, Janet gasped.

"Surely she doesn't believe that?"

Dominic lifted an eyebrow. "Why shouldn't she? After all, she's been gone for four years. She only has my word for what I've been up to in that time."

"Yes, well," said his father. "I'll go and see her if you want."

Dominic let out a mirthless laugh. "Thanks, but I need to convince her myself."

Silence fell and they all sipped their wine while Dominic picked at the snacks. After a few minutes, wishing to bring back the earlier positive mood, he broke the silence.

"Anyway, I intend to get her out first. One way or another, I'll get her free and safe."

"Will she be carrying a baby when she's freed?" asked Janet.

"Actually, I can't be sure. Not if she's out before they've done a successful insemination."

"I see. That would be a shame." She turned an intense look on his father.

"Yes," said Dominic. "I won't adopt an atelier baby from a captive mother. I can't bring myself to put somebody through that."

His dad returned Janet's intense look, then turned to Dominic. "Dom, would you get another bottle of wine from the kitchen?"

Dominic went to the kitchen. He usually drank beer, so picking a wine from the rack of someone who was more of an expert was challenging. He made his selection and went back to the living room. On entering, he found his father and Janet deep in conversation. They stopped as he came in.

"I chose a Corbières. Is that okay?"

"Splendid, Dom. Thank you." His dad took the cork from the bottle. "Dom, if Fru's not carrying a child when you get her free, what will you do? She'll want to start a family."

Dominic had so far pinned his hopes to her being pregnant and didn't really want to consider the prospect of being childless. "I don't know. I suppose I'll have to wait for your cure to be available. I just don't know if I'll be able to get a treatment."

His dad smiled. "Well, if you need a treatment, let me know.

I can't do it legally, but I'm willing to treat you – as long as you're careful that nobody sees Fru pregnant. After the next few weeks, I can treat you any time you wish."

Dominic stared. "You'd do that for me? I don't want you taking a risk like that for me."

His dad nodded. "Thank you, but honestly I can do it without any real risk. Trust me, nobody will know."

Dominic's heart pounded. This was his chance to become fertile. Every man's dream and some men's worst nightmare. It was no nightmare for him, though. Considering his plans, he'd never hoped for such good luck.

"Wow, Dad. Thank you."

They toasted each other with Corbières.

"Are you going to Brett's re-enactment on Saturday?" asked Dominic.

"He's invited us," said Janet. "But we won't be able to make it. He says they're doing the Bataille Pas de Calais."

"Oh, yes," said his dad. "If you poke a sleeping tiger, you have to stand and fight. Very apropos."

Dominic frowned. "I suppose so."

Later, when Dominic left, Janet gave him a warm hug. His father shook his hand and Dominic walked out into the rain. Despite the weather, he decided to walk home. The rain had eased since he arrived, and it fell in a fine drizzle, pleasantly cool, dampening his face and hands.

He had to let Fru know that he would be fertile. He wouldn't risk even an encrypted message for his dad's sake. The new cure would soon be in the news, though. He would do a charcoal sketch of himself, with an exaggerated grin, receiving an injection in his backside from his father. She would understand.

19

"Get off." Craig Drake slapped the young woman's bare thigh. She got up from his lap and walked to the door. "I may want you later. Be available." Trish nodded and left the room.

Irritating little woman really, but she had a great body and knew what to do with it. She had opinions, though, and liked to make them known. Maybe he'd get Mog to cut her tongue out.

He tapped his com-pak. "Mog."

"Yes, Baron."

"Get Gurt and come here."

"Yes, Baron."

The great thing about Mog was he didn't express any opinions other than occasionally praising Craig. Gurt was the same. They did as they were told and mostly did a good job.

The door chime sounded and Gurt and Mog walked in. Craig indicated the burgundy red seats and they sat.

"What's the status of the Knatchbull woman?"

Gurt's face creased into a pained expression, but Mog replied. "Our contacts tell me she's the one who formulated the Nationalist Party policy on..." He pulled a scrap of paper from his pocket and read from it, "...*austerity and ethnic purity for atelier breeding programme management.*" He grinned. "She wants the ateliers to be more like a farm and less like a luxury hotel. She wants to maintain racial purity."

"She still has her committee position in the party?"

"Yes, Baron."

"And she's still after a position as a member of their National Executive?"

"Yes, Baron."

"Good. As long as her government bosses don't know about her little political exploits, she's in my power." He watched Gurt and Mog for a few moments to let that sink in. Mog, at least, would understand the consequences of Knatchbull losing her job now. It would be disastrous, and he would hold Mog responsible.

"We don't have any of the other Cavendish staff working for us. We need to change that. Knatchbull will no longer be enough."

"Yes, Baron." Gurt and Mog both replied.

"Any leads on who we can use?" He looked from Gurt to Mog.

"We'll get right on it, Baron," said Mog.

"Good. You will recruit at least two more members of the atelier staff."

"Yes, Baron."

"I don't want this costing me. Use the usual methods. I'm not paying them."

"No, Baron."

Gurt and Mog left his office. He stared at his bridged hands. This would take careful planning.

Back in his private suite, he went to the bedroom. The scent thrilled him as he entered. Dahlia, who always said all the right things at the right times. She was there when he wanted her and absent when he didn't. There would definitely be a suite for her on the yacht when he bought it.

He lowered himself onto the bed beside her and kissed her lips. "I'll need to do some preparation for tomorrow's hearing."

Dahlia stroked his cheek. "I took the final documents to

Gilmour this morning. The prosecution is relying on luck. They haven't a case. He says their real motive is to give you bad publicity."

Craig didn't trust most lawyers, but he trusted Gilmour. "Champagne?"

"Thank you." She smiled, but he saw sadness in her eyes.

"There's something wrong. Is it your mother?"

"No, really, she's fine. Champagne would be lovely."

"Tell me."

Dahlia lowered her eyes. "She's not doing well. They can't seem to stabilise her after the fall, and she's getting worse. I just think they don't have the resources to care for an old person who's broken her hip."

Craig gazed into her eyes for a moment, then sat up and tapped his com-pak.

"Mog, call the Midfield Central Hospital and have them put Mrs. Claren, who is on the Ballentine ward, into a private room. Tell them she's to have full twenty-four hour care. Call Mr. Avery at the Grosvenor Street clinic and engage him to take care of her. Tell him she's my personal friend."

"Yes, Baron."

20

Wednesday 1st September, 12 noon

Walking home after class, Dominic found two messages on his com-pak. Maybe Fru had finally relented. A message now would be wonderful.

Querying his com-pak, he found one cancelling his evening tuition session. The other asked if he would help a child who was set to fail his maths exam. Nothing from Fru. His heart sank. He decided he would try to call her later in the morning. For now he sent a message. "I love you. I hope you are all right. Miss you. xx."

Yesterday, Hannah hadn't called back as promised, and he wasn't going to pressure her. She was in a difficult situation, and he wanted to be as friendly as possible rather than make her life awkward. If nobody would speak to him, he was fumbling in the dark. If only there was another way to get information from inside the Cavendish.

Back home, he called his friends to see if anyone was free. Tim said he would come straight around. Gerald said he would see him in the evening, and he couldn't contact the others.

After half an hour of fretting, he heard the door chime. He made coffee and told Tim of the latest developments – that he'd be turned away from the Cavendish.

Tim sighed. "Bloody hell, mate, I just realised you don't know.

I'm dating Hannah."

"Hannah? You mean Hannah from the Cavendish?"

Tim nodded.

"Christ, Tim. That's fantastic!"

Tim chuckled. "We had our first date last Monday. She's really nice." He reddened a little. "I haven't seen her since Thursday, though. She's had extra shifts, so she said we could meet this week. Hopefully I'll see her tomorrow."

Dominic frowned. "Extra shifts? I wonder."

"Well, it sounded okay when she said it, but after what you just told me, do you think she's avoiding me?"

Dominic slumped into his chair.

"Come on, mate," said Tim. "Come to the Share and Coulter and have some lunch. It's on me."

They walked to the pub. The bar was quiet, so they ordered sandwiches and beer and took them into the Snug Room. Dominic couldn't hold back what was on his mind.

"I was wondering. I don't want to ask anything you're not comfortable with, and I wouldn't take advantage of your friendship with Hannah, but if there's some way for you to find out why nobody at the Cavendish will talk to me… I don't know what else to do. I'm desperate."

Tim thought for a moment. "It's okay. I don't mind. Hannah might not be able to talk about it, but she'll want to help. I just hope she's not having a hard time, whatever's going on."

"Me too. I like Hannah."

Dominic contemplated his beer. How could something so bitter taste so good? There was nothing good about the bitterness of rejection.

"I know I can't back out of paying Drake what I agreed to, or he'll kill me. But I intend to get her out myself. Before he does. All I've done, paying him, is make it more urgent. He's dangerous."

"What made you change your mind?"

"A lot of things. I told you about Martin, didn't I? My friend at work."

Tim wrinkled his brow. "Er…was he the one who put you in contact with the Baron?"

"Yes. Well, last week, when he came in to work, he wouldn't talk to anyone. He seemed depressed. Anyway, he hasn't turned up at work since then, so he's lost his job. He's disappeared. Doesn't answer his calls or anything. It's just not like him."

"You think that might be something to do with the Baron?"

"Seems likely, doesn't it? Honestly, I think I had a vision of Drake as the new Robin Hood. You know, making his fortune from the wealthy and helping the needy."

Tim's voice was gentle. "I know you did."

"Now Martin's disappeared and Drake is blackmailing officials and stealing atelier babies. Fru won't answer my calls, the atelier staff are stonewalling me, and Drake is in the news evading justice and murdering people. I thought I could trust him, but I just don't believe it anymore. I have to get Fru out before he gets to her."

"You've been talking about getting her out for years," said Tim. "What can you do now you couldn't do before?"

Dominic thought for a moment. "It will need careful planning." He stared into his beer. "Look, Tim, I'm going to need all the help I can get. Will you help me?"

Tim smiled. "Any way I can, mate."

"Let's start by trying to find out what Hannah knows. Meanwhile I'll come up with some ideas. I know the Cavendish pretty well, and I know the people and the security. I just hope I can find a way to get around the security and get her out."

After eating, as they finished their beer, they agreed that Tim would talk to Hannah. Dominic would start planning.

Back at home, Dominic took out his diagram of the layout of the Cavendish. On it, he marked all the security cameras he had seen. He made notes about the security doors, the control panels he knew of, and the route from the front doors to Fru's room.

He knew he couldn't get Fru out without help. Hannah was

his best chance, so he needed to work towards getting her to talk to him.

He also knew he had allies on the outside. Tim and Brett had already offered, and he was sure the others would want to play their parts.

He pulled out a fresh sheet of paper and sketched on it. He drew a cartoon of a small group of people, himself and his friends, running along carrying Fru over their heads. Behind them, standing powerless in front of the atelier and shaking their fists, he drew an angry Craig Drake and Mildred Knatchbull.

Five willing friends were a great encouragement, but without strategy and planning, there would be no hope. Maybe when he met Gerald later he would get more ideas. He needed them.

21

2 pm

Francesca stood as close to the foyer as she could. Any closer and her identity chip would trigger the alarm. A small crowd of queens and lords stood behind her. They all watched through the glazed doors as a convoy of police cars stopped in the driveway. A group of armed pekays came into the foyer and met Mildred Knatchbull who, together with Ingrid, arrived from the corridor with Kelly Walton in handcuffs. The queens and lords behind Francesca talked in low murmurs.

Kelly stared at the floor, ignoring the assembled crowd. The pekays surrounded her and marched her to one of the cars. The convoy pulled away and Kelly was gone.

One of the queens spoke. "Mrs. Knatchbull. Where is Kelly going?"

Mildred Knatchbull turned and fixed the girl with an icy stare. The crowd fell silent. After what seemed like an age, Mildred smiled. "Ms. Walton has been transferred to a penal atelier. She will be one of the first." She turned and walked away, the remaining staff following in her wake.

A tear ran down Francesca's cheek. Ignoring the chatter from the queens and lords, she hurried back to her room. Kelly, the sordid photos and the escape plan dominated her thoughts, and keeping it from her friends had become an unbearable strain.

Life had changed already, and the escape was still beyond the horizon. When would it happen?

Now, with her parents due to visit, she would have to avoid the same subjects – the very things that preyed most on her mind. She hated that she could no longer share the most important things in her life with them.

With that thought, a pit opened in her stomach and sucked her in. Mum and Dad! Why had she not realised before? After the escape, they would be under police surveillance. If she visited them, they would all be arrested. They might end up like Kelly's family. Killed by pekays on the way to a detention centre. She would never see them again.

Francesca dropped to her knees and sobbed, tears running over her hands as they covered her face.

There must be a way.

She went to the bathroom, rinsed her face, and studied herself in the mirror. She needed to lift her mood before they arrived, so she went to the glass-fronted book cabinet. There she carefully removed a small copy of *The Rubáiyát of Omar Khayyám* with uncut edges to the pages, one of two hundred and fifty copies of the first edition. The delicate binding crackled as she opened it to one of her favourite stanzas.

The Moving Finger writes; and, having writ,

Moves on: nor all thy Piety nor Wit

Shall lure it back to cancel half a Line,

Nor all thy Tears wash out a Word of it.

Some, she thought, would take these words as acceptance of defeat, but that wasn't the message. The meaning of his words was very different.

It was about the future, not the past. If she wallowed in

the mire of how she arrived here, then she would focus on recrimination and redress. If she planned for the future with the secure knowledge of the lessons she'd learned, she would make a better life. That was what he said with those beautiful, eloquent words.

A message arrived on her com-pak to say her guests were waiting in the visitors' lounge. She took one final look in the mirror, straightened her clothes, and left her suite.

"Hello, Mum, Dad."

Her mum gave her a lingering hug, followed by her dad. Despite her earlier reservations, she was glad to see them. Their presence made life better even at the worst times. She relaxed and smiled.

They chatted about what Francesca had been doing since they last came, and they talked about what her parents had been up to. Soon they came to the subject of Dominic.

"How is he, darling?" asked her mum.

Francesca's stomach jumped. This was just what she was hoping wouldn't happen. She couldn't hide the unhappiness in her face.

"Sweetheart, what's wrong. Have you and Dom fallen out?"

"Oh, Mum." Francesca sniffed and wiped a tear from her eye, looking away from her parents. "I just don't want to see him for a while."

Francesca forced a more upbeat expression into her voice. "Have you heard my news?"

Her dad raised his eyebrows and glanced at her mum. "News?"

"Yes. I've got a free stay." She forced a smile.

"You don't look very happy about it. I'd have thought you'd be over the moon," said her mum.

Over the moon! The same words Dom had used on his sketch. Over the moon would be out of here, with Dom, making a new home and a new life. Would it really happen? Could she stand the consequences? If the escape attempt failed, she would end up in a penal atelier. If it succeeded, she would never be able to see her parents again and wouldn't be with Dom if he'd been unfaithful. It was hard to imagine what she really wanted now.

Her mum gave Francesca a warm hug. "Darling, if you want to have another baby, it's quite natural. I know these aren't ideal circumstances, but you can't fight your instincts. I know that if I were able, I'd be having babies all the time." She glanced towards Francesca's dad, but he was looking at Francesca, concern in his eyes.

If only it were that simple though. It felt wrong not to reassure her poor mum that she did, indeed, have those maternal instincts, but that the whole process was hateful. It felt as though she was doing her mum an injustice. But to attempt to tell her would be like wandering into a mine-field littered with things she couldn't say.

Her parents stayed for a while. When they left, Francesca went directly to her suite and shut herself in, turning off her Axis and her com-pak. How much did she want to be free? Was the price worth paying? To never see her mum and dad again? Maybe she should tell Mr. Drake she just wanted to call it all off.

22

8 pm

Alex was tired. More so than he remembered feeling for a long time. It wasn't lack of sleep. It was, he was sure, a result of two factors. With the success of Jake Roseberg's treatment, he and his team were working long hours, and there was little hope of a day off, even a Sunday, for some while. His headaches were now compounded by persistent pain in his back and neck.

He called to give Robyn yesterday's good news and expected her to be pleased. Her contribution to the work had made a breakthrough possible. Robyn's reaction, however, was subdued.

"I see. So let's get this straight. Your Priapus drug works, and the process to make it relies on my contribution?"

"Yes. That's exactly right. Together we'll have our names on a colossal breakthrough."

After a moment of silence, Robyn replied. "You're not thinking straight. You really aren't. You know you can't publish any results that use that stuff."

"Surely you don't think I haven't thought that through? You'll have to find a way to make the serum without harming your patients. If you can't, then we'll have to find a way to legalise this and convince the public it's for the greater good."

"The greater good? You haven't seen what this is doing to my patients. They're vulnerable, sick people. This is stealing their lives away. Leaving them without hope."

Alex leaned forwards. "I don't like this any more than you do. But have you thought what would happen if another company made the same discovery? Some people won't think twice about using Bartrev-Moskalet's patients to source a cure. If we patent this technique, nobody else can use it. The whole process would be under our control. Your control, Robyn."

Robyn remained silent.

"If you can find a way to make the serum without harming your patients, this won't even be an issue. Re-double your efforts. Find a way."

"We're doing everything we can, but we may be years away from a useful result. We're doing this research for our patients, not for you."

"What can I do to help?"

"You can stop putting pressure on me. You can accept that your research needs the results of ours, and you'll have to wait."

Their conversation ended on an uneasy note. Robyn would continue her efforts, but she might not come up with a better way for years. He couldn't hold back on announcing the discovery. If he waited, someone else would get there first, and the future of his work, his lab, would be jeopardised along with the lives of many more Bartrev-Moskalet's patients. Maybe all of them.

He hoped for a miracle, but he couldn't rely on one. His one consolation was that Robyn was one of the best researchers he'd ever met. If anyone could do this, she could.

Alex had met some of Robyn's patients, and his knowledge of their genetic disorder was deep. A combination of physical and mental disabilities made it difficult for them to function in society. That alone would make his team's work an emotive subject with the public.

If they could get the serum from a different source, they would. They had to find a way to make it without harming the patient, but the real harm was minor when considered alongside the benefits of doing so.

After the call, he breathed a deep sigh and went home for dinner. Janet must have noticed that he was quiet, thoughtful, rather than his usual self, but she waited until they'd eaten to interrupt his reverie.

"Penny for your thoughts."

"Oh, just thinking about work. There's a lot to do, and time is of the essence."

"I was wondering…" Janet didn't finish the sentence.

"Wondering what?"

"Well, now you know how to make an infertile test subject fertile, when do you think you'll try the gene therapy drug on yourself? Is it safe?"

He'd known this would be coming and had given it plenty of thought.

"Soon. We're monitoring Jake Roseberg to watch for undesirable effects, but we won't know for sure whether it's safe until we've completed the clinical trial. That'll take two and a half years."

"But at some point, you'll have enough confidence in it to be sure for yourself, won't you? I know that doesn't satisfy the requirements of the clinical trial, but you'll be sure long before the regulators are, surely?"

"To be honest, I don't see any risk. I wouldn't have treated Jake if I did. I don't mind having the treatment any time now. We could be trying for a baby within days."

Janet, her expression thoughtful, picked up her wine glass and took a sip, then another.

"I've waited for this moment for years, wondering whether it would ever happen, dreaming that it would. I can't pretend I'm patient about this. I want a baby, and I want it as soon as I can possibly have it. When you said you didn't want me going for a black market insemination, I felt a combination of disappointment and hope. I've lived with that hope ever since, and now I see it happening. The world is changing in front of my eyes and I'll be one of the first to benefit from it."

She sipped her wine again. "I want to be a mother, but I want our child to have a father too. I don't want to take any risks with you. I love you too much to lose you or to have you crippled by some unexpected side effect of the Priapus drug."

"It's okay, darling. I'm confident that it's safe. I'm not going to end up with two heads or father a child who's born inside out." He immediately regretted his words.

Janet sat up straight. "I hadn't thought of that. What if the cure for infertility causes genetic mutation in the children? That would be awful."

Alex sighed. He was tired, and he knew, deep down, that it wouldn't be a problem. He couldn't prove it, but he intuitively knew. It was as simple as that. She'd picked up on the one issue that could extend the clinical trial by another year, maybe two.

"You have to trust me on this. I shouldn't have made light of it, but that won't happen. I understand genetic disorders and inheritance better than most people alive today, and I can tell you with complete confidence that this process is safe." He'd rarely lied to his wife, but the confidence she would gain from this white lie made it worthwhile.

"I do trust your judgement," she said. She'd sipped her way through her glass of wine, so he leaned across to pour more as she carried on talking, "But we've waited years for this. A few more days isn't going to hurt us."

"A few more days?"

"You're going to be monitoring your patient for any adverse effects, right?"

Alex nodded.

"Give it a couple of weeks. If he's still okay then, I'll feel a lot more confident that you'll be safe to take the treatment."

The truth was a couple of weeks would make little difference to judging how safe the procedure was. But he was confident enough to do it even now, so if waiting two weeks made her happy, it was good enough for him.

23

After his early tutoring session, Dominic worked at his dining room table. First he checked his bank balance and made sure he'd earned enough to pay Drake, then he worked through the escape plans, methodically thinking through every step.

Nobody at the Cavendish would talk to him, and not knowing why made him vulnerable. He had to know, and the only way to find out was to go there. He called a taxi.

Arriving at the Atelier Cavendish, he strode through the large glazed double doors. As usual during the day, Aaron was the greeter. He looked up and visibly flinched. "Hi, Dominic."

Dominic walked to the desk. "Aaron, we've known each other for a few years now, haven't we?"

Aaron's face flushed and he looked away.

"Aaron, there's something happening. I know it's not your fault, but I hope you understand I can't just walk away. I won't do that. I don't want to make anything awkward for you, but I have to find out what's going on with Fru. One way or another I intend to find out."

Aaron cast his eyes down to the reception desk, then without a word he pressed a button on the console. There was a pause while he listened to something in his earpiece, then said, "Hi, it's Aaron." He paused and listened. "Yes, you need to come out here.… Sorry, but yes. Dominic Fadden is here and somebody has to talk to him." He listened again. "Let me know." He pressed another button on the console.

"Aaron, I'm really sorry to put you through this. Thanks."

Dominic went to the waiting area and sat down. This wasn't just Fru in a bad mood with him. There was something much bigger going on, but what? Aaron pressed a button and listened again. After a few seconds, he said, "Thanks."

He turned to Dominic. "Ingrid's coming. She'll be here in a moment."

Dominic racked his mind. His recollection of Ingrid was vague. He remembered a slim lady, nearing retirement age, kindly disposed but very matter of fact and efficient.

Within minutes, the door to the interior of the atelier opened and Ingrid came through. She was tall with long, greying, blonde hair. Dominic stood and shook her hand. She led him into the building to a small room where she offered him a seat.

"What can I do for you, Mr. Fadden?"

If the formality was intended to keep him at a distance, what chance was there of finding anything out? It dawned on him why he knew her.

"We've met before, haven't we? Wasn't it Fru's eighteenth birthday? Didn't we plan some of those surprises together?"

Ingrid shifted uneasily in her seat. "I think so, yes."

"Yes. Yes, I'm sure we did.… She was so happy! Good times, eh?"

"Mr. Fadden, why are you here and what can I do for you?"

"You can tell me what's going on. Ingrid, I love Fru and I won't go away until I know why I can't get through to her. There may be a good reason why she doesn't want to talk to me, but that doesn't account for the fact that everyone else is stonewalling me. You can shut me out, but I won't go away."

Ingrid didn't speak for a full minute. When she did, it was in a softer voice. "Dominic, there are things you can't control. Things you won't get around. I can't help you. It has nothing to do with what I want or what anyone else wants for that matter. It's just the way it is. If you decide to wait here, we'll make you comfortable, but please don't take that as an indication you will get any more. You won't."

"I know you care about what happens to Fru," said Dominic. "I know you can't tell me what's behind all this, but I'd like to ask one thing of you."

Ingrid didn't say anything.

"Please do everything you can to make sure Fru comes out of this all right?"

Ingrid's eyes hardened. She levelled her gaze on him. "Dominic, I assure you Francesca's welfare is foremost on my mind. I will do whatever is necessary, and I will do it willingly irrespective of whether you ask for it."

She was hard to interpret. Was this hostility or passionate intensity that showed her love for Fru? In the end, it didn't matter which. She would look out for Fru and that was what mattered. She clearly wasn't about to tell him what was going on, but at least he had that assurance. It was more than he had when he arrived.

Ingrid stood. "Goodbye, Mr. Fadden."

Interview over. She'd given nothing away whatsoever. He walked towards the entrance foyer, and in the corridor saw Hannah approaching.

"Hi, Hannah."

"Oh, hello, Dominic." She didn't slow down.

He stopped as she passed. "Hannah, it's okay. I'm not going to put you under any pressure. I just want what's best for Fru. I know you're in a difficult position."

She turned to him, visibly relaxing. "Fru's okay, Dom." She glanced at the security cameras. "I can't talk. I need my job." She gave him a look that seemed to say, "I'm sorry. I'd like to help, but I'm too scared."

"See you, Hannah." He walked on towards the foyer. There was no point making her feel awkward, and anyway, she gave him more information in three seconds than Ingrid did in her whole interview. *Fru's okay.*

He knew what he had to do now. With Tim acting as go-between, he would get messages to Hannah and hopefully to Fru. When was Tim planning to meet her again? Tonight?

Dominic would talk to him first.

Calling for a taxi, he walked out into the fresh air. A light breeze, comfortably cool, barely disturbed the leaves. He glanced back at the atelier. Mildred Knatchbull was watching from her office window, arms folded, severe eyes taking in his every move.

24

11 am

Francesca put a cup of coffee on the small table by the sofa and sank into the soft cushions. The sofas in the shared lounge were bigger than the one in her suite, with huge, enveloping cushions that made them the most comfortable sofas in the atelier.

She tried to put the sketch out of her mind. It arrived in the morning post from Dom and depicted him bent forwards with his trousers down and somebody – it looked like his father – brandishing a syringe. She had no idea what it was about and couldn't imagine why it might have amused him to send her such a picture.

Jen was already sitting at the other end of the sofa, and Liang lowered herself into the space between as though her tiny bump made the process difficult.

"Hey, Darlin," said Jen. "So you've come out of your shell for once."

Liang nudged Jen. "Leave her alone. She's alright." She leaned across to Francesca and put an arm around her shoulders.

One of the lords sitting across the room from them smiled.

"Well, look at you. Pretty girls all in a row."

Jen's lip curled. "Shut up. None of us is interested in what you think."

The lord picked up the Axis controller and switched on the

large screen dominating the room.

Liang groaned. "Not the news. Put something else on. I hate the news."

The lord grinned. He turned up the volume and put the controller out of reach of the sofa. A woman newscaster spoke.

"In the news this morning, the pharmaceutical company Progenetics announced a major breakthrough in the treatment of Metzner's Disease, the affliction that makes most men infertile. Researchers in the Midfield West Research Laboratory have treated an infertile volunteer with a new gene therapy drug called Priapus." The announcer's eyebrows rose. "And they claim he is now fertile. From the scene, our science reporter has the story."

The scene switched to show a young news reporter in front of the research lab. She turned to someone who stood out of the picture. "With me is Dr. Alexander Fadden, head researcher in the Metzner's Disease lab here in the Progenetics research facility."

Alex approached and stood beside her.

"Dr. Fadden, this is a momentous discovery. What our viewers want to know, of course, is when they can start to take this treatment."

Alex addressed his answer to the reporter rather than the camera.

"Yes, of course. This is, indeed, a big day for us, but we must be patient. The drug used in this treatment is manufactured in a very complex process, and we don't at this time have a way to make the process repeatable. First we have to solve that problem. Then we can begin a full clinical trial."

"So, what you're saying, Dr. Fadden, is that you don't know when the treatment will be available to the public?"

"That's exactly right, yes. Because of the nature of the treatment, the clinical trial will be of the most complex kind." He smiled. "It does, after all, make genetic changes to the patient. Even when we've created a repeatable process, the trial will take three years or more, depending on the regulators."

The interview continued, but Francesca stopped listening. Her mind was in a spin.

"So," the lord sneered, "still not interested in the news?"

Liang put her tongue out. "You'll be out of a job soon."

"Yeah, and I'll be able to leave this place. You'll still be stuck here, though. Just thought I'd mention it." He laughed.

"Hah. You know Knatchbull," said Jen. "You don't seriously think she'd let you go, do you? You'll be stuck here too, and you'll be even more useless than you are now."

Francesca had heard enough. She could see Dom's sketch clearly in her mind. His father treating him with the new cure? Maybe she would never know, but the picture was dangerous. She had to destroy it now. She got up and walked to the door. She heard Jen say, "Darlin', are you –" and the door shut.

25

12 noon

What a mess. A bloody, bloody mess!

Robyn paced her office, then jabbed her com-pak to make a call.

"This is Robyn Harland." She listened to the PR manager's greeting but wasn't in any mood for it. "Listen. You're running a PR department, not a *piss off the staff* department. What the hell did you think you were doing making the Priapus announcement without first informing the senior researchers?"

There was a pause at the other end of the line.

"Er…we normally send a memo, but it didn't get sent out. Why, what's the problem?"

Robyn contemplated the worst swear words she knew but wrestled enough self-control to keep it moderate.

"Bloody problem? You've no idea."

She hung up. So that was it. Plain, straightforward incompetence. Not even an apology. Anyway, he couldn't undo his blunder now. One little memo lost, and with it went her opportunity to stop the disastrous announcement.

She poised her finger over her com-pak to call Alex but thought better of it. She was angry, and talking to him now wouldn't help anyone.

The announcement took the whole situation out of her

control. Had she really ever had control? Yes, to some degree. If she'd said no to Alex, he'd have had to go along with it. Now, if she didn't supply him with serum, she'd be sabotaging what the whole world saw as their big hope for the future.

She could do that – silently sabotage Alex's plans by saying no. Or do it publicly by telling the media what was going on. Or just carry on and damn the consequences to her patients.

If she tried to silently sabotage Alex's plans, what would be the result? He was a persuasive man who knew her well. He knew exactly what buttons to push to get her to cooperate, so however much she said no, eventually she'd end up saying yes, and it would all start again.

That left just two options. She could publicly discredit the work by telling the media about the true cost of the serum, and in doing so, she could raise awareness of the disease she wanted so passionately to fight. Alternatively, she could keep doing what she'd done to Kevin, hurt even more patients, and still not have a real solution to Alex's need for a reliable supply of the serum.

If she chose to just carry on, she would be harming the lives of twelve people she'd grown to love. People who were vulnerable, who trusted her.

If she went to the media, the cure for Metzner's Disease would disappear into a mire of bad publicity for Progenetics. The newly discovered hopes and expectations of the world would be dashed.

She would be implicated, and as a result her own research would be jeopardised. She might even lose her job. Then how could she help her patients? Or those used in competitors' research?

When Robyn agreed to take this job, assuming responsibility for the twelve people who would be both patients and research subjects, she'd seen the potential for conflict between the needs of those two roles. Even so, she'd never anticipated how heartbreakingly difficult it would be when the conflict arose.

Now she had to choose which way to go, but when she tried

to weigh the alternatives, the immense implications of her decision, she couldn't think straight.

26

1 pm

Dominic leaned over the papers, adding detail to his escape plan. He started a list of questions he wanted to ask Hannah if he had the chance. The door chimes sounded. He gathered up the papers and thrust them into a drawer, then went to the door where two men stood, a little too close. Both were tall and broad, wearing black suits, tight around the muscles of their arms. Dominic recognised them. The one with the pock scarred face and the giant.

"Mr. Fadden, we're here for your payment." The giant's face contorted into what was probably intended to be a smile but was the kind of expression that would give children nightmares. He handed Dominic a small piece of paper with an account number on it.

There was no point arguing with them, so as Dominic made the payment he asked, "So, what's the latest news about Francesca?"

The two men stared at him. The giant maintained his ghoulish expression as if it were fixed. When Dominic completed the transaction, they both turned and walked away.

"Bye then." Dominic pulled a sarcastic smile at their backs. "Nice to meet you. Thanks for coming." He glared at them as they disappeared from view.

27

6 pm

Francesca's mind was in a whirl. She'd destroyed the picture of Dom receiving an injection from his father. She tore it into tiny pieces and flushed it away. Her heart beat a little too fast as she thought back to her mum and dad's visit. She could have either a life in the atelier or a life free of the atelier but with a man who might be sleeping with another woman, and she'd never be able to see her parents again. What if she was freed tonight? She would already have seen them for the last time. Ever. She made a call on her com-pak. "Hannah, are you too busy to come over for a few minutes?"

Hannah promised to be there in ten minutes, and when she arrived, Francesca greeted her at the door.

"Thanks for coming over." They hugged. "I just needed to speak to someone, and you're my best friend."

Hannah smiled. "I thought Dom was your best friend."

Francesca frowned. "I suppose that's what I wanted to talk about."

"Are you sure this isn't just a misunderstanding?"

"Not very easy to misunderstand what Craig said."

Hannah sighed. "Perhaps he doctored the photos. Why do you believe a man like him?"

"Why? You sound as though you know something I don't."

Hannah's eyes widened. "No, no nothing like that. It's just that…I don't know, Fru. There's something about him. You've heard the stories. You know what people think of him."

Hannah's com-pak beeped. She inspected a message. "Well, talk of the devil. It seems I have to set up a meeting room for you to receive a visitor. You'll have to eat dinner later. He's arriving in half an hour."

"Craig?"

"Yes, Craig Drake." Hannah frowned. "Look, I don't know what's going on, but nobody here's allowed to talk to Dom. We've been told he has to be kept away at all costs. I don't understand it."

"What? Told by whom?"

"It came directly from Knatchbull. He's to be kept away from here and from you."

"Nobody told me that." Francesca frowned. "But then they didn't need to, did they?"

Hannah's eyes were sympathetic. "We've been threatened with losing our jobs if we tell him anything or let him in. Nobody knows why. Everyone's scared to talk to him."

Why on earth would the atelier management be interfering like this? "So this is nothing to do with me not wanting to see him?"

"I don't see how it can be. Knatchbull doesn't know how you feel about him."

Francesca pointed to Dom's sketch of a house, lying on the table. "I got this from him. Look. It's beautiful, isn't it?"

"'Over the Moon.' That's lovely." Hannah gazed at the sketch for a few moments, then checked the time. "I'd better go and get a visitor room ready. I'll see which room I can use and send you a message."

After Hannah left, Francesca settled into the sofa. Why was nobody allowed to talk to Dom? Her problems with him were no one else's business.

Maybe Knatchbull had discovered his dealings with Craig

Drake. But how? Anyway, if that was the case, Craig wouldn't be allowed to visit her, but here he was. This was her chance to tell him she'd changed her mind about escaping. To tell him she'd rather stay and be able to see her parents than escape and never see them again.

This time, approaching the door of the visitors' room, she knew who to expect and walked in confidently. When she saw Craig, her heart skipped. He was immaculately dressed. His shoulder length hair gave him a slightly dangerous look, particularly with his dark penetrating eyes. He stood as she walked in and held out his hand to her.

"Hello, Francesca."

She took his hand, expecting a handshake, but he raised her hand to his lips and kissed it, all the time holding her gaze. The corners of his eyes showed the same smile she'd seen before. Her face flushed hot. Nobody had ever kissed her hand, and she enjoyed it. She held his eyes and smiled.

His face had a weathered look, his skin darker than hers, his features hard and strong. She felt physical warmth radiating from his body. Breathing in, she inhaled his aroma, faintly sandalwood and citrus mingled with the natural scent of a man's body.

Craig's voice was kind. Gentle. "I've booked us a table in the Cavendish Restaurant. Will you join me?"

"The Cavendish? You're kidding. That's the best restaurant in the atelier. It's almost impossible to get a table. They're all usually used by senior staff and their visitors." She knew she was babbling, but the reputation of the restaurant was legendary in the atelier, and here was Craig, her visitor, taking her there for dinner. "Did you know they serve real alcohol? Every table is in its own alcove. And they aren't monitored by microphones. I could never have got a table there."

"Come on." He offered his arm and they walked to the restaurant. Francesca smiled inwardly at the envious stares she received from the other queens in the corridors. He was a few inches taller than her, and she knew they looked good together. She'd enjoy herself tomorrow. Her friends would bombard her with questions about the mysterious handsome man, and she'd be enigmatic and keep them guessing.

When they arrived at the restaurant, Craig spoke quietly with the Maître d', who guided them to their table. Craig held her chair while she sat, and as he came around to the chair opposite, she watched his eyes. He suggested martinis and she happily agreed.

The décor of the restaurant was mostly a warm red with low lighting. Each table stood in its own intimate alcove, and a delicate smell of fine cooking permeated the room. Most of the tables were occupied, but Francesca didn't recognise many people. She craned her neck to see who else was there but only recognised some senior staff.

"You're absolutely beautiful tonight." Craig's smile broadened. "Lovely." He was even more handsome than before, and his expression had a flirtatious twinkle that made her stomach flutter.

Should she be enjoying this? Considering everything, Dom could hardly complain if she took pleasure in Craig's company. "You're looking pretty good yourself." Her heart jumped as she wondered if she'd been too forward, but the look in his eye told her he was pleased.

The waiter came over and Craig ordered food. He didn't ask what she wanted but glanced across for her approval as he ordered.

She'd never seen such calm assertiveness before. How should she react? What should she do? She picked up her glass and took a large sip of martini. She glanced at him, wiping the resulting drip from her chin, thankful that he was still occupied with the waiter.

He ran his finger down the wine list and made a suitable choice to accompany the food.

When the waiter left, Francesca said, "There's something

really weird going on with the staff here. They're refusing to let Dom in and won't give him any information."

"Oh?"

"I can't think why that might be. I don't want to see him, but most of them don't know that. Anyway, Hannah told me they were instructed to keep him out."

The Baron frowned. "Who's Hannah?" His voice was sharp.

"She's one of the staff. We're good friends."

"Really?" His smile came back. "That's nice. Anyway, I wouldn't worry about Dominic if I were you. You need to keep your mind on our plans."

"I don't really know what you have in mind. What do you have planned for me, Craig?" She smiled to show she was being cheeky rather than rude.

"Well now, what would you like?"

With a flush of excitement she wondered, if this man fancied her, what kind of future would that hold?

The thought left her warm, compounded by the effects of a large martini with no food.

"Well, I can think of all sorts of things that might be fun, but we should start off with the practicalities, don't you think?"

"That's what I'm being paid for, but I think now I've met you I'd do it whether I was paid or not. You're a very special woman."

She gave him a bashful look. "It's a pity about all this…" She indicated the surroundings with her eyes.

"The restaurant? I'm afraid it's the best one here, sorry."

She laughed. "No, I mean the atelier. The fact that I'm in prison. The fact that I can't choose who comes back to my suite for a coffee later on. Things like that."

"Yes." He studied her for a few moments "Yes, I think so too. Things will change, though."

Things will change. She tingled all over when he said that. Everything he said and did left her knowing she could rely on him. She couldn't put her finger on why, but Craig took away her worries just by being there.

And what was Dom doing now? While Craig was here paying attention to her, was he off with that woman? Doing what?

"I've been given a free stay. Was that anything to do with you?"

"Francesca, I can't answer questions like that. Any answer I give would cause problems. If I say no, you'll think I don't have any influence. If I say yes, someone will overhear and I'll be sent to jail. I'm damned whichever way I answer it. I don't want either of those outcomes, so I'll just leave you to believe whatever you choose."

"They don't snoop at these tables. There are no microphones here. I think you're avoiding the question because you're toying with me, Mr. Craig."

He laughed loudly. "Miss Francesca, I think you're the one who's toying with me."

She laughed. The waiter came over with their food. They sat in amiable silence while he served Parmesan pheasant breasts with crisply cooked prosciutto ham in a bed of vegetables. Craig thanked the waiter.

As they ate, Francesca felt a flutter in her chest at the thought of what all this meant. If Craig really felt something for her, she would be safe. Maybe the escape would be all right after all. He would set her free, and if Dom didn't want her, Craig would look after her. If there was any danger, he'd take care of it. He had his methods that obviously worked well.

She couldn't figure out whether Craig was behind Dom being shut out by the staff, but it seemed likely. He clearly didn't trust Dom, and from what he'd said, there might be good reason. The smile never left the corners of his eyes.

If Craig were to fall in love with her, it would be a real, mature relationship. Seeing him here, gazing at her across the table, her love for Dom felt more like a childhood infatuation. An infatuation with the only boyfriend she'd ever had. How could she know for sure that she was in love if she'd only ever had one boyfriend?

She took a large gulp of wine, and when she put the glass back on the table, it clinked against her water glass. She suppressed a snigger – she didn't want Craig thinking she was drunk.

Craig's com-pak beeped and without looking at it, he tapped it to deny the call. She found herself gazing into his eyes.

She wasn't hungry, but she would continue to pick at her food so the meal wouldn't be over too quickly. He'd probably leave then. She'd be left to read alone. This was heaven compared to the solitude of her room.

They drank wine, ate, and eventually went on to dessert. Her stomach complained at the prospect of more food, but she ordered a dessert anyway, more than a little tempted by the raspberry soufflé with hot chocolate sauce.

Light headed from the martini and wine, she imagined herself back in her room, head on his chest, drawing in the scent of his body while he stroked her hair.

With a jolt, she remembered she was going to tell him she didn't want to escape anymore. Maybe she'd hold off for now. Maybe next time.

Finally, with dessert finished and coffees emptied, she knew their time together was over.

"I don't want this evening to end," said Craig. "But I'm afraid I have some business to attend to. Can you forgive me?"

"Thank you for such a lovely evening. It's been perfect." She paused for a moment. "Craig?"

"Yes?"

"Have you heard about the new penal ateliers?" He nodded. "They terrify me. It's really nice here and those places…they're inhuman."

"Francesca, I give you my personal guarantee that you will never be in one of those places. Trust me, it won't happen."

She relaxed, and after a moment, she smiled. "Thank you. I couldn't bear it."

His hand moved across the table to hers and lightly touched

it. "No. Nor could I."

Her whole body tingled at his touch. "Some of my friends think penal ateliers are there because the Nationalist Party wanted them. I don't really like the sound of that."

The smile disappeared from Craig's lips. "The Nationalists aren't very nice people, Francesca. If they had their way, they'd put me against the wall and shoot me. They'd keep you in conditions that would make penal ateliers look like luxury hotels."

"And they're influencing the government?"

"They're gaining some influence, but they're still a minority. Considering our plans, you don't need to worry about them."

Francesca relaxed as the smile returned to his lips and his eyes danced over her. She'd made their evening together last as long as possible, but it was over now.

At the door to the restaurant, he kissed her hand before walking away. She stood and watched him until he was out of sight, then headed slowly back to her suite. It was late. Their dinner had taken most of the evening.

Back in her room, she poured some blackcurrant vodka. She was already tipsy, but what the heck? This moment was exhilarating. He seemed really taken with her. He was strong, handsome, powerful, and well connected. Best of all, he would save her from this place and take her where she would be safe.

She'd forgotten to ask him about her mum and dad. Anyway, he'd make sure she could see them. He had the power and influence. He would even find a way to get the miraculous new fertility treatment. The prospect was intoxicating.

It was early morning in Sydney Harbour. On her Axis, a huge cruise liner steamed into port with a flotilla of tugs and service vessels in attendance.

Francesca imagined herself in the boat on the ballroom deck. The four-piece band played as a crooner sang the old jazz standards. The ballroom was large, with tables at the edge. Each table had jackets and drinks scattered with no apparent owners because almost everyone was dancing, swaying to the gentle voice and the timeless beauty of the tunes.

On the dance floor, Francesca and Craig held each other close, stepping lightly to the music. He was poised and elegant, his arms around her waist. And she, her arm around his neck, head upon his shoulder, hoped the moment would never end.

28

Friday 3rd September, 11 am

Walking along Midfield high street towards the café, Alex pondered his imminent meeting. His last call with Robyn had been difficult, and he wasn't looking forward to meeting her. She'd made a moral judgement about his actions, and although he disagreed, something deep inside troubled him. What if she was right? What if this was all a huge mistake? This very breakthrough that should make him the most famous name in genetic research could backfire and turn him into a monster reviled by the public.

What if he went into the history books as the man who harmed vulnerable people just to get fame and fortune? Of course it wasn't like that, but the news media knew how to drum up a popular sentiment when they wanted to. If not properly handled, this would make him an irresistible target. Somehow he had to make sure his efforts would be perceived for the success they were.

The Patagonia café was quiet with only three other customers. Two were together, deep in conversation, and another sat alone. Robyn wasn't there, so Alex selected a table where they could talk without being overheard and settled with a coffee to wait.

He enjoyed watching other people. Spending so much time in the lab, he didn't often have the chance to do so, but he found a fascination in strangers that he couldn't explain. He wondered what kind of life they led. What sort of work they did. Whether they were happy like he was with Janet. Whether they worked long hours like he did or had straightforward nine-to-five jobs.

The café door banged open, and Robyn walked in. Her demeanour was brash, which didn't bode well considering that she was such a gentle person. She approached the table and sat opposite Alex without speaking.

"Hello, Robyn." Alex didn't want the meeting sabotaged by barriers between them. He had to get through to her. "What's on your mind?" he asked. "Why meet in the café rather than the lab?"

"You know why, Alex. We have to get this out in the open."

"Out in the open? That sounds ominous."

Robyn sighed. "I just mean we have to discuss it openly, the two of us. You're going too quickly. The news announcement, talk of a cure. People have expectations now."

"I had to go to the media. You know that," said Alex.

"You're forgetting what people are like. Most don't understand the difference between Metzner's Disease and Carrick Syndrome. Telling them you don't have a repeatable process doesn't stop them believing they'll be making babies any time now."

"I can't help it if people don't understand the English language. I told the truth."

"This isn't about the truth. It's about public perception. Do you know what they'll say if they ever find out what I'm doing?"

"I know," said Alex. "I have the same worry. I just have to be careful."

"You?" Robyn frowned. "You'll be the hero and I'll be the villain. That's how people will see it. The truth is, I'm taking all the risk, and you'll take all the credit. That's not fair, is it? You'd have got nowhere without me."

"True. I owe it all to you, and you'll be getting joint credit for this. Believe me."

"Oh? Don't you dare. I can't possibly take credit when what

I'm doing is both illegal and immoral."

"You'll find a way to do this without harming your patients. Don't worry, you'll get there soon. I have faith in you."

"I hardly sleep anymore. I'm never at home. My husband is forgetting who I am. I sometimes think I'm forgetting who I am. Do you think I'm in a fit state to make headway with one of the most difficult research tasks I've ever undertaken?"

"I know you can do it."

"That's just a cop-out. You're just dumping the responsibility on me so you can dust off your hands and go on with your glossy publicity." She took a sip of coffee. "You're going to be famous, Alex. Progenetics will promote you. They'll give you huge bonuses, and you'll get a percentage of the sales of Priapus. You're going to be rich and famous, and here I am killing myself to make it all possible."

Alex took a deep breath. "What are you saying?"

"I'm saying I won't go on with this unless I see a good reason to."

"Such as?"

"Such as a worthwhile payment."

Alex leaned back in his chair and gave himself a moment to take in what Robyn had just said. "So, let's get this straight. You want money as an incentive to carry on with this?"

"Yes." Robyn scribbled a number onto a napkin.

Alex tried to cover his shock. It wasn't just the amount Robyn wanted, it was the fact that she'd asked at all.

"So it's come to this. We're to barter with peoples' fertility."

"Put it how you like. I've made my decision."

"I'm doing this research so we don't have to do that anymore. Over the years, fertility has become the root of too much corruption and greed. I'm trying to put an end to all that. Not start doing it myself."

"That's a pretty speech." Robyn gave a sardonic smile.

Alex couldn't think of a suitable way to respond. He needed her contribution to the project, but their conversation left him with a feeling of dread. This could so easily get out of control if it wasn't already. What Robyn had asked amounted to blackmail, but he couldn't say it in so many words for fear that she would walk away from the whole business.

He rolled his shoulders to ease the pain.

Paying her would be wrong. Ironically it wouldn't be hard to do. Alex had considerable budget responsibility and frequently made large payments for supplies or equipment. If he sent a payment to Robyn, as long as the account wasn't traceable, Progenetics would never know what was going on.

But that didn't make it okay. It didn't make blackmail acceptable, and he couldn't bring himself to pay for something that should be offered freely.

Alex stood up. "You have a decision to make. You can be part of the biggest scientific advance in our lifetimes or you can be the one who sabotaged it. Let me know when you've made up your mind." He walked out.

29

11 am

Mildred strode along the corridor, staff and fertiles moving aside in her wake, her eyes unwavering. It was gratifying to see how people reacted. Respect. Such a little word, but so important. Few people showed disrespect in her presence, and on the rare occasions when they did, she made it her business to correct them.

She sensed a mood of expectancy. If Progenetics really had a cure for Metzner's Disease, people would expect the release of the lords from the atelier and for the whole repopulation model to change. In reality, of course, little would change. Despite the lords being a necessary part of the process, they couldn't bear a child. Everything hinged on the queens.

So what if men outside of ateliers could sire a child? The atelier still had to maintain a reliable supply of male seed of appropriate quality and genetic diversity, and they had that with the lords. Anyway, without a fertile partner, who would take the treatment? Probably few, particularly if they might end up in an atelier as a result.

The most likely outcome would be that naturally fertile men would still be sent to ateliers, and nobody would be stupid enough to volunteer for the Progenetics treatment. If the supply of lords became short, suitable men would be conscripted and treated, then taken to an atelier where their work could be properly managed and monitored.

Change would come if and when Progenetics, or some other company, came up with a cure for Carrick Syndrome. Such a cure would be the end of the ateliers. The end of her career. Thankfully that was still a pipe dream.

Turning into the mahogany row corridor, she felt the tension ease as the noise of chatter and footsteps dwindled. Such a peaceful place to be. She passed the executive staff lounge, conference room and bar before arriving at her objective.

The door swished open in response to her com-pak. Before her, the deserted Cavendish restaurant awoke as the lights responded to her presence, providing a warm glow. As the door hissed closed behind her, Mildred crossed to a dining alcove, reassured she wouldn't have to look over her shoulder as she worked. The alcove curved around a spacious table for two.

She put her hand under the table-top, feeling the underside for the device she'd placed there. Her heart skipped a beat. She moved her hand with more urgency, feeling around the area where she'd positioned it. How could it not be there?

She breathed a sigh of relief as her hand made contact with a hard object, smaller than a com-pak, clinging to the underside of the table-top. She grabbed it and pulled. She pulled again, and it came free from its adhesive, falling into her hand.

Without another glance, she put it in her pocket and walked to the door, ignoring the peaceful solitude of mahogany row. She wanted to get back to her office and find out what she'd recorded.

After closing her office door, Mildred placed the small device on her desk and pressed a control. Activated by sound in close proximity, it hadn't recorded until the diners were seated. She listened to the scraping of chairs, anticipating with pleasure the sound of the young Napier girl and Craig Drake conversing in what they believed to be a secure place.

She sat in her unyielding chair to discover the truth of what was going on between Mr. Drake and Ms. Napier. A voice cut across the rustling of napkins.

"Take your time with the menu, my dear. I'll have a look at the wine list."

Mildred leaned forward, listening carefully. That wasn't Craig Drake's voice.

"Oh, how lovely. I shall start with the foie gras."

Mildred slammed the device with her hand, silencing it. She would listen to it later. After all, any conversation might produce interesting intelligence. But what had gone wrong? How did she record the wrong conversation? The wrong couple. Had Craig Drake changed tables? Surely he knew nothing of her intentions. Anyway, why should he anticipate eavesdropping? He would only take such precautions if he had something to hide.

Maybe it was simply bad luck. Perhaps the Maître d' had swapped the table assignments for a purely innocent reason.

She called him on her com-pak. "When Mr. Drake arrived last night, did he ask to have his table reassigned?"

"I usually have to make some last minute adjustments, Mrs. Knatchbull. Has he complained? Mr. Drake and his guest seemed to enjoy their meal."

"Complained? Of course not. For goodness sake, I asked a simple question. Please answer it."

"I'm sorry, Mrs. Knatchbull, but I thought I did."

She hung up. It was a waste of time expecting a straight answer from the Maître d'. He would keep that up all day. If the table was swapped at Craig Drake's request, it would suggest he had something to hide. It would also suggest that he had some foreknowledge of her intentions unless he did it simply as a precaution, but that would be bordering on paranoia.

Mildred stood by her office window, barely noticing the autumn sunshine, the soft breeze in the tree tops. She'd been foiled. Instead of valuable intelligence about Craig Drake's intentions towards Ms. Napier, she had a recording of a conversation that was probably of no use at all.

She opened the daily reports on the Napier girl and looked through them yet again, starting with the earliest. Somewhere in here there must be a clue, but however much she read them, she saw nothing new. There was a series of encrypted messages, but they were all from Mr. Fadden. Mildred didn't have the means to crack open someone's encrypted messages, nor did she have the authority to do so. It was a petty and rather ridiculous rule, but she was bound by it. Anyway, it was clear from the reports that Napier was refusing to see Mr. Fadden, so it wasn't surprising that he was sending plenty of messages. They were unlikely to be anything other than sentimental nonsense.

Apart from that, the report showed nothing out of the ordinary. Mildred wasn't sure why the Napier girl didn't want to see Mr. Fadden, but it suited her that way, so she wouldn't interfere. If Napier knew what Craig's motives were, she showed no sign of letting on.

None of that helped Mildred to understand why Craig had sat at a different table. Was he one step ahead of her, or was this just a coincidence? Mildred Knatchbull didn't believe in coincidences.

30

2 pm

Craig contemplated his forthcoming meeting, oblivious to the view through the tinted window of his limousine. Dr. Fadden was a menace. Even more so than his snivelling son. The genetic science industry provided secure employment for large numbers of people, soaked up vast amounts of funding, and produced little. Now, just when Craig's business was growing into a healthy industry of its own, Dr. Fadden had come up with a result that would spoil it all. A cure for male infertility.

As though that wasn't bad enough, there was now talk about the other Progenetics lab soon coming up with a cure for female infertility.

Craig needed to take action, and he needed to do it now. His livelihood was at stake. He blessed his own wisdom for the move he'd made three years ago to sponsor the Guardian Agency. It was inspired. Not only did it open up new business opportunities, but it had allowed him to push for a position on the Midfield Council Advisory Committee.

He'd enjoyed the creative process of securing that position. He so loved to find new people over whom he could exert influence. In this case, a stranglehold. Gratifying and rewarding.

Now, having been a member of the advisory committee for nearly three years, he was known as someone who liked to be involved. Particularly on matters relating to the Atelier Cavendish and the Guardian Agency. It was under this guise that he would soon meet with Dr. Fadden.

The limousine pulled into the visitors' drop off for the Progenetics Midfield West laboratory. He stood and took in the building. Modern construction. Plenty of architectural glazing. Impressive.

When he reached the entrance, the doors hummed open. He cast his eye around. Two guards behind the foyer desk. Security devices on all doors – the kind that needed a com-pak for ID and an access code. What you have and what you know both needed to gain entry. Effective security.

One of the guards paid close attention to him.

"Can I help you, sir?"

"I'm here to meet with Dr. Fadden. Craig Drake. He's expecting me."

The guard pointed to a row of seats and made a discreet call. After two minutes, a white-coated man came through one of the doors and approached him. His badge said *Sam Gibbons*.

"Mr. Drake? Please come with me."

He led Craig into a corridor that bustled with activity, passing laboratories, offices, and storerooms until they reached a door with a wooden plaque labelled *Dr. Alex Fadden* in gold letters. Sam knocked and a voice inside bade them enter.

Dr. Fadden thanked Sam and turned to Craig. "Mr. Drake. Please sit."

Craig nodded and smiled. "Thanks for seeing me."

"Thank you for your interest in Progenetics, Mr. Drake. I'm sure you and your colleagues at the Guardian agency have been following our recent developments with interest."

"We certainly have," said Craig. "As my secretary explained, I hope for a tour of the laboratory. And I'd like to get an overview of the directions your research will take you now that you've reached this milestone." Not bad. Should be convincing.

"I see." Dr. Fadden tapped his com-pak and spoke into it.

"Ralph, would you come to my office in five minutes, please? We have a visitor from the Guardian Agency here for a tour of the lab."

"I was hoping to take the tour with the great man himself," said Craig.

"Sorry, but I'm afraid that won't be possible. As for directions, there's not much I can tell you at the moment. We're fully focussed on solving our process problems with Priapus and lining up everything we need for the clinical trial. After that, we'll need to put Priapus into large scale production. That in itself will present us with many challenges."

"I see you still have a lot to do. Anyway, I'm sure you'll be disseminating the details of this breakthrough to the scientific community. Won't it be wonderful for this research to be public knowledge so that people all over the world can benefit?"

"Mr. Drake." Dr. Fadden smiled. "I work for Progenetics. We have not shared our technology with anybody, nor will we be doing so until it is fully patented and we can see ways to license it for our own profit. Progenetics is funded by shareholders, and it's our job to protect their interests."

Craig returned Dr. Fadden's smile. "Of course." That was the best news so far in this visit.

There was a knock at the door, and a young man walked in without waiting.

"Thank you, Ralph. Mr. Drake is ready." He leaned across his desk and shook Craig's hand. "Good day, Mr. Drake."

Ralph led him back along the corridor to one of the labs he'd passed on the way in. Ralph pushed the door open and led Craig inside. The huge room hummed with the activity of a dozen people. Along the wall, white-coated researchers attended a confusing array of equipment littering a long bench under the window.

Equipment and benches occupied much of the floor space. In the far corner, facing the window, stood an unoccupied hospital-style bed surrounded by small trolleys, monitors and equipment stands. A curtain rail, hung with an open curtain, surrounded the bed area.

The lab was a hive of activity, both mechanical and human.

"Here's the main lab where Dr. Fadden's research takes place. There are others, of course, where specialised processes are set up, and a separate computer facility provides all the computing power for our work."

"So all your data is on that computer?"

"Most, but not all. Most of our equipment is linked to it via data acquisition nodes, but there are a couple that store their own data." He frowned. "Why?"

"Oh, just curious. We're considering modernising our own business, and it's fascinating to see how the experts do it." He favoured Ralph with his most charming smile. He'd have to be more careful with his questions.

Ralph seemed satisfied with his answer and continued to show him the main lab. Not really much of interest here, so he said little and allowed Ralph to move on as soon as he was ready.

They viewed four more labs, each smaller than the first, and each one a hive of activity. Two of them had specialised equipment that didn't connect to the main computing facility. He studied both rooms carefully, making a mental note of the manufacturer and model of each machine.

"Well, Mr. Drake, you've seen all the labs involved in Dr. Fadden's research. Can I answer any questions for you?"

"Actually, I was hoping to see your computing facility."

Ralph didn't seem to mind and strode off in the direction of a large room with blanked out windows. He led Craig around to a small adjoining room and took him inside. One of the walls was all glass, and it overlooked the dimly lit computer room – a massive room with rows upon rows of equipment racks.

"This," said Ralph, "is a clean environment with temperature and humidity control. Five years ago, there wasn't this much computer power on the whole planet."

Craig didn't care how powerful it was. He was looking for metal shielding or any evidence of strengthened walls. There was none he could see. As far as he could tell, the designers of this facility had paid no attention to the prospect of a malicious attack. No doubt the computer security was strong, but the building was no match for well-chosen explosives.

"I suppose we're deep in the centre of the building?" he asked.

"Oh, no. It's confusing without windows, but that wall there is the edge of the building next to the reception area."

Perfect.

Ralph carried on. "All the data is mirrored to our sister lab, Midfield East."

"Mirrored? I don't understand."

"Oh, it's a simple concept even if the technology is complex. It just means that any time data is stored here, it's automatically copied to the computer at Midfield East using remote hardware mirroring. We also keep a copy of their data."

Not so good. "Ah, I see. That sounds like an excellent safeguard. What a loss to humanity if the data were lost."

Ralph laughed. "Not much chance of that, as you can see."

"No." Unless, of course, both buildings were destroyed at the same moment. To every problem there was a solution.

"Ralph, thank you so much for your time. I really shouldn't take any more. I know you're all very busy here. This has been a most instructive visit."

Ralph took him to the foyer, and they said their goodbyes.

Climbing back into his limousine, Craig considered his next move. He'd get Mog to bring the explosives here in a stolen car, then walk away. It would have to be enough to kill the researchers as well as get rid of the data. He'd need to make sure it was done on a day when the whole team worked. Enough explosives to take out the whole building.

31

2 pm

Dominic took the papers for the escape plan from a drawer and spread them on his dining table in front of Gerald. He checked the time. Tim, Brett and Al would arrive soon. "So, what did your contact in the police Intels find?"

Gerald smiled. "Drake has a dirty secret that would put him away for good. He'd be in a top security penal atelier in no time."

"Penal atelier?" Dominic frowned. "So he's a bolter."

"Right. So, if he's a bolter, Craig Drake isn't his real name, right?"

Dominic sat upright.

"And if the police knew his real name, you'd think they could prove he's a bolter, and that would be curtains."

Dominic picked up his coffee. "Gerald, I love you."

Gerald laughed. "And now we know his real name. It's Frank Lenfield. When he was fifteen, he helped his father break into an atelier to steal a newborn baby. His dad was killed and Frank Lenfield disappeared. He re-surfaced a while later as Craig Drake."

"Bloody hell!"

"Anyway, there's a problem."

"Oh? What?"

"The police have good evidence, and there wouldn't be any difficulty putting him away except for one thing. This is the same old story. Someone very senior in the Corps is keeping the key evidence suppressed. I haven't been able to find out who, but it's somebody senior enough and powerful enough to keep it covered up. Whoever it is obviously is in the Baron's pay, but what can you do?"

"Christ! They're all on his payroll. The police, someone at the Cavendish, maybe the atelier headquarters, there's no end to it."

"I see what you mean."

"How do we find out who's suppressing the evidence? We have to expose them."

"Not much chance of that. There are loads of people in the Corps who'd love to do that and believe me, they've tried. They have suspicions about who it is, but it's being skilfully done."

"I suppose he didn't tell you who they suspect?"

"No. Too risky."

They sat in silence and sipped their coffee. This important information would help if they were not missing the key piece.

"Anything else?"

"Not really," said Gerald. "There are loads of cases against him just languishing. Violence, extortion, even murder. Somebody is doing a good job of keeping them out of court and out of the media."

"Hmm. Not surprising. Mind you, he's just been in court. It was on the news."

"Yes, with jurors threatened and witnesses killed. He'll be acquitted, so even when he does go to court he wins. The police just let it happen."

The door chimes sounded, and Dominic let Tim in. "Tim, if I didn't know better, I'd say you were looking rather dapper today." He laughed. "I'll get my eyes checked later."

Tim looked sheepish. "Hannah said I need to spruce up my wardrobe. She took me out shopping and made me buy clothes. Loads of them. I think she would have thrown out my old clothes if I'd let her. I've managed to save them for the time being."

"You've been dating her for a week and now this?" said Dominic. "So soon? Sorry mate, but I reckon you're a goner."

"Yeah, well, I do have some good news."

Sitting, Tim exchanged greetings with Gerald, then turned back to Dominic. "Hannah says she'll meet you, but she has to be careful. She wants to be able to claim it was a chance meeting."

"Fine by me. When?"

"She's got tomorrow afternoon off. She'll be at the Patagonia Café at two thirty. I'm giving up a shopping trip so she can meet you, mate."

"That's fantastic. Thanks, Tim. I'll be there." This was the best news he'd had so far. Finally a small foothold. A chance to turn his embryonic plan into something more concrete.

They agreed they would not put Hannah in any danger or at risk of losing her job. She might also be able to get cooperation from other staff, and Dominic would explore the possibility when he spoke with her tomorrow.

"We'll need someone who knows the security codes who can disarm the system at the right moment. Night is best because most of the staff will be asleep." Dominic scowled. "Also, that bloody Knatchbull woman isn't there at night. Most of the fertiles will be in their suites, and only two security guards should be on patrol."

Gerald's eyes narrowed. "The guards are from Landsdowne Security, aren't they?"

"Yes," said Dominic. "They have offices in the High Street. Why?"

"I was thinking. They have quite a high staff turnover. People are always leaving. I see their job advertisements all the time."

"I think their biggest problem is burnout. It's a stressful job."

"Well, there's only one of us who doesn't already have a job. Steve could work for Landsdowne. If he was a guard at the Cavendish, we could get in easily."

Dominic leaned back. "I wonder if he would. He doesn't need

the money."

"Why don't you ask him?"

Dominic tapped his com-pak. "Steve, are you free to come over? I'm at home."

He glanced at Tim. "Fru's another problem. She's not responding to any of my calls or messages, so I'm not sure how she'll react to me showing up in the middle of the night to take her away."

"Hopefully, Hannah can help," said Tim. "She'll talk to Fru for you, I'm sure."

The door chimes sounded again, and this time Brett and Al walked in. Steve, who stood a head taller than either, arrived a few steps behind them. While they settled, Dominic poured coffees from the jug.

Steve hung his linen jacket over the back of a chair. Sitting, he looked across at Tim. "I didn't know we were dressing up. What's the occasion?" His eloquently formed words carried little of the posh intonation Dominic knew from Steve's parents.

Tim rolled his eyes. "Gerald had an idea, and it involves you."

"Oh? How exciting." Steve's eyes went to Gerald.

Dominic sat. "I want you to take a job with Landsdowne Security. I need you to work as a night guard at the Cavendish."

Steve frowned. "Me? Why?"

"We need somebody to disable the security while we get Fru out. The guards are our biggest hurdle."

Steve stared. "Oh."

"This is really important, and you'd be perfect. Will you do it?"

Steve sipped his coffee, then grinned. "You know, that could be fun. I've never been an undercover agent before."

Gerald winked at him. "You've never been anything much at all before, mate." Laughter rippled around the table.

"Will I have to be armed?" A cheerful expectancy accompanied Steve's grin.

"Good question." They hadn't talked about the possible use of force. "And the answer is no. I don't want any violence."

"I don't believe this." Al's eyes were fierce. "You've paid Baron Drake to do the job. He's the best person to do it."

"Sorry, Al," said Dominic. "I don't believe that anymore."

He turned back to Steve. "So Landsdowne will issue you with a gun, but it won't be necessary for this."

Brett sat forward. "What will you do if it is needed?"

"Come on, Brett, I know you're spoiling for a fight, but it doesn't have to be that way."

"Whatever you say." Brett pulled a face, aping disappointment.

Enthusiastic about his role, Steve called Landsdowne straight away. They gave him an appointment for the next morning.

Dominic felt a real lift from this. His friends would help, and with Hannah willing to talk, he had the beginnings of a workable plan. "They're not likely to turn you down for the job unless you make a real mess of the interview."

Steve laughed. "Aren't they always desperate for new staff? I'd have to be rather useless." His face straightened. "They will want me.… Won't they?"

Brett patted his shoulder. "Of course they will, man."

"You'll get the job. Don't worry," said Dominic. "You know, for four years now I've been struggling to dream up a scheme to get her out. Now it seems so simple. I wish to God I'd never gone to bloody Craig Drake. It would have been much easier if I'd done this to begin with."

"It's too late to worry about that now," said Gerald. "Drake's a menace and you have to get Fru out before he gets to her. I wish we knew when he was planning to make his move."

Al stirred in his chair but remained silent, staring into his beer.

"I've wasted so much time." Dominic heard the anger in his own voice. "Why didn't I just do it while I was still in favour with the Cavendish staff? What if they know I'm planning a breakout?

What if Fru's said something?"

Brett's eyes were intense. "It's no good talking like that. If you don't expect to succeed, you won't."

"That's reassuring. Anyway, it's all down to timing now." Dominic turned to Steve. "As long as you get the job, we'll wait till you're assigned shifts, then pick a night. Hopefully we'll have her out of that damned place before Drake can do anything."

"You're making a mistake," said Al. "Anyway, I agree with you on one thing. The whole atelier system is a social injustice. People allow it to happen because it's their only hope of getting a family. As long as the fertiles are in the ateliers, people can put them out of their minds. Most people think it's their right to have a child to turn up, as if by magic, when they're ready for a family. The fertiles can't vote, and there's nobody to speak out for them."

"I've got an assault rifle at home that would speak out for them," said Brett. "You know how much damage that can do to a pekay? Bring it on, I say."

Dominic laughed. "Brett, you're mad, but quaintly so. At least, it would be quaint if it wasn't a little scary. How many strange and wonderful weapons do you have these days?"

Dominic knew Brett and his Combat Society friends all had serious collections of real weapons. They used replicas for historical re-enactments, but most of them also had modern weapons – expensive and hard to find. They must have an effective network of contacts.

Dominic raised a concern with Brett. "We're going to need somebody outside while we go in to get her. If anyone shows up, particularly if it's pekays, we'll need a decoy. Something to distract them. Any thoughts?"

Brett's grin almost reached his ears. "Man, I have just the thing. I'll bring a grenade launcher."

Dominic sighed. "I've told you. No violence."

Brett bounced in his seat. "No, no, no, no. Really, man, no. It's not violent. I can launch a *flashbang* over the wall into the garden.

It just makes a lot of noise and a lot of smoke. It won't do any damage. They'll have a rapid succession of loud, smoky flashes in their walled garden and they won't have any idea why."

Dominic considered this. "Brett, you know, I think I've been doing you an injustice. That's bloody brilliant!"

After coffees, the conversation turned to the wrongs of the political system. Dominic brought out the Afterburner and six glasses, and his friends didn't leave until the bottle was empty.

With an unsteady hand, Dominic tapped a message into his com-pak.

"Don't worry, honey, I shall have you out of there soon. I've got it all planned. Can't go wrong. You won't have long to wait now. I love you."

He sent the message.

32

Saturday 4ᵗʰ September, 2 pm

Dominic usually enjoyed walking in Midfield High Street on a Saturday afternoon. The town centre was free of traffic during weekends, enabling a new kind of life to emerge. For two days each week, Midfield High Street became an impromptu festival, bringing out the colourful buskers who loved to show off for the crowd.

There were musicians, playing alone or in bands, and clowns, some on stilts or unicycles. They juggled, played instruments, and performed tricks for the crowds. There were mime artists, sword swallowers, fire breathers, even someone who walked on burning coals. Today, none held Dominic's interest.

He pressed his way through the crowds and strode towards his destination.

Street musicians played as he arrived at the Patagonia Café. In front of them, a brightly dressed young man climbed onto a tall unicycle and balanced while juggling flaming clubs. A few people stopped to watch him. The unicycle swayed back and forth, and four flaming clubs hurled through the air in patterns that formed and changed too quickly to follow.

Dominic made his way to the Café door and went in. Most of the seats were taken, and the staff buzzed around making the most of the Saturday crowd. Dominic saw Hannah across the room at a table near the wall and walked over to her.

"Hi, Hannah. May I join you?"

She indicated the seat and he sat opposite her. When a waiter approached, Dominic said to Hannah, "What a lovely surprise to see you here." If anyone questioned the waiter, Dominic wanted him to think it was a chance meeting. They chatted for a few minutes, then Dominic made sure nobody was listening and came to the point. "This means a lot to me. Thank you."

She held him with a steady gaze. "Fru's a good friend."

"Things haven't gone well lately. I've done something very stupid." Hannah's eyebrows rose. "I paid Craig Drake to get her out." He was committed now. She could report him to the police. "I shouldn't have done it, and I think I've put Fru in danger."

"I know all this. Tim trusts me."

"I don't know what's going on at the Cavendish, but I can't get anyone to talk to me, and Fru won't even return my calls."

She studied him before answering. "There's something weird going on. We've all been warned to keep you away and not give you any information. We don't know why, but we've been threatened with dismissal if we don't comply. Knatchbull is even more of a tyrant than usual."

"Fru wouldn't let that stop her getting a message to me."

"No. The fertiles don't live in fear of Knatchbull like we do. They can't be dismissed." She grimaced. "There's something else. Craig has told her about you sleeping with the pekay's wife. How could you? Fru trusted you."

"Hannah, you've got to believe me. I've never even met a pekay's wife, let alone slept with one."

Hannah held him with a steady gaze. "She showed me the photos. Are you denying it? Drake gave her photos of you and the woman. You weren't exactly walking on the beach."

"Drake? So it was him." Dominic breathed deeply to steady himself. "I don't know what Drake's up to, but he's lying."

"And he says, as a result, you're under police surveillance, so you can't be trusted."

"Look, I'm –"

She held up her hand. "That, together with you getting her a free stay –"

"Free stay?" Dominic frowned.

"What's going on? Why the free stay? She's pretty confused how she feels about you." She folded her arms and watched him.

"Hannah, I don't know anything about another woman and I don't know anything about a free stay. If she has a free stay, it's nothing to do with me." He spoke quietly, failing to suppress his irritation.

Hannah studied him for a moment, then frowned. "If it wasn't you, then there aren't many possibilities, are there? The atelier wouldn't give up her cycle without good reason, but Drake may have coerced them. Why would he do that? What's it to him whether she's carrying a baby when she comes out?"

Dominic felt sick. "We found something about Drake that Fru might not know. He's a bolter. He's a fertile."

"A fertile! But…" Hannah pondered for a moment. "Are you thinking what I'm thinking?"

His head swam. "God, yes! It all fits. He's trying to take her away from me to start a family. Telling her lies. Discrediting me."

Hannah stared at her hands clenched together on the table. "There's something you should know."

"Oh?" He waited.

"I shouldn't tell you this, but on Thursday he visited. They had dinner together in the Cavendish Restaurant." Hannah met his gaze. "She's been a bit dreamy since then."

Dominic's heart sank into his stomach.

"This is so messy," said Hannah. "I don't trust Drake, and I don't know what to think anymore."

Dominic sat up, checking for eavesdroppers. "I do. I'm getting her out before Drake gets to her."

He told her about his plan and explained what he needed.

"Will you help?"

"Yes. I'll do everything I can. I can get work somewhere else if it comes to it. Are any jobs going at the teaching agency?" She gave a wry grin.

He laughed. "Maybe, but it won't come to that. I've promised Tim I won't put you or your job in danger." Maybe there was some hope.

Her gaze hardened. "This has nothing to do with what you promised Tim. She has to get out before Drake gets to her, and it's more important than my job. Fru is my friend, and I'm afraid for her. Drake's a liar and a crook."

They talked details for a while with occasional interruptions from the street musicians. Dominic kept his voice low. "The more people who know, the worse danger to Fru."

Hanna nodded. "I can get the person who does the duty rosters to cooperate without knowing of the plan. During the night, two staff are always on standby. I'll make sure I'm on duty with a friend when the day comes. I have an idea who I can trust but need to talk to her to be sure."

Dominic swept his gaze around before continuing. "Get as much information as you can about the security system, including the security codes, even though that may not be necessary with Steve on guard duty."

Hannah nodded. "I'll do what I can."

Then there was the delicate part. "Hannah, you'll need to help Fru see that Craig lied, and I'm an innocent victim."

"My next shift is tomorrow. I'll talk to her then. This afternoon she'll be getting ready for tonight's Autumn Ball."

Dominic let out a long breath. Finally he had a chance to convince Fru of the truth. "Thanks." He frowned. "One more thing. On the night of the escape, we'll need a way to communicate. We can't use com-paks, even encrypted. It's too easy to track. But I'll need a warning if we're discovered."

Hannah sipped her coffee in silence before answering. "We can do that by setting off the fire alarm. If you're discovered it'll help create confusion while you escape."

Dominic smiled. "That'll do it."

He paid the tab and left. The street musicians were in full flow, and the unicycling fire juggler had been joined by a clown and someone on stilts with very long trousers. The crowd of onlookers had grown, and Dominic had to make his way around it to head along the High Street towards home. So much eye-catching entertainment, yet all he could see was Fru dressed in a revealing ball gown, dancing with Craig.

33

4 pm

Bright sunshine scattered from the faintly rippling water of the Greenwich Marina as four people stepped from the limousine. Craig held out his arm. Dahlia, dressed in a short black, slim-fitting skirt with high heels and white blouse, put her arm through his. They walked towards the Marina entrance and into the boat show. Gurt and Mog, in dark suits, followed two paces behind.

Few people were able to afford the boats on show during this event, but many came to see them and dream. Craig had no time for dreamers – wasters. He'd never had difficulty taking what he wanted.

He led the way to a small, elegant boat. He liked the look because the whole boat was shiny black. As they walked onto the deck, a salesman approached.

"Good afternoon sir, madam." He nodded, a faint excuse for a bow. "The Black Diamond is a fine example of our compact, high speed vehicles. The best." He smiled.

Without acknowledging him, Craig turned and walked off the boat.

"Compact!" he sneered. "It's smaller than my wardrobe."

Dahlia smiled. "Judging by the lack of a sun deck, I'd guess the designer likes fast travel rather than cruising."

Craig held out his arm for her. "And what do you like?"

Dahlia inclined her head. "As long as it does what you need, I'll be happy."

Good girl. She would have her sun deck.

They viewed several more boats before arriving at a large ocean-going yacht. This was more like it, similar to the ones in the catalogue. Craig led them on board.

The salesman on this one had more sense. He kept a respectful distance and watched with attentive eyes.

Dahlia ran her hands over the upholstery of the recliners on the sun deck. Smiling, she started towards the door to the lounge, then checked herself.

Craig turned to Mog and spoke quietly. "Get the salesman's card, then call Kirk. Find out what you can about him."

He led the way into the lounge and they peered around. Gurt looked uncomfortable, standing back as though afraid he might break something, and Mog tapped his com-pak.

Craig paged through a brochure on the small screen that stood on the table. In addition to crew quarters, the boat boasted five large cabins, one of which was a stateroom. Perfect! It accommodated a crew of four. Captain, engineer, chef and steward.

The salesman walked into the lounge and stood by the door. Craig turned to him. "Leave us."

The man nodded and left.

There was a bar in one corner. Craig went to it and opened the fridge. Smiling, he pulled out a bottle of Champagne and popped the cork. He poured two glasses and handed one to Dahlia.

"Promising," he said.

"Delightful." She grinned.

Behind him, Gurt's com-pak beeped and he stepped away to take the call.

"We'll take a look at the rest." Craig led the way down a companionway to a lower deck where they found the stateroom.

The windows overlooked a balcony on each side. The bed was emperor sized and all the fittings were polished wood. Every inch of the room exuded luxury. A marble clad bathroom, a walk-in wardrobe, and a deeply carpeted lounge area completed the suite.

Gurt approached Craig respectfully, and after giving Dahlia a deferential nod, spoke quietly in his ear. Craig let out a belly laugh. He turned to Dahlia. "It seems the Fadden creep has a Judas among his disciples." He roared with laughter. "Another sap in love with the emotionally stunted Napier girl." He turned to Mog.

"Talk to the double crossing little shit. Find out everything he knows and get the date and time they're planning to hit the atelier. Make sure he'll continue to keep us informed. The usual methods. If he lies, you know what to do."

"Yes, Baron."

"This gets better all the time." Craig laughed.

The lowest accommodation deck was close to the water line. It contained two small cabins, each with tiny portholes near the ceiling and no other windows.

In the second one, Craig smiled at Dahlia. "Gurt and Mog will share this one." He pressed down on one of the two single beds.

They took their time looking over the rest of the boat and finally returned to the upper lounge.

Craig called Mog over. "What did you find out?"

Mog spoke softly in his ear. Craig smiled and led the way out onto the sun deck where the salesman waited. "Good afternoon, Mr. Neville." He smiled. "How's Trixy?"

The colour drained from Mr. Neville's face.

"I thought I might call Mrs. Neville later," continued Craig. He lifted his com-pak and showed it to Mr. Neville. "I do have the right number, don't I?"

Mr. Neville, perspiring, swallowed hard.

"But enough! We can talk social niceties after we've done

business." Craig smiled and slapped the salesman on the back. "You should be able to do me a very good deal on this yacht, don't you think, Mr. Neville?"

He indicated one of the plush sun deck seats, his smile broadening. "You look like you need to sit down."

34

4 pm

Alex watched from his office window. He hadn't anticipated the campers outside the lab, but he should have seen it coming. They cared about what was being done here. Everybody cared. They wanted to see him, the lab and everything associated with it.

They hounded all the staff. It was in good spirit though. People saw them as saviours. The human race would survive. Most didn't even understand that only half the problem would be solved. Female infertility, Carrick Syndrome, still stubbornly resisted the Midfield East team's efforts to find a solution.

The campers created a festival atmosphere with mobile food stalls, temporary toilet facilities, even a stage. They had their own entertainment! A tedious succession of inexpert musical performances and rants that would bore a brick wall.

The Progenetics PR team, for the first time in their cosseted professional lives, had been called in on a Saturday to deal with the problem.

Alex didn't mind the crowd. As long as the bad music didn't get too loud. When it did, he called the PR office and they dutifully went out, yet again, and negotiated to have the volume turned down. They must have thought the task demeaning. Alex grinned at the thought.

Public relations. He'd fed them the biggest PR gift of their careers, and since then they'd had a field day. But wouldn't the public be impressed anyway? Alex was the one who did the media appearances. He decided what message Progenetics would convey. What did the PR department do? At least they kept the volume down.

After pushing his way through the crowd in the morning, he'd found an unusual message from Robyn, a piece of paper in an envelope. No words, just an account number. He did an Axis search and found it to be a numbered account with no holder's name. Anonymous.

He wasn't sure whether the numbered account or Robyn's blackmail worried him most. He'd never heard of an honest use for a numbered account. This was the first time he'd been blackmailed, and it hurt that it came from someone he'd called a friend.

He thought back to those dinners for four. Robyn and her husband would invite Alex and Janet for the evening. They'd open a couple of bottles of wine, chat about everything but work, spend their time together in amicable companionship. Then a couple of weeks later, Alex and Janet would invite them back and they'd do it again.

Happy memories, now consigned to the past. Their friendship was over. Alex had a decision to make. Would he risk all his work, everything he'd achieved, by ignoring Robyn's demand? Could he? What of the consequences?

He'd feel better, that was for sure. He could proudly say he didn't give in to blackmail. But who to? Not even Janet. Apart from himself, Robyn and maybe some of her researchers were the only ones who knew how to obtain the serum. The whole point of the blackmail was that he couldn't talk about it to anyone.

What about the research? If he refused to pay Robyn, she would expose their deeds to the media, and his career would be over. Progenetics, shamed, would close down the research. And his reputation? Alex would be the world's most hated person.

Robyn would redeem herself by exposing him, and he alone would take the blame.

On balance, he didn't have much to gain by holding off with the payment. Or did he? If he paid Robyn, he'd compound the offence. He would just dig himself deeper into the mire. He'd heard of scientists throughout the ages who had ruined their own careers with ambitions beyond the plain workings of their research. There had always been researchers who were willing to engage in criminal activity to achieve something that would be otherwise unreachable.

Was he one of those people? Would he go down in history as the promising scientist who, on the verge of changing the world, had slipped into the abyss? The mire of criminality and deceit?

Maybe it was too late to turn back. He'd conspired with Robyn to make the serum available from the research on her patients, and in so doing he'd already crossed a line. Sacrificing the interests of the few to benefit many, he'd already strayed into criminal deeds. Deeds that would catch up with him if he tried to back out now.

Making a firm decision, Alex headed for the Admin office. The corridors were nowhere near as busy as during the working week. The admin people didn't work on Saturdays. Good. He wanted to use their office in privacy.

He closed the door behind him and went to the secure admin terminal. From there he could access all of the procurement and accounting functions. He signed on to the payments system.

He entered Robyn's account number and typed in the figure she'd scribbled on the napkin. This would make a significant dent in his budget. He selected *confirm payment* and entered it. Done. The point of no return.

He leaned back in the chair. He felt sick, as though on a slippery slope, heading down with nothing to grab hold of. The beginning of the end.

35

4 pm

Dominic's meeting with Hannah had left him with mixed feelings. She would help, and that was positive, but the news of Fru's free stay was another matter. He hoped the Progenetics cure would make him fertile. He had his father's word that it worked, but it was too much to take in. He would never expect Fru to take a child from an atelier queen, so now all his hopes for a future family rested with his father's cure.

His com-pak beeped.

"Hello, Dom. Steve. Just wanted you to know. I met with the folks at Landsdowne this morning. They checked my credentials while I was there. I do a day's training on Monday and start at the Cavendish on Tuesday night." Then with a hint of pride mixed with surprise. "I've got a job!"

"Blimey, they don't hang about!"

"I was rather shocked, actually. I need to cancel some social engagements, but I'll be up and running in no time."

"Brilliant. Well done, mate. Thanks for doing this."

"Oh, no need to thank me. I'm rather enjoying myself actually."

"I reckon that clinches it," said Dominic. "Hannah's agreed to help, and with you as a guard the plan's going to work."

"They'll give me the security codes for the Cavendish before my shift. I'll have another guard with me, though," said Steve.

"Don't worry. I'll get you some benzodiazepine to put in his coffee. Brett will know where to get some. Then you can disable the security cameras."

Steve laughed. "I'll be like James Bond."

"You'll just need to stay put and keep watch. We've got two decoys in case of problems. One inside and one outside. Hannah will watch the corridors and signal if we're discovered. She'll press the fire alarm if needed. Brett and one of the others will wait outside with the grenade launcher and some flashbang grenades."

"And you'll be coming in for Fru?"

"Yes. I'll go in with Tim. We'll wear balaclavas in case we're seen going to Fru's room. Hannah will warn her we're coming. We'll bring Fru out, and as long as there are no problems, we'll be back in the car and away long before the alarm goes off."

"What car? You can't call a taxi."

"No," Dominic laughed. "We'll use a stolen car. Once we're away, Hannah will go back to bed as though nothing happened, and you can take some benzodiazepine. That way they'll think you're one of the victims."

"Sounds like you've got it all pretty well figured out," said Steve. "How exciting!"

"The plan's complete now. We're all set for Tuesday."

After his conversation with Steve, he sent two encrypted com-pak messages. The first was to tell Brett they would need benzodiazepine before Tuesday night and someone to give them new identity chips early on Wednesday morning. No more payments to the Baron and no risk that Fru would disappear – or be found all over Chessington Common.

The second message was to Hannah to let her know they would carry out their plans on Tuesday night.

36

5 pm

Mildred's apartment displayed the same qualities of spartan décor and absent comfort as her office. In the small kitchen, she chopped some fresh mint leaves, scraped them from the cutting board into a small teapot, and waited patiently for the brew.

Her com-pak vibrated on her wrist.

"Yes?"

"Mildred, Stan. There's something I have to tell you. Can I come over?"

Stifling her irritation at the intrusion, she responded with as much civility as she could muster.

"Yes, Stan. Please do. I'll see you in…what? Fifteen minutes?"

"Good. Fifteen minutes." He called off.

Mildred loved her mint tea and hated her enjoyment to be disturbed by a bombastic ex-military bore. Four more minutes and she would pour it, but she'd only have time to take a sip or two before he arrived. He'd want beer, of course, and he'd be as pompous as ever, but she needed him on her side. Now was not the time to say no.

Not only was Stan a fellow committee member in the Nationalist Party, but he was doing some research for her – special research. She needed to know if he'd come up with any results. She'd have more tea later, after he left.

She knew without looking that she had five bottles of Stag's Hoof beer left in her cupboard. He liked it at room temperature, not chilled as was the modern trend.

"God, no!" he would say, "Only chill a beer if it tastes like shit when it's warm. Dulls the taste, see? Had to do that during the Norman campaigns. All they had, you see. Shit beer. Anyway, don't want to do that to a decent bevy. No sir."

Sir, indeed. She'd only made that mistake once.

She poured her tea and waited. It wasn't so bad really. If he had some real news, she'd be glad he'd come, and if not…well, he was well intentioned. If his company was a little draining, it was a fair price to pay for a loyal ally.

Her tea cooled enough to sip, and she enjoyed the aroma, the taste. As she took a second sip, a soft chime sounded at the door.

Stan shook her hand vigorously. "Had to see you today. Don't know how important it is. Got some intelligence for you, old thing."

She resisted an urge to slap him. "That's good. Do come in."

She poured him a Stag's Hoof and they sat in the living room. She enjoyed his pained expression while he manoeuvred himself into the narrow, upright seat and squirmed as though trying to find a comfortable position.

Considering the reason he'd given for his visit, she decided to put him at his ease. "I do appreciate the trouble you're going to over this. It's very kind."

"Oh, don't give it a second thought, old thing. It might be nothing anyway. Don't know, really. It's just that someone has been buying rather a lot of explosives."

"Explosives?"

"The worst kind. Military grade stuff. Large consignment."

"Who told you this, Stan?" Mildred was fascinated, but unsure why it was relevant to her.

"Can't possibly tell. Wouldn't be right. He's well placed,

though. Old Brigade boy. Bit shady now though, must say. Trust him with my life, even so." He took a long drink from his beer.

"I see."

"The explosives. Thing is, they're going to somewhere in West Midfield. Don't know where, though."

"And?"

"And what? What do you mean?"

Mildred sighed. "I'm sure there's a reason why you're telling me all this."

"Well, yes. My friend believes they've been bought by Craig Drake." He raised his eyebrows. "Too important to miss, really. The link to you through the advisory committee and all that."

"Are you sure about this?"

"Well, no. That's the damnable thing. These people cover their tracks pretty well you know. Bloody hard to tell anything, to be honest. Anyway that's what my friend thinks, for what it's worth."

Mildred needed time to think. She thanked Stan and exchanged pleasantries, leading him to the front door.

"Thank you again, Stan. Please do let me know if you find anything more."

"Good night then."

Once the door was shut, she boiled more water and went through the chopping and brewing process again. This time she would savour her tea.

Craig Drake buying explosives? What on earth for? Surely there was a mistake. There must be someone else in West Midfield buying them. She needed to confront him. Find out for sure.

Mildred composed a message on her com-pak asking Craig to visit her office on Monday morning.

37

7 pm

Francesca left the cafeteria after a coffee with Liang and Jen. Their plans for tonight's Autumn Ball had dominated the conversation. In the corridor behind her, she heard footsteps and turned. Joseph Cranston quickly caught up with her. She sighed.

"Fru, may I have a word?"

This was the last thing she wanted. "What is it Joseph?" She forced a smile.

"Would you come with me to the Ball tonight?"

"Joseph, you already have a date. You're going with Jane, remember?" She tried to keep the sarcasm from her voice but didn't succeed. He ignored it.

"I'd rather go with you. Please, Fru, would you?"

"Joseph, Jane is my friend."

She walked away as he stood, his expression confused. Turning the corner, she heard "Wait –" before she was out of earshot. She breathed a sigh of relief. What a creep! She walked towards her room but soon heard footsteps behind her.

She quickened her pace, but the footsteps came closer. Panicking, she ran but heard Joseph's heavy breath. He grabbed her arm and pushed her against the wall. With his other hand, he brushed her hair from her eyes, stroking her cheek as he did so.

She tried to pull her arm from his grip, but he tightened his hand and pushed his body against hers, thrusting his hips forward, his face close to hers, his lips parted as though ready to kiss her.

"Joseph. Get away from me or I'll sound the alarm." He released his grip, shock in his eyes. She lifted her arm and poised a finger over the com-pak. "Just one move and you'll be sorry. Try me."

Joseph tensed as if restraining himself, his breath heavy on her face.

She spoke more softly but with passion. "You're a vile turd, Cranston." Her eyes burned into his, her finger poised, ready to press the alert control. His expression of shock turned to fear.

"Get away from me," she snarled. Joseph took a step backwards. After a few moments, he turned and walked away.

Francesca watched his back until he was gone, then started to tremble. Her eyes filled with tears and she leaned against the wall. Why? She'd never flirted with him, or with any of the lords, yet this? What a bastard.

She made her way back to her suite and locked herself in. Still shaking, she poured a large glass of blackcurrant vodka and sat with the Axis controller, paging through the virtual windows. She chose a view overlooking Port Hercule in Monaco. As usual it was beautiful, and she loved to watch the wealthy people come and go.

When she saw a luxury boat, she tried to guess whose it might be. They might be industrialists, politicians, media stars, or maybe a wealthy baron. She smiled. Maybe one day she would sail into Port Hercule with Craig. She would lounge on deck in the sun while people looked on with envy.

How could she think such a thing? She loved Dom. She really did. She was so confused. She shouldn't be thinking this way about Craig, yet he preyed on her mind. Those dark eyes gazing into hers, those smiling lips that would be so easy to kiss.

At least she had one reassurance. Once she was free, if Dom didn't want her, Craig would be waiting in the wings. He'd take good care of her.

It was time to get ready, so she put on her ball dress for the first time since the fitting. She quickly realised she needed another pair of hands to do up the lace at the back, so she called for help. It was a pity Hannah wasn't working. Francesca would have loved to chat with her while she got ready. Instead, Deirdre came. She complemented Francesca on her appearance. She wasn't chatty like Hannah, but she was friendly and kind.

Francesca stood in front of the mirror. She did the dress justice, and she'd probably have to fend off plenty of people asking her to dance. As long as that creep Cranston kept away, she'd enjoy herself.

Every year at the Autumn Ball, she had a wonderful time. Many of the queens smuggled alcohol in and enjoyed it discreetly. Some of the staff, like Hannah, even helped. This time Francesca filled a water flask with blackcurrant vodka and put it in her handbag. The bottle was a colourful opaque material, hiding the deep red of the liquid inside.

Warmed by her drink and ready to go, she left her suite for the ballroom. It buzzed with activity. Several couples were arm in arm while staff monitors stood in strategic places to watch for inappropriate behaviour. This had a dampening effect early in the ball, but as the room became more crowded, and the illicit alcohol took effect, people would forget the monitors.

As Francesca walked into the room, she was given a cocktail glass containing fruit punch. She sipped as she tried to spot her friends. Around a large dance floor, tables were set with white cloths. Most already had people sitting at them, saving seats for friends. Francesca spotted Jen waving, so she walked across the dance floor, amid the admiring glances of the lords, to the table where Jen sat with Liang and Toulla.

She tried to see where Joseph or his friends might be. She wanted to sit facing away from them. Otherwise the whole evening would be intolerable. Some of his friends sat at a table across the room, but no Joseph.

Spirits were high among her friends. They all complemented each other on how they looked, and talked in animated voices while the ballroom filled. They watched people arrive. Some were in small groups, talking and laughing, and some posed like models.

When the room was nearly full, Jane walked in arm in arm with Joseph. Her eyes sparkled as the couple walked across the dance floor, surveying the jealous glances of the crowd.

Francesca frowned. They came straight towards her table. With shock she realised they meant to sit with her and her friends instead of his. Her face flushed hot with anger.

Jane and Joseph sat down and smiled around the table. Joseph leaned across and said, "Hello Fru, you're looking totally radiant tonight. Beautiful."

Francesca stared in disbelief, unable to bring herself to answer or even smile.

"Ooh, jealous girl!" Jane muttered under her breath and smirked.

Needing to gather her thoughts, Francesca rose and walked towards a nearby table. She was too late to move, but chatting with someone else for a moment would help to get her balance back. Joseph's presence would ruin the evening, but she couldn't think of any way to get rid of him.

After a few minutes, as she returned, Joseph came towards her. He put his hand on her arm as if in a friendly gesture. "I trust you're going to dance with me tonight. Especially when the slow ones get going." His smile bared his teeth.

"Get your hand off me, creep." She made no effort to keep her voice quiet. "I've told you before, don't touch me." People nearby turned to see what was happening, and those of her friends within earshot stopped to stare.

With his hand still on her arm, he leaned close to her ear and spoke quietly. "Just think. We may already have had a baby together."

"Ugh! You pig. Let go."

She tried to pull her arm away, but he tightened his grip.

One of the lords at an adjacent table stood. "You heard what she said, Cranston. Take your hands off her or I'll do it for you." More people were watching now.

"What, you and your limp friends?" Joseph laughed. "Bugger off."

The lord's punch was too fast to dodge. Joseph reeled backwards, doubled up. The lord strode forward, grabbed his jacket collar, pulled him to his feet, and brought a knee up. Joseph fell to the ground with a loud cry of pain.

"Watch out for me and my limp friends, Cranston. And stay away from her." The lord pointed to Francesca.

She shook violently as Jane approached. "What the hell have you done? I thought you were my friend!"

Liang and Jen crowded in. Liang glared at Jane. "Back off, Jane. Joseph was at fault, not Fru."

Jane turned abruptly and sat back at the table, glancing at Joseph with a disgusted look.

Francesca turned to the lord who had rescued her. She didn't know his name. "Listen, thanks… Thank you." She didn't know what else to say.

He smiled. "Don't worry. We'll watch him this evening. He won't bother you now."

Back at her table, she took a long drink from her flask. The talk was serious, and Jane had a concerned frown. "Fru, are you going to file a complaint?"

Francesca forced a smile. "He's done this kind of thing before. I might make a complaint, or I might find a better way to deal with him." Her friends laughed, and the mood lightened.

All except Jane whose dark expression lingered.

Several monitors arrived at the scene and asked what had happened, but the women feigned innocent looks and said they didn't know. After a few minutes, the monitors lost interest and wandered back to their posts.

"It's a pity we can't bring visitors from outside to the ball," said Liang. "If Dom were here, that wouldn't have happened."

"No. No, I suppose it wouldn't." Taking another drink from her flask, Francesca didn't try to hide the glum look on her face. She loved Dom so much, but why the free stay? If he was planning to have the fertility treatment from his father, maybe he really had arranged it. If that wasn't bad enough, now he was sleeping with another woman and being watched by the police. If he lied about the free stay, did he also lie about the pekay's wife?

"Oh dear. Tell all. What's wrong?" asked Toulla.

"Oh, I don't know. It's just been a bit of a bumpy ride recently." This elicited sympathetic looks from Liang, Jen and Toulla. Jane stared at the table.

Francesca made sure the monitors weren't watching before taking a drink from her flask. Pushing the lid back on, she grinned. "He's hatching a plan to get me out of here. You just see."

The sympathetic looks changed to shock.

38

Monday 6th September, 10 am

Craig strode through the foyer of the Atelier Cavendish without a word. The young man behind the reception desk at first looked startled, then fumbled the control to allow Craig into the administrative corridor.

Without breaking his pace, Craig headed for Mildred Knatchbull's office.

Mildred Knatchbull – who had summoned him like a wayward servant. To make it worse, he had to keep up the charm with this intolerable woman. She was too valuable a contact. She remained blissfully unaware that he was behind the blackmail over the Napier girl's free stay, and he intended to keep it that way.

Maybe she wanted to ask about his interest in the Napier girl. She would have seen his visits and must have speculated about his intentions. He had a satisfactory story.

Maybe Mildred thought him a lecher who took an unhealthy interest in a vulnerable girl. He didn't mind her thinking that. She would never have the effrontery to say so. All the better if she thought of him as a man with impulses.

Ready for whatever she might say, he knocked on her office door. The catch released and he entered as Mildred crossed the room to greet him.

"Craig. I'm so glad you came." She offered him her hand.

Craig blessed her with his warmest smile and took her hand. He pressed it to his lips and lingered only a fraction over the kiss. It always worked. She must have been unaware of the flash in her eyes because she would never willingly betray her inner emotions. The warmth he knew was there, buried under countless layers of armoured defence. The warmth that made her vulnerable.

"Mildred, it's a pleasure as always. You're looking well."

He maintained his smile through the icy glare he received in response and followed her to the desk. He'd never figured out why she had such terrible chairs, but he sat casually, making sure he showed no sign of discomfort.

"It's come to my attention," said Mildred, "that someone in West Midfield is purchasing a large amount of illicit explosives."

Craig's senses rebounded. How could she possibly know that? Someone had a loose tongue. He would make loose with that person's life as soon as he found out who had been disloyal to him.

"I see." He feigned concern. "Is there some way I can assist you?"

"I hoped you might be able to shed some light on the matter. After all, you seem to have your finger on the pulse of most that happens in Midfield." She inclined her head. "More so even than me."

Craig prided himself on his ability to think quickly in difficult circumstances. "As a matter of fact, I can. I've heard the same rumours –"

"The uncertainty of their destination does not miraculously turn these explosives into rumours."

"No." Craig notched one more onto the scoreboard. She would pay for that rudeness. "When I heard about the explosives, I had one of my men make some inquiries. The destination is not uncertain."

She leaned forward. "Oh?"

"The consignment you referred to has been acquired by someone called Dominic Fadden. I believe you know him. His father is the famous Dr. Alex Fadden."

Mildred's eyes darkened. "My source gave your name as the recipient. Are you telling me he was wrong?"

Craig had a fleeting vision of his hands around her neck, her life fading. He smiled. "If that's what you were told, somebody is lying. I'm sure your source is usually reliable, but I assure you that on this he is wrong."

"Really?" Mildred's face hardened into a mean, calculating expression. "I need facts, not words. Can you prove the explosives are destined for Mr. Fadden?"

This was too much. The smile was becoming harder to maintain. "Not without revealing my own sources, and I'm afraid I can't do that. Of course, I can only speculate why he would want it."

"Oh, so can I," said Mildred. "If what you say is true. Now, perhaps you can enlighten me on one more topic."

This was beginning to sound like an inquisition. "Certainly. Anything I can do to help."

"Quite. What is your interest in the Napier girl?"

It was just like Mildred Knatchbull to be so direct. It was none of her business, but he'd satisfy her with an answer anyway. "As you know, I take my responsibilities with the Guardian Agency very seriously."

She frowned. "Indeed."

"Part of my role is to ensure that the adoptive mothers of the atelier babies are appropriate for the babies we choose. They have to be a suitable psychological match. That is not a simple matter and takes research. I'm convinced I can carry out my role more effectively if I have an understanding of the natural mothers of the children we place in families. To that end, I selected a random queen, and I am educating myself with a first-hand professional insight into their lives. In time, I shall talk to others."

She sat for a moment without responding but didn't seem disturbed by what he'd said. He knew it would make sense to her because she'd talked enthusiastically about the placement of the babies on many occasions.

She stood. "Well, Craig, this has been most instructive. Thank you for coming."

Craig recoiled at the abrupt dismissal. One day he would take great pleasure in repaying Mildred for the casual way she'd treated him like a serf during the time he'd known her. When he finished with her, he'd give Gurt an opportunity to take his revenge for whatever she'd done to him on the night of the blackmail.

39

Craig pushed open the door to the small room. None of the basement rooms had windows, and that suited him. He didn't want inquisitive eyes peering in.

Mog stood, patiently waiting, and nodded to Craig as he walked in. He'd already unpacked the explosives and laid them on the table.

Seeing the explosives reminded Craig of the terrible power they carried. Enough for both of the Progenetics laboratories. "This won't leave much standing. Unfortunately the crowds camping around the laboratory – potential customers – will also be killed. But it's an acceptable price to pay. There's too much at stake."

"Yes, Baron."

"If the scientists at Progenetics succeed in their goal," said Craig, "society will crumble. Then what?"

Mog grunted.

"People hate change. Every time something big changes their lives, whether it's a new government policy, an advance in science, anything, people rail against it. They might think they want Dr. Fadden and his associates to succeed, but they won't like it." Craig eyed the pile of explosives. "Let's get started."

Mog picked up two objects from the floor and placed them on

the table with the explosives. Each was a frame. An approximately eighteen-inch cube with two compartments. He put explosive packs into the lower compartment of the first frame while Craig took wires and tools to assemble a controller.

"You see that?" Craig pointed to the frame Mog was working on. "It gives structure to our work, just like infertility gives structure to society. It's the basis of most government policy, most laws. With that gone, the old laws will no longer be adequate, and the new ones will meet with resistance."

Mog was attentive, but gave no reaction.

"Infertility companies will be put out of business overnight. Fertility testing, fertilisation equipment manufacturers, atelier construction companies. All of them. The supporting industries will collapse too, from adoption agencies to the legal specialists in fertility cases. The list is endless. Even Progenetics will no longer serve a purpose once the cure is out there. Their patent will be overruled by the government in the interests of society."

Mog looked up. "Yes, Baron."

"Just think. If I don't do this, institutionalised atelier queens and lords will be set free. The floundering government won't be able to continue paying them, but they wouldn't cope with the outside world. They have no skills, no job prospects. People who can't be cured will be resentful. They'll become a reviled underclass."

Mog smiled.

"Society," said Craig, "is organised around a dwindling population. Employment, social welfare, medical care, every aspect of life relies on it. There will be a population explosion, and society won't be able to cope. Poverty will sky-rocket. There might even be civil war. I'm merely fulfilling my social responsibility."

Finished, he stood back and surveyed their work. All the explosive packs were neatly tied into the bottom compartments of the two frames. Each frame had a small controller mounted beside the packs, connected to detonators, one pushed into each explosive pack.

"Perfect. This small act of destruction will bring the world back into balance," he said. "Most importantly, it will save my business."

Mog peered at the two assemblies, frowning.

"These are ready to be primed," said Craig. "What's the problem?"

"No problem, Baron. What about these?" He indicated the empty upper compartment in each of the two frames.

"Ah. That's where my plan is so brilliant." Craig grinned. "Do you know what a disruptor bomb is?"

"Er…I think I know what a disruptor grenade is."

"Well, the bomb is just a much bigger version of the grenade. The grenade will take out one or a few people – the bomb will take out everyone in a half-mile radius. It creates an electrical storm that disrupts the central nervous system. Most victims survive, but few keep their sanity. The beauty of it is, though, it will destroy any data as well. The data becomes gibberish."

"Er. Okay."

"I scoped out the Midfield East laboratory after my visit to Dr. Fadden and found the computer room there too – behind a blank wall with too many air conditioning vents. As in Midfield West, the visitor drop-off is alongside it. So, we'll detonate a car bomb in both visitor drop-off areas. One of these for each of the labs, triggered simultaneously. The disruptor bomb goes off." Craig smiled. "It disables the people and destroys all the data. A couple of seconds later the explosives detonate, and the building is destroyed. No data, no people, no Progenetics. No cure."

Mog's face broke into a hideous grin.

40

Tuesday 7th September, after midnight

Brett stopped the car among the trees in a rest area. It was a large, dark blue family car with three rows of seats. Dominic opened the door and peered into the darkness, but he couldn't see the road. The thin crescent moon, with little cloud, gave a weak light. They were a few minutes' walk from the entrance to the Atelier Cavendish, but not visible from it. This was the perfect location.

Three days had passed since Dominic met with Hannah at the Patagonia Café, the day of the Autumn Ball. Three nervous days, waiting in anticipation of Steve's first night shift at the atelier.

Dominic shivered. The temperature had dropped at sundown, and now, many hours later in the dead of night, the soft breeze in the autumn air held a sharp chill that cut to the bone.

He sent a message on his com-pak while his accomplices sat in silence. Dominic and Brett were in the front, with Al, Gerald and Tim behind them. A few minutes later, Dominic's com-pak beeped, and he peered at the response.

Steve was in position, making coffee. He would disable the cameras, then put the benzodiazepine in the other guard's coffee.

They waited without small talk. They'd gone over the plan so many times they knew it backwards. The consequences if this went wrong were unthinkable, but the plan was simple and the risks minimal.

The silence dragged on. Eventually Dominic's com-pak beeped.

He read the message carefully. "That's it. Steve's ready." He looked at Al. "If anyone you don't expect shows up, keep out of sight."

Al appeared nervous. "All right."

They climbed out of the car. Gerald and Brett both carried bulky backpacks. They made their way across the undergrowth in the shade of the trees. Soon they were close to the lighted entrance of the Cavendish.

"You know what to do." Brett and Gerald nodded and headed off towards the perimeter wall. Dominic watched from the shadows until they reached the wall's shade a hundred yards from the entrance.

They unpacked their backpacks, and Brett prepared the flashbang grenade launcher. While he worked, Gerald paced, watching the entrance doors and the approach road.

Satisfied, Dominic tapped his com-pak to put it in silent mode. He indicated Tim to do the same. They pulled on balaclavas and headed for the entrance door.

Steve was standing over an inert figure slumped on the reception desk. After a moment, he looked up and saw them. He went to the control console behind the desk, tapped in some commands, and they heard a quiet clunk from the doors.

Dominic pushed open the door and walked in, Tim behind him. All three briefly acknowledged each other.

Without a word, Steve went back to the control panel and released the latch on the door to the interior of the building. Dominic and Tim went through into the dimly lit corridors.

Dominic's chest pounded with every heartbeat. He was light headed. They were inside the atelier. Inside the secure compound. The prison. If they were found, they would go to jail.

They followed the corridors until they were close to Fru's

room. Dominic felt the elation of adrenaline coursing through his body. Reaching a junction of the corridors, he heard footsteps around the corner.

They dashed to the shelter of an alcove and pressed themselves against the wall, but it was no use. If the person turned towards them, they'd be seen.

The footsteps came closer. Hannah appeared with someone by her side. She gave a thin smile. "If that's your impression of a flower pot, I've got news for you." She indicated the girl next to her. "This is Deirdre. You can trust her."

Dominic let out a long breath. "You scared me! We had nowhere to go."

"Listen, there may be a problem." Her smile was gone. "Fru's scared. She thinks she'll end up in a penal atelier, or you'll get her out and tell her you don't want her after all."

"For goodness sake!" said Dominic. "What kind of person does she think I am?"

Deirdre rolled her eyes. "Ask her that when you've got her free."

Hannah led them to Francesca's door, then whispered, "At least she knows we're coming." She turned to Deirdre. "Keep a watch, okay?" Deirdre nodded and walked away.

Hannah placed her com-pak close to the door and tapped in a security override code. The door latch gave a soft click, and she pushed it open. Fru sat on the sofa, her arms wrapped around her body. She was shaking violently, staring at the floor.

Dominic's heart lurched. She wasn't just scared, she was terrified.

Fru's voice broke the silence. "It'll go wrong. I'll never see my parents again. And what if someone gets hurt?"

As she spoke, several loud bangs came from outside the building.

"Oh, bloody hell!" Dominic's eyes met Tim's. "Brett's decoy." He turned to Fru. "Fru, there's no time. We've got to go. Come on, let's go."

She sobbed. "I can't. I can't bear it." She lay down and curled up on the sofa, crying.

A loud siren rang out in the corridors, adding to the cacophony. They started as the shrill alarm picked up in each wing, one at a time. Tim stared at Dominic, terror in his eyes.

Dominic knelt beside Fru, trying to keep his voice gentle. "Come with me now. If we don't leave now, it'll be too late."

Tim grabbed his arm. "Dom, we've got to go. Come on." The sounds were getting closer, and the fire alarm jarred.

Dominic looked at Tim, then at Hannah who stood with her mouth open. Fru lay sobbing on the sofa, ignoring them all.

It was too late. He couldn't drag her out, and whatever had happened, there was no time to argue. He'd already stayed too long.

He saw the understanding in Tim's eyes.

Tim touched his arm. "If we try to force her, we'll all get caught. We have to go."

Dominic and Tim ran along the corridor. *Damn, damn, damn!*

Turning the corner, they saw two men in pekay uniforms.

They ducked back, waited for the pekays to pass, and set off more carefully to the foyer. When they got there, the second guard was fast asleep on the desk. Steve was nowhere in sight, so they rushed towards the exit door.

Dominic heard gunfire outside, but who was shooting at whom? They would need to run for cover. As they reached the door, he heard a loud noise behind them. Two pekays burst into the foyer. Dominic turned to look as one of them fired.

With a flash of intense pain, his limbs froze and he fell, hitting his head on the glass of the exit door. He vaguely felt an arm grab his as he regained his feet and staggered out into the night. Everything was a blur.

The cold air hit him like a bolt. The night was alive with ear-shattering gunfire. The arm jerked him towards the shadows of the tree. Crumpling into a bed of leaves on the ground, he moaned. The pain shot from his arm into his chest.

Someone pushed him onto his side and prodded his shoulder. Pain stabbed him and he came to with a loud cry. A hand clamped over his mouth and he struggled.

"Bloody hell." Tim's voice floated among the sound of guns, alarm bells, and loud explosions. "Someone'll hear you. Shut up!"

Dominic struggled to get the hand off his mouth, but the effort caused too much pain. He slumped and gave up. Then the hand relaxed and left him free to breathe easily. He groaned again.

"Dom, we have to get to the car. Can you make it?"

He tried to nod his assent but cried out as a surge of pain ripped through him, down his arm and back up to his head. The arm scooped him up again and guided him farther into the shadows. Stumbling over roots and shrubs, Dominic heard shouts and the sound of gunfire behind him. It seemed as though every pekay in Midfield had turned up and was shooting.

As they made their way into the darkness, the noise and pain confused Dominic. He couldn't see much and kept stumbling. Tim led him, but kept stopping to look around, then setting off again in a different direction. Several times, he re-traced his steps.

Dominic needed to get his wits together. They needed to find the car soon. He stopped Tim and sat down, glad of the rest. Painfully, he entered an encrypted message into his com-pak and sent it to Al. "Shine light into woods."

He rested for a moment to catch his breath, then got Tim to help him up. He was shivering and weak, but starting to think straight. A glance back in the direction of the atelier told him that it was now completely floodlit.

He estimated which direction would take them towards the road. It must be to the right. Tim had taken them too far into the woods. They needed to turn towards the road a little farther up to find the rest area. He squinted in that direction but couldn't see a light. He looked around, but still there was no sign of it.

He pointed the direction he thought they should go, and they set off, stumbling over shrubs and rocks. Every minute or so they stopped and searched for the light. Eventually Dominic saw it farther to the right than he expected. Breathing a sigh of relief, he shuffled on.

As they emerged into the clearing, Al rushed up to them. "What happened to him?"

Tim led Dominic to the car. "He's injured. It's his shoulder. Bloody pekay shot him."

"Damn." Al squinted into the darkness. "Where's Fru?"

Tim shook his head.

Helping Dominic into the car, Al said, "We have to get him to the hospital."

Dominic raised his head. "No. Wait for the others. We're not leaving them here. Brett knows someone who'll fix me up. I can't just walk into a hospital with a bloody gunshot wound."

"Dom, you're losing blood –"

"No. Wait." Dominic grimaced. "See if there's a first aid kit."

Tim and Al searched the car, but neither found one.

Al took the light and shone it back into the woods. A few minutes later, Dominic heard rustling in the trees, and Gerald appeared, trying to run but stumbling. He climbed into the car, breathless. "Brett's coming. I think he's actually enjoying this. Did you know he had a gun with him? He's been with Steve shooting back at the pekays."

"Oh, God! This is a bloody disaster." Dominic's heart sank. A shoot-out with the pekays, Fru still inside the atelier, and people injured. The worst possible outcome for everyone.

A commotion came from the shrubbery. Brett and Steve burst into the clearing, running. Both looked high on adrenaline, and Brett carried a rifle. They scrambled towards the car, talking in loud voices. Al switched off his light and followed.

Al grabbed Steve's arm. "You were supposed to stay behind."

"Not a chance. Not with everyone shooting each other."

Brett said, "Man, we really gave it back, didn't we?" He opened the back of the car and put the rifle in, then sat next to Tim.

Steve was shaking but hadn't lost his voice. "You were amazing!"

Brett carried on. "They were expecting us! How the hell did they know? Somebody must have told them. Bloody hell!"

Dominic interrupted. "Brett, what's the address of your medic? I need help and I can't go to the hospital."

"Oh man! Go to Bridge Street. Number eleven. What happened?"

"Pekays. Bastard shot me in the shoulder."

Steve got into the driving seat and started the car. As they pulled away, Brett tapped a message into his com-pak. "Did you see his face? I'll find him." His face was grim.

"No. And why did you bring a gun?" Dominic was tired and didn't want any more violence.

"It's the grenade launcher. It mounts under the barrel." His expression was awkward and unhappy. He turned to Tim. "Man, I…erm…"

Tim seemed confused. "Brett? What's wrong?"

"Man, it's Hannah." Tim's eyes widened. "It was a bloody pekay. I don't think he meant to, but, well –"

Tim grabbed Brett's shoulders. "You bastard, what happened?"

"Tim, she went down. There's no way she survived that. I mean, it was –"

Tim slumped back into his chair and put his face in his hands. His shoulders shook as he sobbed.

"He paid the ultimate price, man. I saw him do it, bloody pekay. I couldn't just walk away." He paused, then spoke quietly, "I thought revenge would be sweet, but…" He turned his face to the window. "God!"

They arrived at the edge of Midfield in silence and turned to follow the ring road. Tim sat, head in hands, and sobbed while Brett put an awkward arm around him. After a while, Steve turned into Bridge Street and pulled up outside number eleven.

All six of them climbed out and Tim helped Dominic to the door. It opened, and a middle-aged woman with short, grey hair greeted them.

She peered up and down the street, then hurried them in, closing the door behind them. She led them along a corridor into what looked like a fully equipped hospital room where she showed Dominic to a bed. She then cut the clothes from around the injury and inspected it, gently touching it with a surgical probe.

"You did the right thing to come to me." Her voice showed no emotion. "You were lucky they hit only your shoulder."

She cleaned the wound, front and back, and dressed it with pressure pads. Having completed this to her apparent satisfaction, she gave Dominic an injection and told him to lie still.

"The injection was a bit of a cocktail. It has painkiller and antibiotic. You will be fit in no time." She smiled, then turned to Brett and nodded towards the door.

The woman left the room with Brett, and the others chatted in muted tones. Dominic paid no attention to what they said. The pain eased and the tears flowed.

Hannah! The lovely Hannah who was always so kind to Fru, who had been so friendly when nobody else at the Cavendish was. Hannah who made Tim so happy. Dominic felt as though he'd killed her himself. He might as well have done. *Stupid, stupid, stupid!*

The door opened and the grey-haired woman walked in, followed by Brett. She picked up a small device from a table and came over to where Dominic lay.

Seeing Dominic's wet eyes, she gave him a sad smile. "If I could trouble you, would you be so good as to let me scan your identity? I will prepare a bill, and it will appear as an invoice to you at Green's Corner Grocery shop. You must go there and pay it soon. Nobody will know you've been here. I will not see your identity myself."

She passed her scanner near Dominic's wrist and took it back to the table, then turned to Dominic. "I recommend you rest for a few days."

Half an hour later, all six of them were outside in Bridge Street, shivering with cold.

Dominic turned to Steve. "You should have stayed there. They'll know you were involved."

"Oh, that's alright. I've thought it all through. I'll just tell them I got scared and ran away. They'll sack me, of course, but I didn't want the job anyway. I suppose the police will want to talk to me, but that's okay. I'll say the same thing. I'll be fine."

Brett took the car to dump it and set fire to it. He insisted on dropping Dominic home on the way, and Tim stayed with Dominic to keep him company. The rest of them walked home from Bridge Street.

Dominic slumped onto his bed. "Tim, I don't expect you to ever forgive me. I'm so sorry."

Tim, sore, red eyes still glistening with tears, sat cross-legged next to Dominic's bed. He raised his hands to his face and talked through his fingers.

"She was so beautiful. So lovely. She used to make up little songs and sing them to me. Silly songs about people at work or about something we were doing."

Dominic said nothing.

"It's not your fault, you know. We all did this together. It was that bloody pekay." He took his hands away from his face, revealing fiery eyes. "What the bloody hell did he think he was doing? He was mad! Shooting an unarmed, innocent woman." His voice quietened. "He deserved to die."

Dominic didn't have anything to say to that. Did anyone deserve to die? Presumably the pekay had a family too. Then again, what he'd done was unforgivable. He'd never have been brought to justice if he hadn't been shot. This was a different kind of justice.

It was nearly dawn when Tim left Dominic's apartment to

go home.

Dominic lay on his bed, eyes wide open. He had no intention of giving up on Fru, despite the way she'd reacted when he came for her. The price was too high already and the Baron was too big a threat.

41

Wednesday 8th September, 6 am

Unable to sleep, Dominic shredded his escape plans, then watched the news, cradling his arm against the pain in his shoulder. When interviewed, the police said little.

"Our investigation is ongoing. There were two fatalities, a member of staff and a peacekeeper."

Yes, and the pekay was the one who killed the member of staff. Poor, sweet Hannah.

"We will release the names of the victims when their relatives have been informed. The murder of a peacekeeper is deplorable. This investigation has our highest priority."

More deplorable than the pekay murdering Hannah? *Bloody hell!*

"The government," said the news anchor, "has vowed to hold the criminals responsible for what they referred to as 'this reckless law-breaking.' The Nationalist Party is holding a protest in Midfield and another outside the atelier."

A clip showed a crowd at the front of the building. One of them spoke. "The government has lost control and are not taking security seriously enough." His eyes burned. "Society has lost its way, and people are forgetting their duty to others."

The news reporter interviewed pedestrians in Midfield town centre. There was considerable sympathy for what the

Nationalists said, and the camera showed a line of people waiting to sign up for party membership. The news reporter interviewed the dead pekay's wife and showed her crying.

A loud bang shook Dominic's front door, followed by a shout from outside. "Police. Open up."

Dominic sighed and turned off the Axis. He didn't hurry to the door. They wouldn't break it down for at least a couple of minutes. Two men stood at the door with a uniformed, armed pekay behind them. The two men showed their identities, an inspector and a sergeant.

"Good morning, officer."

"We have a warrant to search your home." They pushed past him, followed by the pekay.

Dominic followed them around his apartment as they worked. They opened drawers and cupboards, leaving the contents on the floor. They stripped the bedding, pulled books from shelves and overturned furniture. The sergeant picked up Dominic's axis controller and plugged a gadget into a socket at the back.

While he inspected the display on the gadget, the inspector approached Dominic. He grabbed Dominic's collar and pulled his face close to his own. "You're going to tell me the truth. Everything you know. Get it?"

Dominic nodded, gulping to avoid crying out at the pain in his shoulder.

"Where were you at one o'clock this morning?"

"I was here, asleep, officer."

Lying turned out to be easy. The hardest part was hiding his pain. The sergeant finished his work on the Axis controller and joined the inspector for the interview. Or was it an interrogation? The armed pekay stood over them.

"Where are the explosives?"

Dominic allowed his confusion to show. "Explosives? What do you mean?"

The inspector held out his hand to the pekay, who handed

him a baton. "Don't act stupid, lad, or you'll get hurt. Now, where are the explosives?"

Dominic was sure they wouldn't hesitate to use the baton on him, but what could he say? "I don't know anything about any explosives."

They spent over an hour questioning him. They bullied and threatened him, repeating their questions until he was exhausted. He offered them no refreshments and when they finally left, he slumped onto the sofa, exhausted.

Now Drake would think he was clear to grab Fru whenever he wanted. Dominic suppressed a vision of Fru in the arms of Craig Drake. *I'll save her first or die trying.*

42

10 am

Alex normally enjoyed the company of his associates in the research lab. Ralph was reliable, intelligent and hard working. Claire was nothing short of brilliant. He knew he would never have achieved such a result in his research without Claire's insights and her grasp of the science that underpinned their work. She should get more recognition. She would, indeed. He would make her the primary author of their next paper. That would secure her future in the research field, especially now. He depended on her heavily but knew better than to hold her back or fail to recognise her contribution.

He wondered what Claire would say if she knew the true cost of the serum they'd received from Robyn. She would lecture him in that judgemental tone, then walk out and refuse to work with him.

Today, he didn't want company, so he stayed in his office. He'd not slept much lately, and the headaches were getting worse, as were the pains in his back and neck. Stress. He'd brought it upon himself, he knew. It wasn't a simple matter to relax, though – to ease those painful muscles, remove the source of the pain, rather than treating it with pills.

He was stuck with a situation he no longer knew how to control. There was so much at stake. Not only his career, his work, but the future of the cure. The future of this major step towards salvation for humanity. He had it in his grasp but couldn't prevent it from slipping away.

Now they needed more supplies from Robyn. He had to call and let her know. Robyn would react badly, he knew, but Alex had no choice. The whole project couldn't grind to a halt just because he didn't want a confrontation with his friend. His ex-friend.

Through the window, he heard the sound of someone singing and playing a guitar. It was badly amplified and he sang slightly out of tune. Alex suspected the voice was better for being drowned by the strumming on the guitar even though the playing was clumsy and grating. About half a dozen people gathered around the stage to listen, but most of the campers ignored it.

Alex massaged his temples. Had he led those people astray by making the announcement too early? They saw him as a hero now, but how would they feel if the project collapsed? If Robyn revealed his dirty secret to the newspapers?

He had to find a way to convince her not to do that, but how? He'd tried appealing to the scientist in her. Maybe he should aim for the conscience this time. Try to convince her she'd be letting people down. Letting herself down. Would that work? She didn't respond well to pressure the last time they met.

Nonetheless, he had to make the call. Coaxing, pressure, what did it matter? Robyn had to do this. The consequences if she turned against Alex now were unthinkable.

He made the call.

"Robyn, Alex."

Silence.

"We have to get past this, Robyn. Please. For the sake of an old friendship, at least talk to me."

"Is that why you called? For a chat with an old friend?"

"Partly, yes," he lied.

"And?"

"And we need more serum."

"You know the price." Robyn's voice had a steel in it he hadn't heard before.

"Yes, and I've paid it. Check your bank balance if you're not convinced."

"You didn't think that was the end of it, did you?"

"Does it matter what I thought? As far as I can see, you're asking me to enter into an agreement for which I don't know the real cost."

"Isn't that what I did when I first agreed to help you? Well it's time to pay up. If you don't want to, then it's simple. I'll just go to the press and do the right thing. Expose this for what it is."

It would be useless to appeal to Robyn's better nature while she was in this frame of mind. Alex had to pay or give up everything he'd worked for. "It seems you're holding all the cards. I don't have a choice, do I?"

Robyn carried on as though Alex hadn't spoken. "In fact, sod it. I think I'll go to the press anyway. I'm not harming any more of my patients for you, and I don't want you finding someone else to do your dirty work. I'll put an end to it now."

"Please. Don't do that. Just one more consignment and I'll get you more funds for your research. As much as you need. I'll just have to find a way to do it without exposing what we've done so far. I'll find a way. I promise. Just one more consignment."

Robyn hesitated. "More funding? And only one more consignment? No more harming patients?"

"I'll find a way, I promise. Please." Alex would go on his knees and beg if he needed to.

"I still have some in storage. I'll courier it over as soon as you've made the payment. If it makes you feel any better, the money is going into a trust fund for my patients. It's a kind of retirement fund for them."

Alex sat down. A trust fund. He'd misjudged Robyn. He'd thought the demands for money were selfish greed. Why had he thought that? He'd known Robyn for years, and never had she displayed any selfishness or greed. He'd jumped to that conclusion and judged her. He hadn't even asked.

"You'll get your money. I'll do it as soon as I can get access to the payment terminal with nobody around. Hopefully it'll be lunchtime. It was easier on Saturday."

"Okay. I'll hold off with going to the press for now. You have a lot of influence in Progenetics, but unless you can find funding… I won't be holding my breath, and I will go public if you don't deliver on your promise."

Alex sighed. One problem temporarily solved, a new one created.

Outside, the singing had stopped, leaving an oppressive silence, expectant, waiting.

43

Francesca stood before a glass-fronted book case and gently touched the door handle with a trembling hand. Was this what it was like to have a broken heart? Hannah dead. How could that be? How could anyone allow such a monstrous thing to happen? How could anyone point a gun at a beautiful person and pull the trigger?

Hot tears ran down her face. Dom had caused this. She knew all along it would end in disaster, and now it had. He'd got Hannah killed. Surely he knew the risks he was taking.

She sobbed.

What if she were to blame for Hannah's death? She hadn't meant it to happen. She couldn't ever forgive herself if it was her fault. Everything would have been fine if she'd just done as Dom said. She'd ruined everything.

But if she had gone with him, the pekays would have taken her to a penal atelier. They might even have killed Dom.

Now, just a few hours later, Fru was being blamed. She'd never been on lock-down before, so she'd never really understood what it meant. Thankfully they hadn't moved her to the lock-down wing yet, but what small liberties she had before were gone.

She opened the bookcase door and carefully pulled out a tall, slim volume from a set of ten. She touched the beautiful tooled leather binding.

The page fell open on a ballad called "The Elfin Knight," telling of two lovers who had impossible challenges to overcome before they could be together. The book contained twelve versions of this ancient song, collected by Francis Child, all of which she loved so much.

She sang softly, reading from the lines in the book, but as she did so a strange noise interrupted her. It sounded like a chant, like one of the sports crowds at the big matches she'd seen on the Axis newscasts. It came from outside the atelier. But they were in the countryside, away from Midfield. Why would there be a crowd in the middle of nowhere?

She tried to concentrate on the words of the song, but soon found herself with the book on her lap, staring at the blank Axis screen. Her tears fell, but she didn't wipe them away. Hannah, poor, lovely Hannah.

A faint click came from the door as it unlatched and Deirdre came in. Walking over to Francesca, she perched delicately on the sofa.

"Fru, it's time for your exercise." Deirdre spoke quietly. "I'm to take you to the garden."

Francesca scowled. "This isn't my fault, you know. I don't see why I'm being punished."

"You're not being punished. They say the extra security is necessary."

"Then why can't I open my own front door? Solitary confinement is it?" Deirdre flinched. "It's all very well, but how do you think I feel?"

Deirdre's eyes were sad. "I know."

"It's not your fault. I just hate this."

She wasn't allowed any contact with her friends or with any of the other fertiles. Her daily exercise had to be taken under supervision. All this because of the failed escape attempt and because Hannah died in such awful circumstances.

Francesca exhaled with a sigh. Was she being selfish?

Immature, feeling sorry for herself while Hannah was in the mortuary, her family in mourning.

She stood and carefully replaced the precious book in the cabinet. As she closed the doors, Deirdre said, "I'd be quite happy to keep your lovely books dusted and clean. I know how delicate they are. I wouldn't do any harm, I promise."

"No." Then realising she'd sounded harsh, Francesca smiled. "Thank you. Really, I like to do it myself. It's part of the fun."

The chanting sounds intruded on Francesca's thoughts again. "What's that noise?"

Deirdre avoided her gaze. "Well, it's a protest. There's a crowd outside. They're protesting about the poor security here and about the way ateliers are run."

"Oh, who? Why do they care?"

"It doesn't matter who they are. They're just crackpots."

Francesca stiffened. "This is about last night. It's about me. Who are they?"

Deirdre breathed a deep sigh. "They're the local Nationalist Party. Once the escape attempt was in the news, they jumped all over it. They say it's a sign of what's wrong with…with everything, really. Like I said, crackpots."

Deirdre led the way to the garden. Every time someone passed, Francesca turned away and blushed. She was the prisoner in the exercise yard.

Last night's events would be the only topic of conversation for everyone, and plenty of stories would circulate about what had happened. Few would bear any relationship to reality. What were they saying? It would be ages before she would be allowed to have a normal conversation with her friends, and when she did, they might not tell her what was really being said. Maybe she would never find out.

They came to the garden as daylight faded. In the chilly evening wind, she was thankful for the shelter of the atelier walls. The autumn leaves formed a carpet, and more leaves swirled in the turbulent air. Outside the walls the chanting continued.

Indistinct words.

Approaching her favourite spot, Francesca saw Liang and Jen, arm in arm. They stared as they passed, barely smiling. Fru's heart sank. If her friends thought badly of her, everyone else certainly did.

On a path to her left, four queens stood deep in conversation. Their eyes followed her as they talked. She averted her gaze. At least that way she wouldn't see the looks in their eyes.

She imagined what it would be like if someone else had been the object of an escape attempt – of a Nationalist Party protest. She would gossip with her friends. They would speculate and probably end up saying uncharitable things about whoever it was.

"The damnable thing is I don't know much about what happened. I don't know how or why Hannah was killed. Only that it was a shot from a pekay's gun." Francesca sighed. "This is the biggest gossip opportunity since Kelly's capture."

They passed the gap in the hedge leading into her usual secluded spot and continued following the path deeper into the wooded area of the gardens. Finally Deirdre spoke.

"Your friends love you, you know. They don't mean it unkindly."

"You don't know them like I do. I know exactly what they're doing. I'd be doing the same in their position." She sighed. "It's all right really. They haven't stopped being my friends. They just have to gossip."

Deirdre frowned. "Maybe you're right." She turned to Francesca. "I'm sorry."

Francesca smiled. "Thank you. It means a lot to me." The tears welled in her eyes.

Exercise time was nearly up, so they headed in the direction of the queens' residential building. Arriving back in the more open, grassy area, they heard a call from the path on the other side of the lawn. "Hey, Francesca."

Joseph walked across the grass towards her. Francesca's

stomach churned. "I really don't want to talk to him." She hurried her step, hoping to get away.

"Running away won't change anything." He raised his voice. "Hey, I want to talk to you."

Francesca muttered under her breath, "Yeah, like you did before."

She knew she couldn't get away fast enough to avoid him, so she stopped and faced him. As he arrived, she kicked hard between his legs.

His breath expelled and he hit the ground groaning. She was reminded of him writhing on the ballroom floor.

He moaned, his voice plaintive, "Why? Why?"

A brief gust of wind came from a different direction and she heard the words of the chanting for the first time. *Here to serve. Here to serve.*

Francesca hurried to the entrance door, away from the moaning lord. Deirdre fell in step beside her.

"Wow, I can't believe you just did that."

"Right, just what I need. More trouble."

Deirdre put her hand on Francesca's arm and they stopped. "Fru, trust me. Other than you and him, I'm the only person who actually saw what happened."

Francesca, unsure of what Deirdre was saying, gave her a quizzical look.

"What I saw was him shouting at you and coming towards you. Then he threw himself down and yelled. You didn't do anything, right?"

Francesca let out a heavy breath. "I can't ask that of you."

Here to serve. Here to serve.

"You're not asking it, but it's what you're going to get. Please don't make me out a liar."

Francesca smiled and put her arms around Deirdre. For the first time, they gave each other a warm hug. "Thank you. Thank you."

They made their way back to Francesca's suite and sat

together on the sofa. Francesca told Deirdre about the events at the Autumn Ball and the other undesirable occasions with Joseph.

"The thing is, I don't encourage him. He knows what I think of him, and he still does it. Is he stupid?"

"Probably." They laughed. Deirdre's com-pak beeped, and she read the message.

"They want me to bring you to the Red Room for a meeting after dinner."

"Ah. So, the trouble starts. Are you sure about what you said?"

"Positive, and we have to say the same thing."

"Okay, thanks. Well, we don't know for sure what the meeting's about yet."

Deirdre's com-pak beeped again. "Whoa! I'm popular this evening."

Frowning, she read the message out. "It's from Joseph. 'Please, please, please. Fru had every right, but I only wanted to speak to her. It's important. Can we meet?'"

Francesca scowled. "I don't trust him, and I have nothing to say to him."

"I'm not sure. He said he only wanted to talk. We took his tone of voice as threatening, but maybe it wasn't."

Francesca wasn't convinced. "When has he ever been not threatening?"

"Maybe we should find out what he thinks is so important."

"And give him a chance to molest me again? He doesn't need any encouragement."

"I'll be there too, you know," said Deirdre. "If he does anything like that, I'll have security here before he takes his next breath. He knows the consequences."

Francesca hesitated for a moment. "Okay. If you'll be there, I'll see him."

Deirdre tapped her com-pak and set up a meeting in the garden for later that evening.

"I'll schedule an evening exercise for you." Deirdre did so, then called for Francesca's dinner and left when it arrived. "I'll come back in a bit to take you to the Red Room. Enjoy the meal."

Francesca picked up a novel. It was one Dom had left on his last visit, and she was halfway through. She read, eating little, absorbed in the romance of the story, occasionally distracted by the chanting.

Engrossed in the story, she was disturbed by the soft click of the door as Deirdre let herself in.

"Time to go."

They left the suite and walked to the Red Room. On the way, they passed several people who, without exception, stared. None tried to speak to her. Reading the romance book had lifted her spirits, but it was a temporary relief.

When they arrived, Deirdre wished Francesca luck. Inside, Mildred Knatchbull's dark, expressionless eyes followed her. "Sit down. I hear there was a fracas in the garden this evening." She paused as though waiting for a reaction, but Francesca had no intention of giving one. It hadn't been a question, after all.

"Ms. Napier, do you understand the gravity of your situation?"

"Mrs. Knatchbull, do you think I am stupid?" She figured she didn't have anything to lose, and anyway, why should she take this kind of bullying?

Mrs. Knatchbull's eyes drilled into her. "Ms. Napier, tread very carefully with me. We have alternative quarters where we can move you. I can choose to do so any time, and you would not be there with your possessions, your Axis, or any of the other comforts you currently enjoy."

So, Mrs. Knatchbull had called her here to threaten her. "In that case, Mrs. Knatchbull, I apologise."

Mrs. Knatchbull nodded as though accepting the apology. "Be sure to keep your tone civil with me." She studied her fingertips for a moment. "I enjoy my job, Ms. Napier." She smiled. "It gives me great pleasure."

The woman was intolerable. She was even worse than that revolting excuse of a man, Joseph Cranston. Francesca's heart sank further to think she would see him later on.

Mrs. Knatchbull spoke again. "Tell me what happened in the garden."

"Joseph Cranston shouted at me, then came towards me. When he got close, he suddenly dropped onto the ground. The next thing I knew he was groaning and shouting." She raised her eyebrows. "I simply can't imagine what it was all about.... Mrs. Knatchbull."

Mrs. Knatchbull said nothing for a few moments. Then she smiled. "Ms. Napier, thank you. You have helped me come to a decision."

Francesca took a mental step backwards. *What?*

"I shall make an exception to our normal policy of discretion about partnering information. When you have finished enjoying your free stay, your next partner will be Joseph Cranston."

Francesca's breath came short. "But –"

Mrs. Knatchbull smiled. "Yes. And there's one thing more." She smoothed a crinkle from the dress on her knee. "It is, of course, our policy to always use artificial insemination. We have many reasons, and it's hard to sum them up in a few words, however, our overriding concern is, of course, protection for all concerned."

Francesca's heart pounded. Joseph Cranston? Carry his monster for nine months? She'd rather die.

Mrs. Knatchbull carried on. "However, on this occasion, I believe a relaxation of that particular rule is called for. Mr. Cranston will procreate with you in the old-fashioned way, Ms. Napier. I shall supervise." Her lip curled into a smile. "I have to be sure you are submissive."

Francesca opened her mouth to speak and almost choked.

Mrs. Knatchbull's face broke into a broad smile. "Ms. Napier, why, surely you have some chirpy retort for me?" The smile disappeared. "No? You're well advised to hold your tongue. Perhaps you're learning."

Francesca threw her head forward and vomited onto the carpet. She sat back up again, the taste souring her mouth, her head spinning.

Mrs. Knatchbull tapped her com-pak. "Please tell housekeeping they're needed in the Red Room. Thank you."

She turned her attention back to Francesca. "That will be all, Ms. Napier." She picked up a small file, opened it, and started to make notes.

Francesca didn't know what to do. She stood to walk out, hoping her legs would carry her. Never before had she been so lost. So hopeless. The photos of Dom with that woman, the disastrous attempt to get her out, Hannah dead, and now this. This monstrous, disgusting…revenge. Mrs. Knatchbull was a sadist. She did whatever she liked and nobody stopped her.

Deirdre was outside the door. Her eyes widened when she saw Francesca.

"Are you okay?" She raised her hand to Francesca's face and wiped away a tear. "What on Earth just happened?"

"I…I don't know. Oh God!" She let the tears flow freely, turning away.

Deirdre put her arm around Francesca. "Come on. Let's get some air."

They made their way to the garden. Deirdre set off in the direction of their rendezvous with Joseph, but realising where they were heading, Francesca put a hand on her arm and stopped.

"I can't go. I'm not seeing him."

"Fru, can't you tell me what happened in there?"

"I don't know. She said…" Francesca couldn't say it. She'd have to start at the beginning. She told Deirdre of her conversation with Mrs. Knatchbull. When she came to the part about Joseph Cranston, Deirdre gasped. When she told her about the "old fashioned way" and Mrs. Knatchbull's plans to watch, Deirdre's expression turned livid.

"What? No. She can't."

Francesca wiped her eyes. "Who's going to stop her?"

"Fru, I don't know what's going on, but surely she won't go through with this. Honestly, she's just trying to frighten you. She wants to get back at you because she thinks you've got away with something. She's hateful."

Somehow, telling Deirdre had helped. At least the tears had stopped now. As someone who worked for Mrs. Knatchbull, Deirdre wasn't necessarily going to be sympathetic, but she'd taken Francesca's side without hesitation, and that meant a lot.

"Fru, I promise I'll be there between you and Joseph. Honestly, he won't get anywhere near you, and this time I'll be the one kicking his pride and joy if he tries anything."

Francesca managed a laugh. "I don't know. Why should I see him?"

"Well, one thing's sure. If Mrs. Knatchbull just made that decision, he knows nothing about it. Honestly, he may be a sod, but what she's doing isn't his fault. Really."

"Huh."

"Think about it, whatever he feels for you, I doubt he'll be any more pleased about this than you are. Anyway, he thinks this meeting is about what he wanted to say to you. Why don't we find out what it is?"

Francesca hated being wheedled 'round. "You're right. He's a complete pig, but he doesn't know what that woman just said, and it isn't his fault."

There were few people around, and they made their way to the rendezvous without being noticed. The chanting outside the walls was losing steam.

Joseph was already there. As they approached, he backed off a little, appearing nervous, and held up his hand as if to stop them coming too close. Francesca was glad. Perhaps he was tired of pain.

He didn't meet her gaze. "I want to apologise. I'm not very

good at this, but I need to say it. I've behaved really badly towards you. I know that. The trouble is I don't want to, but it's just what happens. My emotions get in the way and my judgement is bad. The truth is I really like you. Despite what you probably think, I respect you as well." He sighed. Fascinated, Francesca waited for him to continue. She'd never heard him use so many words all at once.

"You know, you're the only queen who won't give me the time of day, and you're the only one I actually respect." He seemed to expect a response, but she gave none.

"Anyway, what I want to say is that in future I'll stay away from you. I won't pester you, I promise. But if there's anything I can do to help you…" He hesitated. "I know things aren't going well for you at the moment, but I'd like to help, that's all."

She waited to see what else he would say, but he seemed to have finished.

"Thank you, Joseph." She kept her voice gentle. She was surprised and touched but wasn't going to say any more. Exchanging glances with Deirdre, she turned to go. They remained silent as they walked back to the suite.

Once inside the suite, Deirdre grinned. "What a sweetheart!"

"Hardly." Francesca's stomach turned at the thought. "But d'you know, I think he actually meant it. Did you see he was trembling?"

"I thought he was going to wet himself. Listen, I'm going to have to go. I've got other stuff I need to do before the end of my shift. Are you going to be okay?"

"Deirdre, thank you so much for everything. I'll be fine."

Deirdre left, and Francesca realised that the chanting outside had stopped. She settled on the sofa with her book. Before starting to read, she tuned the Axis to display a picture window overlooking San Francisco Bay.

The view was over the water, towards the Golden Gate Bridge, with the museum island of Alcatraz in the foreground. The sun shone over the bay. The beauty of the scene didn't change the chill Francesca always felt when she saw the crumbling remains on the museum island. Its bleakness stood out among the beauty.

The prisoners had earned their places in that ancient jail, yet she'd done nothing to deserve her fate here.

A tourist boat pulled up and docked on the Island. Visitors to Alcatraz, not giving a second thought to their own freedom.

44

The meeting room echoed to the sound of voices. The bare walls and high, vaulted ceiling emphasised the emptiness of the space. The long table, seating seven grey-uniformed people, seemed tiny, situated as it was, close to one end of the large, otherwise bare hall.

Mildred studied the frustrated faces of the other committee members.

"No. Certainly not." Her voice echoed around the empty space. "As principal of the Atelier Cavendish, my membership of the Nationalist Party's Midfield Regional committee must not be public knowledge, likewise my associations with the party's National Executive. Particularly now, considering recent events at the atelier."

Stan came to her defence. "Quite. Quite." He banged his fist on the table and glared at the assembled members. "Somebody else will have to do it." His eyes lit up. "I wouldn't mind –"

"No." Theresa, a gaunt, androgynous woman with lank hair and grey skin to match her uniform, held up her hand. "Thank you, Stan, but as chair, it is my duty. This will be one of many press announcements, and since Mildred is unwilling to speak in public, I shall do so myself."

Nods of agreement and a few murmured words of assent settled the matter.

Mildred understood why they wanted her to do the public speaking. After all, she had such a commanding presence, and people listened when she spoke. She was also the only committee member with any experience of public speaking. Nevertheless, she was glad the matter was settled. Theresa would read out their statement at the press conference.

"You have my full support, Theresa," she said. "I'm sure you will be splendid."

Stan snorted, then coughed as though to cover it up. Theresa offered a weak smile, and the other four committee members studied the table.

They were at the end of today's agenda and Theresa asked if anyone had other business to discuss. Mildred answered before anyone else had the chance.

"Yes, I do. As you are aware, there has been an attempted breakout from the Atelier Cavendish. Unsuccessful, I might add. The attack was orchestrated from the outside, and it is supremely important that the perpetrators are brought to justice."

The other committee members gestured their agreement.

"I've acquired some information that implicates a friend of the queen who was the target of the attempt. His name is Dominic Fadden. Of course, I've passed that information to the police, but that will not be enough. I would like instructions to go out to all party members in Midfield. I'd like Mr. Fadden and his friends watched closely."

"Certainly," said Theresa. "I'll send encrypted instruction messages to all the members after the meeting."

Stan rubbed his hands together in undisguised glee. "I'll organise the duty rosters and assignments." He beamed at Mildred.

Mildred thanked them, and the meeting drew to a close. She excused herself from the customary small talk and left.

Something bothered her. It seemed logical that Fadden had attempted to free Napier, but if he was the recipient of the explosives, why were they not used in the attack?

45

9 pm

Dominic winced. Every time he did anything with his right arm or hand, the pain gripped his shoulder and shot down his arm.

He took out a sheet of paper and some charcoal, but when he tried to draw, he only managed a shaky scrawl. His hand shook, and the pain in his arm caused jerking movements. He brushed the paper aside.

He hadn't slept for over twenty-four hours, but there was no time for slacking. He needed to decide what to do next. His friends would be in on the process from the start. He called each of them in turn and told them to meet him in the Share and Coulter. He was in no mood to be told he should be resting and ignored the advice.

He walked to the Share and Coulter and bought a pint of beer. Typically for a Wednesday evening, the bar was almost deserted. He took his beer over to the usual table in the Snug Room and waited.

A few minutes later, Brett and Steve arrived together. Brett said, "Dom, you look terrible." He wasn't laughing and displayed none of his usual flippancy. Sitting down, he carried on. "Listen, man, you walked in there like a bloody lamb. You weren't prepared, most of us weren't armed, and we were massacred. It was stupid."

Dominic peered into his beer. He couldn't argue with that. It was stupid, and Hannah's blood was on his hands. He looked up. "And?"

"And you can't leave it at that. She's still in there and you're still out here." Brett waved his hand towards the door. "And the fucking pekays are out there celebrating another victory and glorifying that murdering bastard as a bloody hero."

Steve put his glass down. "I suppose I've always thought of pekays as just *there*, you know, necessary checks and balances and all that. But what I saw last night… We were outnumbered, and they were so brutal. It didn't have to be like that. Horrible."

"What is it with pekays?" said Brett. "They're quick enough to use violence against innocent people, but when anyone fights back they cry 'shame' and complain that hurting a pekay is the worst crime ever. Why is it worse to kill a pekay than for them to kill Hannah? Eh? Where's the sense?"

"It seems to me the pekays want it both ways," said Steve. "Violence is okay if they use it but not if anyone else does."

Brett sighed heavily. "Do you know they're planning a pekay funeral procession right through the middle of town? They want maximum news coverage and they're going to make us out to be scum." His eyes glared. "Are we going to just sit back and say 'Okay, we tried our best, never mind'? I can't do that, man."

Dominic suppressed an urge to thump him. Give up? Of course he wasn't giving up. His voice trembled as he spoke. "No, Brett, nor can I. We're not going to do that."

Sipping his beer, he saw that Brett and Steve were watching him carefully.

"Look, I screwed up, and Hannah was killed as a result. That's my fault, but Fru won't be staying in there. If I wait for the Baron to get her out, then her life will go from bad to unbearable or worse. I'm not waiting for that to happen. Will you help me do this job properly?"

They both said, "Yes."

Brett said, "Dom, this time it has to be decisive. No messing.

No being squeamish."

"Quite." Steve nodded.

Dominic frowned. "Brett, there's been too much violence. You want to use force and I don't. We have to get her free, but I can't risk getting more people killed."

Gerald walked in, closely followed by Al and Tim.

Brett's expression turned serious, and he looked around before speaking more quietly. "I never killed anyone before. Trust me, you don't want to have to do that. I still feel sick." Pain darkened his eyes.

Steve, Al and Tim sat down with their beers, exchanging subdued greetings.

Al's voice shook. "Last night was shit. I never want to live through anything like that again." The others nodded and murmured in agreement.

After a few minutes of conversation about the disaster, Gerald asked, "So what have you guys decided? You looked as though you were hatching a plan when we came in."

Dominic checked through the door to the main bar, but nobody was near enough to listen. "Not much so far, but we're in agreement that we have to get Fru out of the Cavendish before the Baron tries, and we have to be decisive about it. We can't risk failure again. It'll be worse this time because security will be tighter."

His friends grunted their agreement. Al was silent.

"Are we all in on this?" Dominic asked, rubbing his shoulder.

Brett and Steve had already answered the question. Gerald and Tim quickly agreed.

"Look, we have to be organised, and we need more collateral if we're going to succeed."

"I know you're not keen on this," said Brett, "but I have loads of friends who are good at this kind of thing. Quite a few of them have experience in active service, and they train the rest how to tackle active service situations. Battlefield situations, man, if you know what I mean."

"I think we know what you mean, but I was serious. Nobody else must die."

"Look, this is important. I know what you think of my Combat Society friends, but if it's war, then we're the people to fight on your side. I'm not exaggerating. The pekays won't stand a chance even if they use their special forces. They won't know what hit them."

"That would be nice," said Tim.

Dominic wished he could do or say something to help Tim feel better. "I can't even begin to know how you must be feeling right now, Tim. I feel bad enough, God knows, but this is so much worse for you. But this isn't about revenge. We can't make it that. Otherwise we'll just be escalating a war. Getting more people killed won't help Hannah, and it won't help Fru."

"Look, I have my reasons for wanting to do this. Let's just leave it at that. I'm helping." Tim glared.

Steve turned to Brett. "I don't suppose I could borrow one of those pistols you showed me, could I?"

Dominic sighed. He just wanted his friends to help him come up with a decent plan to get Fru out. Now it was getting out of control. Brett wanted to start a fight with the pekays, and Steve and Tim wanted to join in. He couldn't risk Tim's emotions getting the better of him. The last thing he needed was a breakout attempt marred by revenge attacks on pekays.

"Anyway…" Brett cut in as though his little speech hadn't been interrupted. "If you're in agreement, I'll get on to my friends and get a campaign plan together. All we need to do tonight is figure out when we want to do it."

Dominic opened his mouth to answer, but Al spoke up first, anger in his voice. "Look, you've already proved you can't do this. You're putting Fru in more danger and getting on the wrong side of Drake. Her best bet is for Drake to get her out." He stood and jabbed his finger towards Dominic. "Don't get her killed. I won't help you do that."

Dominic's heart did a somersault. "Any escape is unavoidably dangerous, but I'll do everything possible to avoid the risk of anyone getting injured. Particularly Fru. I'll get her out, but I'll make damned sure she doesn't get hurt."

Al glared at Brett, then at Dominic. "What's the matter with you? Don't you see what you're doing? You've paid Drake, and he'll get her out. That's dangerous enough, but at least he's equipped to do it and experienced enough to succeed. But you… all you'll do is mess up his plans and make it all go wrong. The pekays will turn it into another bloodbath, and whatever happens, Fru will be the victim. Worse still, you want us to help you do it."

The strength of Al's words hit Dominic. "You're backing out. I don't want anyone to feel under pressure." He wanted to make it easier for Al. He couldn't ignore the danger to Fru, but it would be worse if they didn't free her before Drake got to her. "I'm really sorry. And thanks for last night. We couldn't have done it without you." He felt stupid saying that. What exactly couldn't he have achieved without Al? "Anyway…thanks."

Al left his beer and walked out.

"It's okay," said Dominic. "I don't want anyone to help with this if you're not…you know, okay with it," he looked around the table at his friends. "Anyway, if you're with me I'm grateful. I'm not doing a great job of figuring out how to get her out, and you're my only hope."

"So, anyone else not in on the plan?" asked Brett.

Dominic's heart sank. Brett was about to turn this into a fully armed attack. "Brett, we're not going to start a war." He put his beer down heavily on the table. "We're not going in there with guns blazing. We're not killing anyone, and we're not getting anyone else killed. Enough!"

Brett put his hands up in a gesture of submission.

Steve spoke up. "I just think if we go in fully prepared, we can get her out without violence. But at least we'd be ready to respond properly if…well, if it goes like it did last time."

"We don't have any better plan," said Tim.

They all turned to Dominic. He was at a loss. "You all seem to favour Brett's idea, but that will just lead to more bloodshed. There must be another way."

Brett cleared his throat. "Well, er…" He reddened a little. "Look, I don't have all the answers, but I'll get together with my friends and we'll make a plan. We won't do anything unless all of you agree. Okay?"

"Brett, I can't do it," said Dominic. "I'm sorry, but setting out with loaded weapons is a recipe for disaster. The answer is no."

Brett sighed. "I tried, man. I tried."

"I suppose that's it then," said Gerald. "You go and hide back under your rock and we all just go home. Right?"

Something snapped inside Dominic. He didn't intend his arm to sweep his beer glass from the table. He didn't choose to stand and turn as the half-full glass shattered on the floor or to walk away from his friends. Away from the shards of glass, the shocked faces. It was as though someone else was inside him. His legs carried him but he wasn't the one moving them. The next he knew he was in the cold evening air, cradling his arm against the pain from his wound, walking home.

A spasm of pain gripped his shoulder. Had he ruined his chance of getting help from his friends?

46

Thursday 9ᵗʰ September, 11 am

Francesca sat in front of her Axis and peered at the screen. The display showed purchase options and she needed to decide whether to commit. Percy's *Reliques* had been first published in 1765, but this was a later edition. She was thrilled to find it because she only had a one volume abridged version, and she'd so far failed to find a copy of the full three volumes of the original content.

Even though it wasn't a first edition, it was very old and an amazing find. She carefully inspected the facsimile on the Axis. The set of books appeared in excellent condition as the seller claimed. Their price was high and non-negotiable, so she had to decide soon whether to pay it or miss the opportunity to acquire this rare and wonderful set of books.

She was probably stuck here forever now. She would need to find a way to distract herself, to occupy her mind. With a shaking hand, she committed her money to the transaction. The set of books would be on their way and should arrive tomorrow. It was her consolation gift to herself.

She crossed the room to the glass-fronted cabinet, taking in the beauty of the books. Such a wealth of history in a small cabinet. Just a few dozen volumes of precious ancient books arranged on three shelves. It was an amazing collection started by her grandfather and much expanded since he bequeathed it to her. There was room for a few more volumes, but then she'd have to find another cabinet. She tried to figure out where she should put the next cabinet, but then her heart sank.

The next cabinet. This one represented four years of collecting rare books. The next cabinet would be what? Another four years of collecting rare books? Another four years of having babies she'd never see, staring into a future of just more of the same? How could she go on with this?

She'd had several messages from Dom since the terrible events of the night before last, and she'd read them all. What was she supposed to think? Maybe he really hadn't been with that woman. Maybe she'd made a terrible mistake, but considering the outcome of the breakout attempt, she thought not. She'd be on her way to a penal atelier and would never see her family or Dom again.

Dom should have left it to Craig. Craig seemed quite capable of carrying it off. On the other hand, what if Dom's stories about him were true? Could they be? They just didn't seem to fit with the person who'd been so kind to her. Anyway, once Craig got her out, she'd never have to see him again if she didn't want to.

There was little prospect of anyone getting her free in the foreseeable future. The security lock-down since Dom's failed attempt had ruined any hope she might have had. Knatchbull would see to it that nobody got anywhere near her if they posed a threat.

No. If she was ever leaving this place, she'd have to wait for things to calm down first. A year or two? Maybe more.

Perhaps, if she escaped in a couple of years' time, the Progenetics cure would be nearer to being a reality, and she would have a real chance to start a family with Dom. Maybe it would all be spoilt, though. After all, her free stay would expire in two years. After that she would be put through the cycle again. If she escaped after that, they would be bringing up someone else's baby irrespective of any cure. Maybe it would be

Cranston's. Maybe by then, Knatchbull would have carried out her disgusting threat. Francesca shivered.

A loud crash accompanied by a deep boom from somewhere in the building made her start. The room shook slightly, and she heard raised voices. Outside her suite, somebody ran noisily down the corridor, and there was more shouting. An alarm sounded, one she wasn't familiar with. She knew the fire alarm well, but this was different.

There were more loud noises from far away in the building. They sounded like explosions or weapons being fired, but she couldn't be sure because the walls muffled the sound.

Nothing showed on her com-pak – no calls. With shaking hands, she tapped in a call to Deirdre but got no answer.

The noises continued, louder, getting closer. She heard running feet in the corridor and someone crashed into her door as they passed. Her heart leapt. She backed into the bathroom and shut herself in.

The latch of her suite door released and someone burst in. She cowered to the back of the bathroom and looked around for something to defend herself with. All she found was a soap dispenser, so she picked it up. The door to the bathroom banged open and Deirdre ran in.

Francesca dropped the soap dispenser and met Deirdre with an embrace. "Thank God!"

Deirdre wrapped Francesca in her arms. "I don't know what's happening, but I'm here now. Are you okay?"

"I think so. I'm scared. I was locked in. I couldn't…" She burst into tears and Deirdre hugged her tighter.

The noises outside grew louder, more confused. Francesca and Deirdre crept towards the suite door and peered into the corridor. It was difficult to make out what was happening. People ran in both directions, some shouting. The bangs and explosions were out of sight, but getting closer. Suddenly Joseph appeared around the corner and ran towards her.

"Fru!" He was breathless, his eyes wide. "Are you all right?"

"Good God! Yes, Joseph, what the hell's going on?"

"I don't know. I heard all the noise. I thought something might happen to you."

Francesca was surprised. "Joseph! You really do care."

The fear in his eyes changed to hurt. "You should get back in your suite. Close the door. I'll stay here and make sure nothing happens to you." She stared at him. "Please, get inside." He hurried her through the door and shut it behind her.

Francesca backed away, fearful. It sounded as though the explosions were happening in her own corridor. She was trapped. Unless whatever it was went by, she would be in terrible danger very soon. Deirdre put an arm around her as they watched the door.

Outside, Francesca heard renewed shouting, more explosions and a loud cry, then a crash. She jumped as the door shattered and fell away in pieces. Four men wearing black body armour and combat helmets stormed in brandishing guns. They rapidly pointed them around the room as if to quell any resistance. One of them came straight to Francesca and grabbed her arm, peering at her face.

She heard him say, "This is her." The other three came over, surrounding her.

Deirdre shouted, "No!"

One of the men hit Deirdre across the head with his gauntleted hand. She reeled across the room and fell over the table. She didn't get up. Francesca barely heard her own scream as the man who had grabbed her arm forced her towards the door.

In the corridor, Francesca gasped. Joseph lay inert on the floor in a pool of blood with one arm bent in an impossible direction. Her legs gave way, but the man picked her up.

The other three formed a protective shield around her as he carried her towards the entrance foyer. They passed more people on the floor and some who cowered in alcoves or doorways, but nobody tried to stop them. As they came into the entrance foyer, Francesca saw more devastation.

The glass entrance doors were shattered and the foyer was wrecked. Aaron lay face down on the floor by the smashed reception desk. His clothes were drenched in blood.

She realised with shock that she hadn't seen a single pekay.

The four armoured men carried Francesca outside and continued until they were out of sight of the atelier. They arrived at a black limousine and pushed her inside. Two of them climbed in with her.

Baron Craig Drake sat opposite, calmly watching her, smile lines in the corners of his eyes. "Hello, Francesca."

The two men took off their body armour and threw it out of the limo. The helmets and gauntlets went, and soon they were just two men in black suits. Both were heavily built, their suits of fine quality but tight over their muscles.

"Francesca, would you do me the honour of joining me?"

Craig held out his hand to her, but she stared back.

"Sit with me," he said. "Take my hand."

She folded her arms. This good looking and charming man was smiling at her across a car, talking about holding hands while the blood of dozens of people stained the floors only a hundred yards away. Something was horribly wrong. Surely Craig wouldn't be so violent?

But she'd seen it with her own eyes. The ruthless efficiency with which his men had cut down anything or anyone who stood in their way. Poor Joseph, slaughtered trying to defend her.

She tried to keep her voice calm. "Take me to Dominic."

He made no reply. He simply watched her as though observing the results of an experiment. He was different. He still had the smile lines around his eyes, but deep inside, his expression was cold, unnerving.

"I want to see Dominic, now." The sooner she was with Dom, the sooner she would get over this rising fear.

"I'm afraid that won't be possible, Francesca," Craig said. "I shall take you somewhere secure now."

"So, now I'm your prisoner instead of theirs." She glared at him.

He smiled. "Oh, come, Francesca. You're a free woman."

"So let me out of here."

"I'm afraid I can't do that. You see, I have a contract to fulfil."

"I see. So I'm free to do whatever you tell me?"

He sighed but kept smiling. "You're a plucky woman, Francesca. I like you. You will be glad of what I have done. You'll see."

So what next? She thought of some of the stories Dom had sent her in those messages. Would she soon be reunited with Dom? Would she end up chopped into small pieces, scattered over Chessington Common? Probably not, it was a long way away. Maybe Midfield College playing fields? Or a trail of bits along the river path?

But why? This break-out was organised like a small-scale war. The pekays must have been kept away. How much had Dom paid the Baron? Surely not enough to cover the cost of such an attack?

If the Baron had spent more on the breakout than he was paid, what was his motive? He seemed to look on her kindly, but these weren't the actions of a kind man. The man she thought she knew. In fact, this was more like the pathological behaviour of a madman than the reasoned actions of a normal person.

Could he really have fallen for her? Could he really want a relationship with her?

Or was he a killer? A murderer? Maybe Dom was right. A horrifying prospect if Craig had fallen for her.

47

3 pm

Dominic sat on his sofa with a plate of bread and cheese and a cup of coffee. Jabbing his finger at the Axis controller, he flicked the display over to the news. He breathed in the rich, strong aroma of the coffee before taking a sip, then picked up a piece of bread with a large chunk of cheese balanced on it.

The news announcer read the main headline. "In today's breaking news, the residents of Midfield are in shock following a military style attack on the Atelier Cavendish."

Dominic stopped, mouth open, bread and cheese poised for a bite.

"So far, few details have been released, but I can confirm that there have been at least four fatalities, and many of the injured have been taken to Midfield Hospital."

The cheese dropped from the bread onto his lap. His mouth hung open.

"The names of those killed will not be released until their next of kin have been informed. Here is our report from the scene."

Dominic closed his mouth and missed putting the bread back onto the plate. The news reporter stood in front of the wrecked atelier foyer and explained what little they knew of the events.

"No one knows who carried out the attack and nobody has

taken responsibility for it. The peacekeepers arrived afterwards to discover a communications whiteout coincided with the attack. Police believe it was caused by a powerful electronic jamming device outside the atelier, but no such device was found at the scene. As a result of the whiteout, nobody was able to call for help until the attack was over."

The reporter interviewed Mildred Knatchbull who was fiercely upright, ready to take on anything he might say.

"I heard the sound of gunfire and explosions but found that my office door would not open. I attempted to notify the police, but my com-pak would not connect."

"How long were you trapped in your office, Mrs. Knatchbull?"

"Only about four minutes. Afterwards, I did a roll-call of staff and residents and discovered four fatalities. Three of my staff and one resident are dead, and another resident is missing." She looked straight into the camera. "The missing resident is the same person who was the centre of a failed escape attempt only thirty-six hours ago. The dead resident was found outside the missing resident's suite door."

"Do you have any idea who might have carried out the attack?"

"No. This violence is shocking. I will launch an immediate investigation into how my security failed to protect us from this callous attack. The perpetrators *will* be caught."

Dominic watched in stunned silence. *Please, God, let her be alive.*

He turned off the Axis but continued to stare at it. He'd left it too late. He'd let her down and now she was in terrible danger. Would Brett have attacked the atelier despite Dominic's objections? Surely not. He sent a message to Brett. "Was it you?"

A few seconds later a reply came back. "No, man. This is not good."

The brutality and the pseudo-military style of the attack

made it clear. It could only have been carried out by the Baron. Whatever Drake's plans were for her, she was completely at his mercy. That was the worst possible situation.

Dominic cupped his head in his hands and groaned.

What now? Would the Baron just hand her over? Maybe, but he'd not contacted Dominic yet. Anyway, given everything that had happened, it seemed likely that Drake had his own plans for her. Worse, Dominic had failed to save her before, so what chance would he have to save her now even if she was still alive? He'd never know whether she was unless she was found dead. Like those other people.

Like those other people! This was his fault. If she turned up dead, he'd signed her death warrant.

So many deaths and they were all the result of his actions. How could he ever face anyone again? How could he even look in a mirror? What a complete, utter and unforgivable idiot.

The door chimes sounded. A voice, as if through a loud-hailer, shouted.

"Police. Open up."

48

3 pm

Craig brushed the damp hair from Dahlia's face. She was flushed, her breath still heavy, chest rising and falling as she lay beside him on the huge, curtained bed.

"What will you call her?" she asked, caressing his naked chest.

"I've been thinking about that. I shall call her The Golden Hind."

Dahlia roared with laughter. "Shall I get you a cutlass?"

Craig smiled. "Only if you have time. Our first trip is in less than a week. We're taking a short holiday to celebrate our new business venture."

"That's great. Maybe we should go to Valparaiso, score ourselves some Spanish gold on the way."

He laughed, watching her sip champagne. "And what would a lady pirate wear for this adventure?"

"Oh, I think they dress the same as the men pirates. You know, big smelly trousers and a shirt with baggy arms. And a cutlass, of course."

"I don't know. I think I prefer a sexy, sweetly perfumed lady pirate. You'd be much better at that."

"That gives me an idea." She gently caressed his face. "I'll surprise you with it on the boat."

Craig leaned back, basking in the moment as Dahlia snuggled close in and put her head on his chest. For a while neither of them spoke. He was pleased with the progress of his plan. Gurt had done a good job leading the strike, and he would have more confidence now. The whole thing was faultless. Craig smiled at the thought of the confused looks on the pekays' faces when they were interviewed by reporters. So rewarding.

Then, of course, there was Francesca. When he first met her, he'd thought she was rather sweet, even if a bit young. Since then, it had become obvious that she was no more than a mouthy, emotionally backward brat.

She'd have to learn that it was in her interests to please him. If she did, he would be kind to her, but if she fought him, he would win, and she would regret trying. On balance, she didn't seem like the kind of person who knew what was good for her, so she would probably fight.

He hadn't anticipated this aspect of his new business venture. He'd have to tame her. What a delightful thought. The new dimension this brought to the endeavour would add spice to an otherwise mundane task. It was a pleasure he could enjoy any time he felt the desire.

"Oh, my!" Dahlia moved her hand down to caress his arousing body. "Again?"

He sat up. "I wish I had time." He topped up Dahlia's champagne glass, but not his own, and kissed her lips.

"I have to go. I have some business to attend to."

Dahlia lay back and closed her eyes, the smile still on her face. Craig put on his clothes and left the room, heading for his office.

There were two doors to his office, one facing his desk and one behind it. He always used the second one when he had a visitor. In the hallway, he stopped to inspect himself in a full-length mirror beside the door. Perfect.

He walked in, and without looking at his guest, went to his desk and sat down. Finally he made eye contact with his visitor, a wiry young man with short, lank, black hair and dark eyes. Al Jones, the slimy Judas.

"Mr. Jones," he said, "you've already told me all I need to

know about your so-called friend Mr. Fadden. Why are you here again?"

He watched the young man twist his hands together and thrust his chin out as though trying to appear strong. "I helped you because I want Francesca to be safe."

"No doubt," said Craig.

"Well, Dom...I mean, Mr. Fadden, is wondering where she is." He appeared to be warming up, "And I'm wondering why she's still here."

Craig considered for a moment before replying, "Mr. Jones, I really have no idea what you're talking about. If you even consider causing any trouble, the consequences to you will be beyond your worst nightmares."

He paused to allow time for this to sink in. Mr. Jones' face went as white as a sheet.

"I hope I've made myself clear, Mr. Jones. I don't intend to repeat myself."

The young man looked nervous, glancing from side to side.

"Goodbye, Mr. Jones." Craig gestured towards the door with his hand. For good measure, he tapped his com-pak, and Gurt came in to show Mr. Jones out.

When the Judas was gone, Craig left his office the way he'd arrived and headed for the obscured basement door. On reaching Francesca's room, he unlocked the door and pushed it open. "Hello, Francesca."

She lay curled up on a small steel framed bed. She didn't stir. Craig sat next to her.

"Francesca, my dear." He brushed a tear from her cheek. "I'm sorry I haven't been able to see you sooner. I hope you like your room."

She stared at the wall.

"It was the best we could do at such short notice." He stood and folded his arms. "Your young man made a real hash of things. By doing so, he forced my hand, and I don't like that. He's done a very stupid thing, Francesca. Be thankful I was able to save you."

Francesca sat up, suddenly animated. "Save me! Save me

from what? You took me from my home to this prison. How many people did you kill, Craig? How many?"

"You really are ungrateful. I may have to punish you if you talk like that."

"Punish me? You're mad." She lowered her voice, no longer shouting, but her voice trembled with emotion. "You really took me in. I believed your lies and deceit. How does that make you feel, Craig? You're an accomplished liar, a murderer, what else? You've taken Dom's money, so you're a thief –"

Craig slapped her face, leaving a bright red welt across her cheek.

"Control yourself, young lady. You're here because that's what you asked for. You will show some respect."

Francesca glared. "What will you do with me? What do you have planned?"

"You'll have to wait."

He smirked and left the room, locking the door behind him.

49

5 pm

The police didn't interview Dominic in his home this time. They took him to the Intel Headquarters and shoved him into a small grey cell.

A uniformed officer stood at the door, stern and forbidding. Two heavyset men in plain clothes came in and wasted no time with niceties. One pushed him roughly into a chair.

"Where were you this afternoon at 1 pm?"

Dominic frowned. "At home."

The officer stood too close to him, tall and threatening. "Were you alone?"

"Yes."

The officer raised his arm as though ready to strike. "You're lying. Where were you?"

"Christ!" Dominic cowered. "I told you. At home."

After another hour of questions, threats and bullying, they hadn't let up.

"You're not going home until you tell us what happened. Where is she?"

Dominic folded his arms. "Who?"

The officer slapped him, almost knocking him off his chair.

"Don't act stupid, sonny boy. We've hardly got going yet."

He lost track of how long they carried on. Despite their

threats and the heavy-handed approach, he stayed surprisingly calm. He knew they had nothing to connect him with the crime, and the disgust he expressed when they asked about the violence was genuine.

At the end of the interview, he'd given them little. They grabbed an arm each and manhandled him into a car. When they reached his home, they stopped.

"Don't leave town. Don't go anywhere. Do you understand?"

"Yes. Yes, I do."

The officer who sat next to him leaned across and opened his door, then shoved him out.

Inside his apartment, he closed the door and leaned against it, breathing heavily. He could no longer think straight. What on earth should he do? After the Baron's performance at the atelier, he didn't relish the thought of trying to get Fru away from him, but he had to do something. She was taken from the atelier six hours ago and there was no word from Drake. The number he originally used to make his appointment with Drake no longer connected, so the only way to contact him was to go to the House of Fun and ask to see him, which would be too risky.

What an unholy mess. The death toll was etched in his mind. Hannah. The pekay who shot her. Three members of atelier staff and one of the lords in today's débâcle. All pointless, stupid deaths. All would have been avoided if he'd never gone to the Baron in the first place. What had happened to Martin? After introducing him to the Baron, Martin had stopped showing up at work, stopped answering his calls. Was he a victim too?

Dominic pressed his knuckles into his temples. Recriminations would have to wait. For now, he needed to decide how he would get Fru back to safety.

The door chimes sounded. He waited, but this time there was no amplified, threatening voice.

The chimes sounded again. He couldn't think of anyone he wanted to see now. Putting his hand on the latch, he hesitated. He didn't have to be at home. He lifted his hand from the door latch and turned back towards his living room. He started as the chimes sounded again, followed by a thump on the door.

Dominic sighed. He opened the door to find his father and Janet standing there.

His dad wore a forced smile and had a large bag in one hand and a bottle of Afterburner in the other.

"Hello, Dom. Chinese takeaway?"

Dominic rushed forward. He hugged Janet, then his dad, and suppressing his own tears, invited them to follow him into the kitchen.

"We've been interrogated by the police all afternoon," said his father.

"I hope they treated you better than they did me."

Dominic's father studied his face for a few moments. "From the look of you, I suspect they did. They took a liking to Janet's home-baked fruitcake. I thought the younger one was going to move in. Quite disturbing really."

Janet levelled her gaze on him. "How about you pour some of that Afterburner while I dish up some takeaway."

Dominic went for glasses while Janet spooned fried rice onto the plates. They sat down and conversation gave way to spicy beef, honey-roast duck and Kung Pao prawns.

After a few mouthfuls, Dominic no longer felt hungry. How could he eat while Fru was in danger because of him? "I have something to tell you."

His dad put his knife and fork down. "You know where she is?"

"I have an idea, but I'm not sure. It has to have been Craig Drake."

Janet raised her eyebrows. "And he took two goes at it? When we heard about the first escape attempt, we honestly thought it was you. After what you told us."

"It was me. It was all my fault. Hannah dying, everything."

His dad stretched across and filled up his glass. "So, what are you planning to do?"

Dominic sighed. "That's the problem. I don't know."

His dad looked enquiringly at Janet, who nodded.

"Do you remember that evening when you asked if we were going to Brett's re-enactment?"

Dominic sighed. "The re-enactment of the Bataille Pas De Calais. *If you poke a sleeping tiger, you have to stand and fight.* That was it, wasn't it? The message of the battle?"

"I want to ask you a question," said his father. "It's a hypothetical situation. Let's say, at some time in the future, you and Fru are happily married and have a child and a home of your own. One night, deep in the darkest part of the night, you hear an intruder. You get up to take a look and find there is a man in the house. He hasn't seen you yet, but he will any moment now. You have no time to make a decision. You have to act instantly."

Dominic drew breath to speak, but his dad carried on.

"He may be armed. If he is, he could easily kill you, rape your wife and murder your child in its bed. You have no idea why he's there, but you know he's bold enough to break into an occupied house in the night. Before he notices you, there's an opportunity to take decisive action. You can kill him there and then or give him the advantage – wait to see if he's a killer and rapist."

Dominic let out a heavy breath.

"Which is it to be?" asked his father, his gaze intense, urgent.

The realisation hit Dominic. "Oh, God! You killed someone?"

His father's face was grim. "It was when you were only a year old. Before your mother and I divorced. I have no regrets. It was him or my family. I couldn't take the risk, and I would do the same again. Your mother never got over it."

"I think I need more of that Afterburner," said Dominic.

"Me too." His dad poured three more drinks. "What are you going to do about Fru, Dom?" His voice was soft but urgent.

Dominic watched his father steadily for a moment, then tapped his com-pak.

Brett answered. "Hey, man. What's up?"
"We have to talk. I need your help.…"

50

7 pm

Alex and Janet drove home, and as they climbed the front steps to their door, Alex heard a voice.

"Hey, I want to talk to you."

He turned to see Robyn appear from the shadows, pointing her finger and walking towards him with unsteady steps.

"Robyn? Are you okay?"

Robyn slurred the words. "Oh, sure, sure. I'm just fine. What, don't I look it?"

"You're drunk. What the hell are you doing? It's only seven o'clock."

"I may have had one or two." She frowned. "Nothing wrong with that."

The last thing he needed was a confrontation with Robyn outside his own home.

"Get in the car, for goodness sake." He opened his car door.

"Yes, sir." Robyn saluted and stumbled into the passenger seat, landing heavily.

Alex turned to Janet. "I'll take her home." He scowled. "I won't be long." He climbed into the driving seat.

"Now, what's going on? Why are you here drunk?"

"Hey, don't you give me a hard time. Anyway, I've made a bold move."

That didn't sound promising.

"What have you done?" Not the newspapers. Please, not the newspapers.

"Aha! Wouldn't you like to know?"

Alex checked the time. "Look, I'm not in the mood for this. You came here to tell me something. Now tell me."

"You," – Robyn leaned forward and prodded Alex's chest – "will be proud of me. Yes, you will."

Alex folded his arms and frowned.

"I've destroyed all the Iaso data. Gone, all of it."

Alex's heart pounded. "Iaso data? What are you talking about?"

Robyn's face cleared a little. "All of it. Equipment parameters, volumes, levels, source datasets. Everything I've used to get that vile serum. Now we *have* to find a better way."

The pounding in Alex's chest echoed in his ears.

"No. Tell me you're joking. This is just a stupid prank. Right?"

"No, sir. Took years to put it together. Now it's gone." She grinned. "Got to do it properly now."

"But –"

"Couldn't do it. See? I couldn't do it and live with myself." She peered closely at Alex. "Surely you see that?"

Alex started the car. On the way, Robyn dozed in the passenger seat. This was a disaster. Once the last of the serum was used, that would be it. Unless they came up with a new way to extract it, they were back to square one. They had a cure in need of a source material that didn't exist. It was as useless as having no cure.

What was going on in Robyn's mind? She must have thought it was the right thing to do. But why? Why do this now when they were so close?

Alex sighed. He knew perfectly well why. What they'd done was awful. Maybe Robyn had done the right thing. Maybe the price was too high.

Whatever the morals, Alex now had a huge problem. It dawned on him what Robyn had done. She'd banked the money, then forced Alex to find a way to get her more project funding to accelerate her research. Nothing was more important now.

51

7 pm

Dominic knocked on the black-painted front door, its gloss long faded and peeling where the wood was rotting. Most houses in the street were built to the same design. Uniform terraces with a single window beside the door and two above it, giving the front rooms a view across the street to another house exactly the same.

His knock triggered a dog barking in the house next door. A large, black dog, jumped at the window, leaving a slime of saliva, bouncing back but coming again, vicious, undeterred, its teeth bared.

As Dominic watched its impotent attempts to reach him, a bolt clicked, then another, and the door in front of him opened.

"Come on, man, you're making Sampson go nuts."

Brett, in his usual combat trousers and camouflage shirt, led the way into the small front room. A huge, ageing, threadbare sofa in an unpleasant light brown colour, "shit by moonlight" as Brett called it, dominated the off-white room. An ancient sideboard, shelves and tables stood around the edges of the room. Books, binoculars, a compass, and many other strange devices, as well as boxes and cartons of various sizes, littered every surface.

Occupying most of the wall opposite the door, arranged in

a fan-shaped pattern, a display of vicious looking knives and swords surrounded a bright metal shield with a vivid coat of arms in a central enamel panel.

A space had been cleared on a low table in front of the sofa, its peeling varnish surface covered in rings from cups and glasses. In the space stood two glasses of beer.

"Expecting someone?" asked Dominic.

"Hah! You're late." Brett pointed to the table. "Have a beer."

They both sat. Dominic was impatient to get down to business.

"I've put this off too long. I only hope I haven't got her killed."

He half expected Brett to laugh, to say he knew it would come to this, that he'd said so all along. But Brett just fixed his eyes on Dominic, waiting for him to finish speaking.

"So, if the offer still stands, I'd like your help. You and your Combat Society friends."

Brett peered into his beer for a few moments, frowning, before looking back up at Dominic.

"Okay." There was no smile, no back slapping. That was it.

"I need advice about a few things too. Logistics," said Dominic. "Particularly money. I'll need to come up with more to pay for this."

Brett's demeanour brightened. "How big a loan can you raise?"

"Loan? I can't afford a loan. I owe Drake a bloody fortune already."

Brett was warming to the subject. "But it doesn't matter. Don't you see? The moment you've got Fru, you'll have a new ID, and any debts you had…well, you won't exist, will you? You won't have to pay anything back because you'll be a different person. Debt ridden Dominic Fadden will have disappeared forever."

That was startlingly obvious. *Why didn't I think of that before?*

"Anyway," continued Brett, "take out as many loans as you

can, as much money as possible, and don't stop borrowing until they won't lend any more. Then go to the loan sharks and get more. I'll give you an account number, and as you get the money, transfer it into the account."

Dominic laughed. "Oh, yeah? And what happens to it then?" He trusted Brett completely, but this was risky.

"One of my friends is a banker. There's a way he can move it to an account in your new name, and it can't be traced back."

Dominic's hand shook as he took a large sip of his beer. He knew that if Brett trusted his friend, then he could trust him too, but what if the money never turned up?

Brett cut into his thoughts. "Do you think you've got anything to lose? It's the only way you can pay your expenses. Anyway, it's borrowed. It's not your money, is it? If something goes wrong, which it won't, somebody else loses, not you."

"I suppose not. I just wouldn't get the money, but you're right. It would be someone else's loss." He sighed. "Can I have another beer?"

After Brett poured more beers, they talked through the logistics.

"I have a friend of a friend who will do the ID chips," said Brett. "He's reliable, and you'll be able to stay with him overnight when she's freed. You can stay there, get the ID chips the next day, and be on your way. Go to a different part of the country where you won't be recognised."

"Recognised? I just realised… Won't they put pictures of us out on the news?"

"Normally they don't, but when they do, it never leads to anyone being caught. You'll just have to keep your heads down for about six months. Anyway, even if the police come knocking on your door, the best they can do is ID you, and if you don't match, then they have to leave you alone. They'll have nothing on you."

Dominic's heart was racing. The risks were enormous, but he didn't have a choice anymore. Fru was in immediate danger, and he had to save her.

"As soon as possible, get together a case of everything you want to take with you. Nothing distinguishing, no family photos or anything like that. Just clothes, toothbrush, stuff like that. Give it to me and I'll make sure it's at the ID guy's house when you get there."

Dominic nodded and took a long sip of beer.

"So where is she?" asked Brett.

"What? Well, at Drake's House of Fun of course. At least, I assume she is. Why, where else would she be?"

Brett frowned. "I dunno, but that seems risky to me. If we wade in at the wrong place, we've shot our bolt. We won't get a second go with Drake."

"Well, it's all we've got to go on, and I'm not giving him any more time. God knows what he's up to, even now. If you've got any better ideas, tell me. Otherwise we go for the House of Fun."

Brett swirled the beer in his glass but didn't drink it and eventually put it back on the table. "You're right. There's no other choice."

They sat in silence for a few moments. Then Brett stood. "Come with me."

Dominic followed him up a narrow stairway and into a back room. Brett switched on the light as they entered, showing faded paint on the walls. A blackout blind covered the window. A bench took up one complete wall, and three tall, grey metal cabinets occupied the wall opposite. Small tables and boxes cluttered the rest of the room, and guns of every imaginable kind lay on every surface.

Dominic gasped. He'd known Brett had a large collection of weapons, but this was incredible.

"I've got out a few examples for you to look at." A broad grin transformed Brett's face.

Dominic said nothing.

"Okay, let's start with this one. Craig's people usually use

AKs. This is the latest AK assault rifle. It's basically the modern version of the old AK47s. It's probably what most of his men will carry."

He handed it to Dominic, who gingerly took it and felt the weight. It was the first time in his life he'd held a gun. The steel was cold in his hands, and the weight suggested solidity and purpose.

"Some of them will have handguns. Craig's guys usually carry one of these." Brett handed him a heavy black handgun, and he put the rifle back on the table.

"That's semi-automatic with an eight-round magazine, but you won't be counting the shots, trust me."

Dominic turned the gun in his hands, and Brett picked up another from the table.

"Now Drake himself, when he wants serious fire power, carries one of these."

He waved the gun in front of Dominic. It was a large, clumsy looking pistol with a long magazine protruding underneath.

"Don't be fooled by its looks. It's a handgun, but it's a fully automatic submachine that can fire 850 rounds a minute. The terrorist's weapon of choice. This, my friend, is evil in the palm of your hand."

"Bloody hell, Brett. You own all these?"

"Well…yes. Anyway, don't get in front of that one if you can help it. In fact, don't get on the wrong end of any of these."

A wave of nausea struck Dominic. His skin prickled. He was committed now, and this was no game. He would carry a gun, and he would probably be shot at. He knew how that felt and didn't ever want to repeat the experience. For the first time, he realised he might die trying to rescue Fru. She was worth it. His only regret was if it came to that, he wouldn't be there to care for her.

"So," he said, "we'll be up against all these guns. Will we have the same kind?"

"No. Most of our guys will carry an HK assault rifle." He

pointed to a rifle on the bench. "It has a higher rate of fire than the AK, but to be honest, once we're up close, it doesn't make much difference which you use. I need to take a long shot. You'll see why. So I'll be carrying this."

He picked up a large, black, military rifle from the bench and held it for Dominic to see. This formidable looking weapon reminded him of newscasts when they showed soldiers in war zones.

"This is another HK, but it's that one's big brother. It's the latest battlefield version." He grinned. "This is mean." He handed it to Dominic.

Unlike the AK, which was cold steel with a wooden butt, this felt more like a plastic toy. "So," he asked, "Will I use one of those?" He indicated the HK on the bench.

"No, man, I've got something special for you. This could have been made for you. It's perfect."

He picked up a shorter rifle from the bench. It looked no less terrifying for its smaller size.

Dominic frowned. "I've seen these. It looks like what the pekays use."

"It is. It's a compact commando assault rifle. Here, have a feel."

Dominic took it and felt the weight. It was easier to hold than the others and lighter.

"I'm going to take you to the firing range tomorrow," said Brett, "and you're going to use it until you're confident with it. It'll be on a sling over your shoulder so you won't drop it. Dropping your gun in a battle is the last thing you'd ever do."

"I'm sure," said Dominic, unsure whether to worry that he liked the feel of the rifle in his hands. What did that say about him? He found he was surprisingly comfortable with the thought of using it to protect Fru. To rescue her.

"Steve and the others will have to come to the range too. However long it takes. You all need to be capable with these if we're going to succeed."

They talked for another hour about logistics and the order of events for the day of Fru's rescue. Brett insisted that Dominic leave the planning of the assault to him and his friends. They knew what they were doing, and Brett would explain it to him once the planning was complete.

"When this is done," said Brett, "you and Fru won't be able to just pop in on the family for dinner. You know that, don't you?"

"Yes, I realise that. But I really need to be able to see my dad, and Fru will be devastated if she can't see her mum and dad again."

"You'll be able to see them, but it'll take some arranging, and you can't risk doing it too often."

"Oh? How do you know about these things, Brett?"

"Man, you've been planning to get Fru out for four years. I've done my research, trust me. At first I honestly thought you'd let me help you get her free, but as time went by I realised you didn't want to do it that way. I wanted to be ready, though. In case you changed your mind." He grinned.

"So how do we see our families?"

"In a nutshell, we're going to agree on a date and place for your first meeting. I'll tell them about it when you're safely away. After that, each time you meet, you arrange the next meeting. Do it verbally and don't write it down. Use a different place each time, and make sure it's a long way from where you both live. Avoid patterns. Don't see them the same time every year, don't see them too often, and make sure the places you choose are dotted around the country. Don't try to see them in the first year, and don't ever send messages to them. That's about it, really."

Brett pondered for a moment. "Oh, and one more thing. Every meeting you arrange, you have a back-up meeting arranged in case it doesn't happen for some reason. That way you don't end up breaking the cycle of arrangements."

For the first time, Dominic had a plan he believed in. Until now he had wanted it badly, needed it, and planned for it. But he realised that deep down, he'd never had a deep-rooted confidence that he'd thought of everything. That his plans would work.

Brett's words were reassuring, to say the least. He'd obviously done his research well, and thanks to his Combat Society, he knew the right people. Now, the more they talked through their plans, the more Dominic realised this was it. Six months ago he would never have believed he could have this kind of confidence in Brett. *Why did I ever doubt him?*

52

Francesca held her trembling hands in front of her. She clenched them into fists before folding her arms, pacing around the tiny bedroom.

Why was Drake doing this? He'd got her out of the atelier for Dom. But then, why all the lies? Why the fake romance? He didn't harbour any romantic feeling towards her, so what did he want? Why didn't he take her to Dom? That was the contract.

There must be something she could do. She was stuck here in a squalid cell with a primitive bathroom and a smelly bed.

She'd make him regret it. Like she did Joseph. She felt a pang of guilt. Poor Joseph. So much blood. He didn't have to die.

She sat on the edge of the bed, thinking through the situation. There was no doubt now about the truth in Dom's messages. If she had answered them, believed them, would this have been avoided? She didn't see how. If she'd gone along with Dom's escape attempt, it would have resulted in a one way ticket to a penal atelier. Drake would still have come to get her, and she'd still have ended up here. But why here?

Perhaps he still intended to hand her over to Dom, to fulfil the contract, but couldn't because of some problem. Maybe he just had to wait until the coast was clear, the police paying less attention.

Her heart clenched. What if Dom had told Drake he didn't want to take her away? What if he was in love with the pekay's wife?

But he couldn't be. Wasn't that all just Drake's lies?

One thing was certain. If she stayed here, it would drive her mad. She had to get away, but how? Would Dom come and save her? He'd tried when she was in the atelier. Would he be more successful getting her out of here? Not likely. Anyway, without her com-pak, she had no way to contact him. No way to ask him what was going on.

She had two rooms – no windows. A bricked up patch of wall in the bathroom must have once been a door. In the bedroom, one door provided a way in or out of her prison. The door Craig had come in by. The door through which her food arrived. She went and tried it. No more luck than last time. She rattled the lock.

Nothing.

She rattled it again, harder.

It didn't move.

She banged the door with her fist. Both fists.

"Let me out of here," she shouted. "Help. Help me!"

Both fists now, banging on the door. Her feet kicking. Bruised hands, bruised feet.

She stood back and took a swing at the door with her foot. A good hard kick. She put all her might into it. Her foot made contact with the door and her senses imploded. Pain shot through her foot, numbing her toes, and excruciating pain from the arch shot up to her hip.

She stumbled back towards the bed but didn't reach it. She fell, hit her head on the side of the steel framed bed, and landed hard on the floor as darkness overcame her.

53

Friday 10th September, 3:30 pm

Dominic checked the time. Later he would meet with Brett and the others, but until then he had some free time. He decided to watch the news, and when the Axis screen blinked into life, the newscaster was already speaking.

"… controversy surrounding Ms. Knatchbull, the ex-principal of the Atelier Cavendish, accused by a member of staff of planning a supervised rape. Since her highly publicised dismissal from the post last night, Ms. Knatchbull appears to have wasted no time." They showed a picture of Mildred Knatchbull standing in the centre of a raised platform, flanked by four other people. She wore a grey uniform with a red, five-pointed star on an armband. She had a grey, peaked cap and stood rigidly to attention.

The newscaster continued. "The Nationalist Party has today entered into negotiations with the government in what they refer to as 'a proposed reform of policy on atelier management.' Mildred Knatchbull has emerged as a member of their National Executive and represents them in negotiations."

The camera went back to the scene on the platform. Dominic stared at the Axis – at Mildred Knatchbull in Nationalist Party uniform. How could she be their leading voice only a day after losing her job? He blinked.

"As a member of a government department, in the role of

principal, my hands were tied. I was bound by government policy, not only on security, but on every other aspect of atelier management. I am, I'm sure you are aware, the best qualified person to formulate reforms to this area of government policy. My proposals are as follows –"

She continued speaking, but the sound faded back to the newscaster who went on to explain. "In addition to atelier security, Ms. Knatchbull's proposals would cut spending on what she refers to as unnecessary privileges for fertiles. Most controversial is the proposal to reform the breeding guidelines to protect what she refers to as racial purity. Despite strong opposition to this part of the Nationalist Party proposal, the government may be forced to consider it in view of the decline of their own popularity. The opposition parties in parliament, anticipating a Nationalist led coalition after the next election, insist on voting for the Nationalist Party reforms as a package. They say a piecemeal approach will only weaken government."

Dominic sighed. How would rejecting any of this nonsense weaken government? Politicians never made any sense. If all this was true, it meant that Mildred Knatchbull might end up with a role in the next government.

The door chimes sounded. Distracted by his thoughts about the newscast, he went to the door and released the latch. On the doorstep stood two large men in black suits. He recognised both of them. He knew why they were here.

In a cautious, low voice he said, "When can I see her?"

The giant, unsmiling, held a small piece of paper out to him. On it were the same bank account details he'd seen before. "The next payment," was all he said.

"Ah, of course." He tapped on his com-pak, then hesitated. "But when will I see her? Soon?"

They both just stared at him. With shaking hands, he tapped in the bank details. He held his hand over the com-pak, poised to complete the transaction. This was his only bargaining chip. Surely now they'd answer. "Well?"

Four hands curled into tight fists. Jaws clenched.

This was pointless. He couldn't bargain with these thugs. He tapped the final instruction into his com-pak.

They turned their backs and walked away.

"Wait!"

They were gone.

54

4 pm

Robyn Harland closed the large double door and walked towards her office, exchanging the peaceful calm of the residential wing for the clamour of activity in the research complex. The care staff would look after her patients until her next rounds, and until then she had time to make sure she hadn't missed anything when she'd erased all the Iaso files from the system. Never again would her patients be subjected to that abominable procedure.

Iaso was gone, and so was the weight that had hung over her since they first discovered its effects. She couldn't undo the harm that had already been caused, not without a significant breakthrough in the research. But she could make sure it never happened again and ensure that her patients were well cared for.

Alex would have to find his own way. If he brought extra funds to her project, the research would progress more quickly, and he would have his serum sooner. Otherwise he was on his own. Either way, no more Iaso – and no more harm to the patients.

She sat at her desk and opened her journal. Every day she recorded her day's work in longhand. Most of the researchers kept their journals on the computer system, but she preferred paper and a pen. The notes, scribbled diagrams and a multitude of other jottings that would be illegible to others were her favoured way to record her daily progress in her work. Yesterday, however, she'd been so stressed by the time she finished erasing all the Iaso files that she completely forgot to write her entry. Today she would carefully record what she'd done.

As she had every day since she graduated.

She dropped her pen and swivelled around to look at the shelf behind her desk. There, among the long row of old journal books, she realised there must be records of Iaso. Records she'd made in her own handwriting as the work took place.

She wouldn't need to get rid of them because they didn't contain the key data and parameters. Those had been stored on the system in the Iaso files, now safely gone. She realised, though, that she needed to read back through some of them to make sure there was nothing that could be used to reproduce the procedure.

She ran her finger along the row of journals, looking for the date of the start of the Bartrev-Moskalet's Disease research project. She spent about ten minutes flicking through the pages but found nothing that worried her.

Half an hour later, deeply immersed in a trip down memory lane, discarded volumes littering her desk, she spotted a margin note that grabbed her attention. The first word was "Shame!"

Fascinated, she read the note, recalling the events that led to its writing.

A research team in the Moscow State University had made some real progress in the area of spinal injuries. They found what they believed would lead to a method to stimulate the spinal cord to repair itself. That research held the promise, she'd noted at the time, to offer them a way to stimulate the regeneration of the spinal fluid of their Bartrev-Moskalet's patients. At the least, it would give them a generous supply of the serum, and at best, it might even lead to a cure.

She'd called the lead researcher in Moscow, and he'd informed her, regretfully, that the research was in its early days and a long way from providing what she needed.

She frowned, tapping her teeth with her pen. That was two years ago. So much for her valuable system of recording her work in her journal. She'd never followed up on the lead. What if they could do it now? She had to find out.

She looked up his name on the system and called him. The conversation took nearly an hour, leaving her head spinning. They hadn't published the results yet because they'd just finished verifying them, but they had succeeded in their mission. They could stimulate spinal tissue to heal itself.

He was interested in her potential application of the result, and after much discussion of the technical details, they concluded it had a high chance of success. All she had to do was verify the process on her patients.

She would need additional funds, of course, but with this potential, fundraising would be easy.

Hanging up, she sat and stared out of the window, unseeing. This was it. The breakthrough they needed. If this worked, if it proved to be safe, they'd even be able to provide Alex with serum.

Or would they?

She'd destroyed all the Iaso data.

She tapped her com-pak to call one of her senior researchers. "Could I have a word, please, in my office? Thanks."

She waited for him. If anyone had a personal copy of the Iaso data, it would be him.

He knocked and walked in.

"Hi, thanks for coming. The thing is, there's a problem."

He raised his eyebrows.

"All the Iaso data has been erased."

"Oh?" He frowned, but slowly his frown turned into a smile. "You erased it, didn't you? You know, I'm kind'a glad you did really. I mean, we won't be needing it again, and it's one of those things the world's better off without. I thought of doing it myself, but –"

"Listen. What if we could stimulate regeneration of spinal fluid in our patients? Then Iaso would be the key to creating enough to work with. Right?" She watched him digest this thought. "Well, we probably can."

"What?" His look was incredulous. "I know you've been working long hours, but if you've cracked this without the rest of us knowing, I'll eat my own shoes. We'd have seen the results on the system. It's not there."

"No, that's not what's happened. It's the Moscow team. Do you remember two years ago, the research into spinal regeneration?"

"Yeah. It didn't lead anywhere."

"Well now it has. They're sending their processes, data, everything over to our system –"

"What, no payment?"

"It's state funded research. They make it freely available. We'll get new funding, validate the results, and be well on our way to a cure. But we need Iaso, and I erased it yesterday."

"I see."

"You don't happen to have a copy of the Iaso data anywhere, do you?" That was the big question. She almost didn't want to ask it in case the answer was no.

"A copy? No. It was always on the system when we needed it, and we haven't used it since we changed our research direction."

"So, that's it. Another two years of painstaking data collection, constructing source data sets, experimenting to establish volumes and equipment parameters. All the research we've done will need to be repeated."

"I bet you didn't erase it all though. You couldn't have."

"Trust me, I was thorough." This was depressing.

"So you went to Midfield West, found the backup disks for the mirror data site, and destroyed them, did you? You'll have some trouble if you did."

She realised she was staring at him with her mouth open. "My God. You're a genius."

55

7 pm

Craig broke open the first of the two boxes. Inside was a large, gleaming metallic, egg-shaped object with a flat base and a small control panel set into the top. There was no documentation, no instruction book, just the disruptor bomb – a darkened silver egg with a hint of sapphire blue.

Lifting it from the crate, he placed it on the table beside the first of the bomb assemblies. The egg weighed more than its mere dimensions would suggest. He now had everything he needed. It would take some work to install the disruptors into the bomb chassis and set up the split-second timing for the detonation, but he would enjoy the challenge. This was important. Too dangerous to hurry.

He had a momentary vision of himself in a care home, dribbling while a nurse spoon-fed him slushy food. Victim of a disruptor detonation. The worst thing would be not even knowing to put an end to his own life. He'd just live on, vegetative, unaware of his loss.

He shook his head to dispel the unwelcome image. No mistakes.

Mog leaned forward to peer at the control panel, a childlike bewildered expression clouding his face. For a fleeting moment,

Craig considered letting Mog take the risk, giving him instructions to set it up, then removing himself to the other side of town before Mog did so. But no. He had to make sure it was done properly. To cause a mistake in the very effort to avoid one would be folly, and he was not foolish.

Craig ran his hand over the cold, mirror smooth surface. "Such an elegant object. So much awe inspiring destructive power resembling the source of life. Beautiful irony, don't you think?"

Mog looked up, his expression confused. "Irony, Baron?"

"Yes. Don't you wonder whether the person who devised this mighty weapon was pleased with his achievement?" asked Craig. "Did he stand back and admire his creation?"

Mog shrugged and glanced at the nearest bomb frame. Craig carefully lifted the egg into the frame's upper segment. He nodded to Mog, who secured it with straps and bolts.

Craig opened the second box and peered into the reflections in the egg's gleaming surface. "Whoever invented this opened a new door to human suffering and invited anyone to walk through. Anyone able to afford the technology. His technology. Was that a moment of pride? Perhaps he believed that force should be met with force. After all, other world powers were busy developing new weapons of their own. It was his duty to keep abreast."

He looked across at Mog. No reaction. He took the second egg from its container and positioned it similarly in the second bomb frame. As Mog began strapping it in, Craig stood back.

"Perhaps, instead, the inventor simply followed where his research led and considered the result to be justification enough." Craig sneered. "The unfailing excuse of the scientist."

"Yes, Baron." Mog finished bolting the second bomb to the frame and stood straight.

Craig removed the panel from the controller on the first disruptor bomb. "Our objective is to kill any member of the research team who might understand the methods used and to destroy all the data. If we simply destroyed the building with explosives, we'd probably kill the right people but risk leaving recoverable data among the debris."

Mog grunted.

"The disruptor bomb," said Craig, "detonated a fraction before the explosives, will wipe out all the data and scramble everyone's minds. The explosives will do the rest."

Mog smiled. He seemed to understand that part.

Craig removed the second bomb's control panel cover. "All I need to do now is to connect this controller with the wiring for the explosives."

He worked in silence. Mog stepped back and said nothing.

Ten minutes later, Craig stood upright and eased his shoulders. He hadn't realised how tense his muscles had become. It didn't matter though. He'd finished wiring both bombs. "I've set each with a delay of five seconds. The disruptor will detonate, and five seconds later the explosives will demolish the building." He turned to Mog. "It's too late in the day now, and tomorrow is weekend, so we'll do this on Monday morning. You'll go to the Midfield West lab and Gurt will go to the Midfield East lab."

"Yes, Baron."

"I shall put one device in each of two stolen cars. You and Gurt will tell me when you have parked them. Then you'll get away as quickly as you can. I'll give you ten minutes."

"Yes, Baron."

"Once you're both far enough away, I'll detonate them from here."

Mog's shoulders shook with mirth.

"Have I said something funny?" asked Craig.

"No, Baron. I just wish I could see it."

56

7 pm

Dominic walked slowly and arrived at the pub feeling lower than when he'd left his apartment. The attitude of Craig's two gorillas didn't bode well. He'd have to be decisive and quick if he ever wanted to see Fru again.

He bought a drink and took it through to the Snug Room. His friends were already there – except Al.

Brett gave him a meaningful nod, so Dominic asked, "All sorted?"

"Yeah, man. We've got a lot of support on this one. To be honest, there's been nothing like this for years. They're all ready whenever you are." Brett raised his beer glass and touched it to Dominic's.

Hearing these words, Dominic felt a flutter of fear. "This mustn't get out of control."

"I'm keeping a tight rein on it, don't worry." Brett frowned and spoke more quietly. "I don't ever want to feel like that again." He gazed into his beer, then grinned. "This'll go like clockwork. All the best people, best gear, best planning. We'll make Drake's lot look like a gang of street kids up against a professional army."

Gerald folded his arms. "Would one of you mind telling me what's going on?"

Steve answered. "I have a pretty good idea."

Dominic raised his hand to silence them. "We're going to free Fru from Drake. Brett and his friends will help. It'll be dangerous, and I'm not asking any of you to help. We'll use any help that's offered, though."

Gerald, Steve and Tim spoke at once, all volunteering.

"There's one possible problem," said Dominic. "Fru's a fertile and so is the Baron. We know from Hannah that he's been coming on to Fru and she's been taken in. She might actually want to be with him rather than me. She might not want this."

"Christ, Dom!" Brett's eyes widened. "You can't be having second thoughts. Drake's a murdering bastard. She's not safe with him. We're not just doing this for you, for God's sake. We're doing it for her."

"Fru might say *I'm* a murdering bastard. Have you thought of that? She'd be right, too."

Tim spoke quietly. "She might, but you haven't killed anyone." He kept his eyes averted from Brett, whose shoulders sagged.

"I'm not saying we shouldn't do this. I'm just saying she might resist us. She did last time, and it was disastrous."

"That wasn't what went wrong," said Steve. "Somebody warned the pekays we'd be there. Otherwise, how would they have known? If she hadn't refused to come, she would be in a penal atelier by now."

Brett took a long drink from his beer before speaking. "There's one more problem. Some of our members are Nationalist Militants. Anyway, I've been told they're planning to be there."

Gerald interrupted him, "So they're going to try to stop us? Betray us to the pekays?"

"No," said Brett, "these people have their own axe to grind with Drake. He's made enemies among their friends, so they won't be telling their party leaders. They're there for the action."

Tim made a wry grin.

Brett went on, "They're Combat Society members. They're showing up for a fight."

Gerald's eyes narrowed. "I hope you're right."

"I'm sure of it. Even so, to be honest, they're our biggest threat. If they find out we're freeing Fru from Drake, they'll want to get her themselves and return her to the authorities. For them, this is about attacking Baron Drake because he's lawless. They mustn't know about Fru."

"Who'd tell them about Fru?" asked Tim.

"In theory, nobody," said Brett. "Apart from us there are only four people in the raiding party who should know about rescuing her, and none of them is Nationalist. The rest are coming for a raid on the Baron. Trouble is we need some key people to know because we have to rely on them. But one careless word and we have a huge problem. If they don't know, our chances go way down." He turned to Dominic. "So what's your decision?"

"Do we have a choice?" asked Dominic. "Is there another way?"

All four of them stared at Brett. "No. To be honest, this isn't a great situation. We don't know how the pekays found out last time, so we're at a disadvantage. Fru might not want to come, and the bloody Nationalists might steal her from under our noses. I don't see any better way, though."

"Tell them," said Dominic. "We're going to do this right. Just make sure they understand."

"Right," said Brett. "Since you said you'd got involved with Craig Drake, me and my buddies have been studying his habits. Everyone has a weakness, so I figured he must have one. Now I know what it is."

Dominic was fascinated. Craig Drake had a weakness? "Oh?"

"Yeah." Brett sat up straight and smiled. "He likes to step out of his office and take a breath of air. He does it several times a day, and he's pretty regular about it. He comes out at the same time, give or take ten minutes. It's priceless."

"Oh, right," said Gerald. "He likes to take a breather. Now I know we're going to be alright." He pulled a face. "Brett, have you been smoking something?"

Brett frowned. "Trust me. It gives us a way in."

Al walked in. He had no drink and stopped when he reached the Snug Room doorway. His hair was dishevelled and his eyes bloodshot. Dominic's eyes were drawn to him as one by one his friends fell silent.

"I thought I'd done the right thing," said Al. "I thought Fru would be pleased with me. Maybe think better of me. I didn't want it to be this way."

Dominic was confused. "What the hell are you talking about? What didn't –"

"Listen!" Al's hands and body shook. "She's being held at the House of Fun, but you won't find her if you don't know where. She's in a basement room. The door to the basement is covered by a wall hanging. It's a picture of a big boat." He turned and walked out.

Brett leapt from his seat to follow him.

"Don't," said Dominic. "Leave him. Christ! I don't believe this."

Gerald glared at Al's back. "We have him to blame for the pekays knowing about our plans."

"I don't think so," said Tim. "He wouldn't have told the pekays. It's not his way."

"Either way," said Dominic, "he bloody well betrayed us to Drake. Bastard."

"I'll tear his fucking head off," said Brett, his hands curled into fists.

"Later," said Dominic. "We can't get side-tracked now. If he hadn't told us, we might not have found her." He frowned. "Now we know what to look for."

"And you trust him?" Brett's eyes blazed. "Maybe he's setting us up. Have you thought of that?"

Dominic sighed. "I don't know whether we can trust what he said, but it's all we've got. He's obviously been through the wringer. Maybe Drake's screwed him over too."

"Your decision, man. Are we going to trust him? It'll either help us or get us killed."

Dominic thought for a few moments. "Yes. We look for the wall hanging and find the basement, but we'll hedge our bets. We'll have other people looking elsewhere, too. Warn your people that Drake may know we're coming."

57

7 pm

Alex accelerated, thankful that the traffic was light after work. That precious last package of serum Robyn had sent was on the bench, ready for work to re-commence tomorrow.

With it, he could repeat the tried and tested process and make a final batch of Priapus. He knew exactly how much of the drug it would yield, and he had uses lined up for all of it. He would put one dose aside for Dom and one for himself, then set up the early stages of the clinical trial. Indeed, the trial wouldn't start if the regulators did not see a demonstration of the technique.

He had data, of course, proving that Jake Roseberg had been infertile before treatment and fertile afterwards. Nonetheless, they would want to see that same test carried out in front of their observers before they would authorise the trial. They had to be convinced that the objective was worthy of the inherent risks.

He also had data to show that Jake continued to show no side effects from the treatment. The next milestone would be getting permission to use Jake's seed for insemination in an atelier queen. She would not, of course, know that she'd participated in an experiment, but if she fell pregnant, they would, quite literally, have living proof of the efficacy of Priapus.

Alex made his way through the evening traffic, reflecting. Not every insemination using a lord's seed resulted in a pregnancy, but they would only have to try two or three times at the most, and the queen would fall pregnant.

What he doubted was whether he could convince Progenetics to fund a new research project for Robyn's work to produce the serum. The whole application process would be clouded by secrecy. If he could produce a convincing argument that it was the foundation of Priapus production, he would shoot himself in the foot. Robyn too. They would investigate how he'd produced the initial batches, and the truth would come out.

If he didn't argue that it was needed for Priapus, how could he give it the priority it would need? He couldn't see a way through the dilemma.

His com-pak beeped, and he checked to see who was calling. Robyn. He muttered a curse before answering the call. "Hi, Robyn."

"Alex, you won't believe what's happened."

Her animated voice was a startling contrast to last night when she was drunk, slurring her words as Alex took her home.

"We've made a huge breakthrough. We think we'll be able to regenerate my patients' spinal fluid."

"What are you talking about?" He swerved to avoid another car. "Last night you told me you'd destroyed all your data. You had nothing left to work with. You can't be telling me you've found an above-board way to make the serum."

"But I have. I know how to do it." The excitement in Robyn's voice was infectious.

Alex knew her to be an experienced and cautious scientist. If she said she'd succeeded, she had. No doubt, Robyn had made a major breakthrough. "But how?"

"Well, this afternoon I went through all my old notes to make sure I'd been thorough. You know, getting rid of all the incriminating research. I found a notebook from the early days. It was there. A lead I had two years ago with a research team in Moscow State University. They didn't have useful results then, and I forgot all about it, but I spoke to them today, and they've made a breakthrough in spinal injury repair processes. We're sure I can use it to regenerate the spinal fluid in our patients. They haven't published it yet, but they're willing to share the results with us."

"Are you sure about this?"

There was no answer. Only silence. Alex knew better than to doubt Robyn's judgement on something like this. She'd never have made the call if she was uncertain.

"Sorry," said Alex. "I'm sure you're right, but... Great Gods! Do you realise what this means?"

Robyn laughed.

"Tell you what," said Alex. "Let's meet over the weekend to celebrate. Only, please, don't let on to Janet. She doesn't know about the serum, and she doesn't know we've been stressed with each other lately. I told her you were drunk because you'd been celebrating somebody's birthday. All she has to know is we might now have a repeatable process."

"Tomorrow night? We haven't had a Saturday night dinner party for too long."

They agreed on the arrangements, and Alex called off. Suddenly, the world was a good place again, as if the sun had emerged from behind the clouds after weeks of oppressive, stormy weather.

He arrived home soon after his call with Robyn, and Janet noticed his elevated mood as soon as he came indoors. Janet had prepared a beef and bean stew, so Alex opened a bottle of Cabernet Sauvignon, and they settled in the dining room for another culinary treat.

"So," said Janet, "what's happened today to make you so happy?"

There were two answers, but he'd only give her one. "I've got everything lined up now. Tomorrow will be a quiet day at work. Saturdays always are. I'll be able to get the next batch of Priapus started, and the process will complete by Monday."

Janet didn't answer but watched him with that cute expression, half a smile with one eyebrow raised. "And? Tell me more."

"I can administer it myself, so nobody else will need to know."

Janet smiled. "You're ready to take it?"

"Yes, I am." Janet was the most beautiful person he'd ever laid eyes on. He only had to look at her and he melted.

"I can do it on Monday morning. I suppose I'm rather impatient."

Jumping up, Janet almost knocked the table over. She ran around and enveloped him in her arms.

58

11 pm

The latch clicked and the door swung open. Francesca's heart missed a beat. Craig Drake stood dressed in an immaculate suit. His eyes smiled as he walked in.

"Francesca, I trust you've been well cared for."

"Well cared for?" Her laugh was dry.

"Ah. I see." He rubbed his chin. "So, Ms. Napier." His voice mocked her. "What can I do for you?"

"You can let me go free."

"Oh. I see. And when I've set you free…" He waved his hand in the air. "Then what will you do? You have an identity chip that will bring the pekays to you within minutes and you have nowhere to go."

"You were supposed to give me a new chip. Anyway, Dom will look after me." She immediately regretted saying his name. He was in enough danger already. She didn't need to put him in the line of fire.

"Ah, Mr. Fadden. Yes, well we've seen how effective he is, haven't we, Ms. Napier?"

Francesca glared at him. "What will you do with me?"

"You have been a queen at the pleasure of the state for too long. From now on, you will be my queen."

"Oh, God! No." Her stomach heaved. She'd rather die. "It's

true then. You're fertile." The tears welled up in her eyes.

"You're not too bright, are you? Let's hope our babies will inherit my intelligence."

"Please, no." She sobbed and sank onto the bed. Somebody new to make her have babies against her will. To rape her.

"Don't worry. I'll be good to you. I shall be a good father."

Father! Her sensations reeled. Her skin numbed and her vision blurred.

The Baron stepped to where she sat on the edge of the bed and crouched. He used his thumb to wipe a tear from her eye.

"Allow me to comfort you." He leaned forward, bringing his face closer to hers. She sensed that he intended to kiss her and ducked away, moving farther onto the bed. He followed and rested his weight beside her. She fell back and he followed, pushing himself towards her and pressing against her body. She struggled, but he put his arms around her.

Francesca screamed as loudly as she could. "Get away from me, bastard!"

He rolled on top of her and she felt his arousal, sickening, pressing against her.

"Get off me!" She tried to kick but couldn't. She struggled to pull free but was trapped.

With a deft movement, he unzipped his trousers. She felt the slap against her thigh as he broke free from his clothes. She screamed again and pushed hard, catching him off balance and giving herself a brief moment of opportunity. She saw the pink, rigid monstrosity as he clawed to get her back in his grasp. She clutched at it with her hand, tightening her grip, resisting the revulsion – soft skin, hard underneath – the urge to pull her hand away. She wanted to tear it from his body, cram it down his throat. His grip weakened momentarily, so she twisted and pulled as hard as she could, digging in with her fingernails.

Craig's arms tightened around her. His hands grabbed, pulling, clawing. He lowered his head and bit hard on her shoulder. She yelled and let go, twisting, and fell to the floor, free of his grip. Sensing a chance, she sprang to her feet and rushed to the door.

Hearing Drake behind her, Francesca grabbed the door handle and prayed. She'd never been religious, but she silently swore that if God answered this prayer she would honour him forever. She gripped the handle and pulled. The door rattled, but didn't move. *God, please!* She tried again and the latch freed – but the door stuck.

Drake was on his feet, moving around the bed towards her. He'd regained his composure and moved quickly. She pulled again but the door didn't budge.

"No!" She screamed at the door and beat it with her fists.

Drake was behind her. She pulled again. Drake grabbed her hair. The door came open in her grasp, and she ran through it. Tears sprang from her eyes as he tore a tuft of hair from her scalp.

She ran into the corridor, not knowing which way to go, not having time to consider the options, just running. The only way forward led her up some stairs to a door. Trying the handle, she turned to see Drake run up the stairs, bruised, pink flesh swinging from his trousers, a manic, angry glare in his eyes.

She turned the handle. *Please, God, just one more thing. Let this open. Let me out.* She pulled at the door and it opened. A sheet of some sort blocked the doorway but, pushing it, she found it was flexible and easily moved aside. She almost fell through with Drake only moments behind her.

Emerging from the doorway, Francesca came face to face with two large men in black suits.

59

Craig knew Mog understood. Of course he did. It was Gurt who really needed the beating, but Craig couldn't do it to just one of them. That would seem wrong. Gurt had cowered as Craig swung the heavy steel chain at him, much like the pathetic teacher, Martin, did near the end. Mog took it like a man. That was the difference between them. Mog was a man and Gurt was still learning to be one. He'd get there.

Craig trusted Mog. Mog had seen him in compromising situations before, but not Gurt. Gurt had to learn that what he'd seen wasn't a sign of weakness in Craig. That he shouldn't have stared, with horrified expression, at Craig's exposed, bruised body.

The bruises Craig had received at Francesca's hand would be repaid with interest.

He roused Mog on his com-pak.

"Get Gurt. Go to the Napier girl's room and wait for me."

Dahlia was comforting last night. She didn't ask about the bruises, she just caressed him, cajoled him, loved him. He felt a stirring now just thinking of her lovely body, the skilled ways in which she pleased him.

The Napier girl would learn to be kind, too. He'd see to it, but she'd never be the equal of Dahlia. Nobody was. Napier would serve her purpose, generating revenue for his business. One undocumented child a year would command a good price. It wouldn't take many of those to pay for the Golden Hind.

His next project was to acquire more queens. The glorious part of his plan was that potential new clients would not know what had happened to the queens of his previous clients. How could they?

The queens would disappear without trace. That the client would never see their precious queen again…well, they could hardly complain to the police, could they? The queens would be safely in Craig's basement rooms, producing valuable babies while the client who had funded the breakout would have no recourse. Perfect.

He might have to silence a few disgruntled customers along the way, but so far Fadden had proved himself a weak, passive fool.

Craig reached the wall hanging with a picture of the boat and stopped to admire it. Beautiful. Not long now and he'd be on the deck, heading along the estuary towards open sea. He pictured the name *Golden Hind* on the back of the boat, then pushed the picture aside and opened the basement door.

When he reached Francesca's room, he found Gurt and Mog standing like sentries outside the door. They both averted their eyes as he arrived.

"Are you clear about what you have to do on Monday?"

Mog nodded. "Yes, Baron."

"Gurt?"

"Yes, Baron."

"I am planning for detonation at 10 am," said Craig, opening the door.

They entered the room, and Gurt and Mog took their places on either side of the door, impassive, watching Francesca sob on the bed.

Craig crossed the room and stood over her, but she didn't respond to his presence. Such a weak, irritating person. Maybe she needed more bruises. "You look a mess. Sit up."

She didn't move.

"She's to have no water or food for the next forty-eight hours," said Craig. "That'll make the little bitch more compliant."

Craig leaned over her and ran his hand along her leg. She whimpered as he gave her thigh a squeeze.

"At the end of that, I want her hands and feet tied to the corners of the bed. No clothes."

Mog nodded. "Yes, Baron."

"Face down."

60

12 noon

Francesca was losing her sense of time. Without a com-pak to tell, without windows to show the days and nights, she had only mealtimes as a clue. She knew that if she were a more diligent prisoner she would be making marks on the wall, one for each day, like they did in the films. But she would probably get it wrong and only end up misleading herself.

She reckoned it must have been about four hours since Drake had issued that terrifying instruction to his men. They even took the bottle of clean water from the bathroom. Without plumbing, she had no other source.

Only forty-four more hours, then she would be tied down by thugs and raped by a monster. She lay on her back and stared at the ceiling, jamming her hands underneath herself to try to stop the shaking. It didn't work.

Since she was sixteen years old, she had been captive, and over the years she'd learned to live with it. But never in her life had she been tied down like an animal. Like she would be soon.

She would fight, but they would win. That would happen again and again until her spirit broke. Until she no longer had the will to fight back. Bruises upon bruises. Perhaps broken bones.

She saw herself in five years with dull eyes, listlessly obeying

Drake's commands, taking whatever he dished out, offering no resistance.

A vision of the future.

She didn't mind much that her books were left at the atelier. She missed them, but she could live without them. She did mind that her atelier friends weren't there to talk to at the touch of a com-pak – a walk down the hallway. She could have survived without them in her new life with Dom, but not like this. Not when she had nobody.

Was Dom looking for her? Had he sold her out, leaving her to Drake's mercy? Left her to be with the pekay's wife? It didn't seem like him, but then neither did the photos. Were they real? If so, she had no hope. Nowhere to go. She couldn't even get to a penal atelier. That, at least, would be civil, if lacking comfort. But to get to one they would have to know where to find her. Drake wouldn't be that careless.

All her daydreams, Dom's promises, the future. All out of reach.

Instead she had this.

Perhaps they would move her to a better room, but why would they care? If she wasn't to be treated like a human being, who cared what the room was like? What did it matter anyway?

The last time she saw Dom she'd been unkind, then refused to go with him. If she had let him take her, at worst she would have ended up in a penal atelier. She might have been killed, like Hannah, but even that would have been better than this.

She tried to lick her lips with a dry tongue. Only four hours since Drake's visit and already she was parched. Forty-four to go before what was left of her world would implode.

Would she have water then?

She couldn't live like this.

Could she survive? Four days ago, Hannah, her friend and confidante, had died. A day later, Mrs. Knatchbull had decided to personally supervise her being raped by Joseph Cranston. The same man who had already attacked her. The next day Drake took her from that prison to this one. This place where she had no one to talk to, no rights, a foul room, and was subjected to unspeakable hell.

Yesterday was her last chance, she was certain, to fight Drake off. She'd succeeded then, in a minor way, but by doing so had sealed her own fate.

What was left? The vain hope that Dom would show up, like a knight in shining armour, just in time to save her from the evil Baron? Even if he wanted to save her, it wouldn't happen in the next forty-four hours. There was no way out. No hope.

Yet…maybe there was a way to end it all.

If this was to be her life, she didn't want it.

She climbed off the bed and searched the room. The light-fitting was not very strong, so it wouldn't take any weight. What would? Tears welled in her eyes as she realised there was nothing above shoulder height that might take the weight of a person.

Had they thought of this already? Had they planned the room to carefully avoid suicide attempts? Had they realised the depths of desperation that would follow their treatment of her? What kind of sick minds did these people have?

She stood on the bed. She could just about reach the light, which she tried to take out of its socket. She needed two hands to do so, but when she raised her left hand, her right shoulder lowered. She could only reach it with one hand.

She swung the light at the ceiling, but it didn't reach. She tried harder and it hit the ceiling, swinging back again. Third time lucky. She grabbed the swinging light and threw it hard at the ceiling. The casing broke and the room went dark.

Without moving her feet, she felt for the broken core of the light. Each time it swung past, it knocked her hand, but without light she couldn't see to grasp it. She grunted in frustration. She'd have to wait for it to come to a stop. She would wait. She had almost forty-four hours, and the light fitting wasn't about to leave the room.

She counted slowly to a hundred, then carefully felt above

her head for the fitting. She found it and gasped in relief. The innards, exposed by the broken case, must be live. She grabbed it.

Nothing.

She felt for the base, where the light connected to the power. She touched metal.

Nothing.

She'd have to put her hand across the two terminals. She groped with her finger. There. Two pieces of metal.

She felt a sharp tingling sensation across the end of her finger.

Is that it? Was this what it was like to die from an electric shock? Just a tingle, and the world seemed to carry on?

The power was just passing across the end of her finger. That was it. She needed it to pass through her body. Preferably her heart. She put her foot out, feeling for the metal of the bed frame, but couldn't reach it.

Damn!

There must be a way. But how? Maybe she could move the bed to bring the bedpost closer. She stepped off the bed. All she had to do now was move it, get back on, find the light fitting in the dark, and that would be the end. The blissful end.

She tried to push the bed, but the broken glass cut her feet, and the bed was fixed to the floor.

With a sob, she dropped to her knees and felt around for a large enough piece of broken glass to cut her wrist. There had to be a suitable piece, so she kept searching in the darkness. With bleeding knees and hands, she eventually found a piece that felt big enough.

Sitting against the wall, she pushed it against her wrist. The wound was soon slippery with blood, but she knew she hadn't cut into the vein. She pushed a little harder, and her stomach convulsed. Faintness swept over her, but she knew it was not from the blood loss.

She recovered a little and tried again. She pressed the glass into her wrist. The blood drained from her face like a cold breeze on her skin, vertigo causing her to reel. Amid the nausea, she realised she couldn't bring herself to do it.

She tried the glass against her neck, but already knew she could no more slit her throat than her wrists. What else could she do? The darkness of the unlit room closed in around her, and one by one her options disappeared.

61

Sunday 12th September, 4 pm

The sun shone through a veil of autumn clouds, making a cold afternoon barely brighter. The light breeze carried a bite that only freezing air could bring. Beyond the trees, the ground sloped down gently towards the road, past which Drake's House of Fun stood, a hundred yards distant, bathed in thin sunshine.

The pain from Dominic's shoulder wound, now five days old, was finally under control. He glanced across at Brett, who lay on his stomach and wriggled to get comfortable on the hard ground. He held the battle rifle firmly and squinted through the optics that magnified his target.

Brett held up his hand in a prearranged signal to tell the others to hold their position. Dominic's face and hands stung in the bitter cold, but the combat armour kept his body warmth in. He watched as Brett squinted through the gun's sight.

Brett became still and Dominic saw him concentrating. Nothing had happened yet down there. All that moved was the trees in the wind, leaves drifting to the ground. Dominic checked the time on his com-pak. If Brett's observations were reliable, Drake would come out soon. He sighed quietly, though it didn't matter how loudly he sighed at this distance.

Two men appeared at the mock portcullis. Brett's rifle moved slightly to sight one of them, but he did no more. This wasn't their target. Nothing would happen until Drake came out. The two men talked together for a few minutes, their words lost on the breeze. They finished their conversation, and one of them walked to the road and climbed into a car while the other returned to the doorway. Brett's gun followed until he disappeared.

A car passed by without slowing.

Finally the portcullis door opened and a man walked out. Brett tensed. Dominic said, "It's Drake. This is it!"

Dominic's chest throbbed, his heart beating against his body armour.

A short burst of rifle fire shattered the silence. Craig Drake's pace faltered. Leaning forward slightly, he slumped, clutching his chest.

Dominic's ears rang from the gunshots. His heart pounded, and his breath was short.

A pool of blood formed around Drake, and the door opened again. A man in a black suit ran out and shouted into the building, dragging Drake back towards the portcullis.

Brett's voice came over the earpiece, this time urgent. "Now. Everybody move."

Fifty people appeared from the trees, wielding guns. They ran purposefully towards Drake's House of Fun. Twelve of them headed straight for the fake portcullis. The rest fanned out around the building towards the other doors and windows.

Dominic sprang to his feet, running. He held the compact assault rifle strapped over his shoulder on a sling. Running down the slope, he saw a group of about fifteen people approach on the road from the south, marching in formation. They wore grey uniforms and carried rifles. A similar group appeared from the north. They would converge on Drake's House of Fun.

Dominic heard Brett's voice in his earpiece. "Christ, they're here."

"Ignore them," said Dominic.

He needed to get down there where the action was. His ankle turned on a small rock, but he paid it no attention. Staying with

Brett, he led the way to the portcullis, the other leaders heading around both sides of the building. As they went, some threw small objects through the windows on both levels. Glass shattered. Shouts and gaming sounds cut through white knockout smoke wafting through the broken windows.

Brett pulled a mask over his face and the others followed his cue. Some fired guns as people staggered from the building. Dominic, his mask in place, went for the portcullis. He knew his way in from here and could get to the corridors, but he didn't know where the concealed basement entrance would be. He heard Brett, barely short of breath, issuing calm commands over the earpiece.

Dominic went through the entertainment hall at a run, ignoring the inert and struggling teenagers falling to the floor, engulfed in white smoke. When he reached the door at the back, two guards already lay across it, unmoving. One of them lay in a pool of blood. The other might have been overcome by the gas.

Dominic leapt over them without thinking and kicked the door. It yielded with a crack. Less smoke and fewer people blocked the corridor beyond. He slowed, not wanting to miss the wall hanging concealing the basement door. As he came to a junction, he said to Brett, "Go left. I'll go right."

He turned right and followed the corridor but soon found another junction. He turned left and broke into a run, looking frantically left and right. After twenty yards, he saw a large banner boasting an expensive looking cruising yacht.

"Got it." He spoke into his throat microphone. "Follow me, then turn left and twenty yards."

Brett acknowledged, "Right behind you."

Dominic pushed the wall hanging aside and tugged the door open over a staircase leading into darkness. Peering around, he found a switch. He flicked it and the lights came on below. He took the stairs two at a time.

At the bottom, he stopped dead. The warren of passages ahead would take an age to search. Maybe too long.

Hasty footsteps on the stairs signalled Brett's arrival. "I've left the door covered. Christ! More corridors."

Dominic touched his arm. "Same routine. Come on."

Dominic took one side of the corridor and Brett the other. They kicked doors open, checked inside, and moved on.

They split when the corridor did, and Dominic turned right. Door after door gave way, and when one was too solid, he took careful aim and shot out the lock. So far nothing, but there were many more to search.

She had to be here. Al wasn't lying, surely? No. That wasn't even worth considering now. He kicked a door, and his steel reinforced boot made no impact. He shot the lock and kicked. Inside, the room was dark. He switched on his headlight. A bed, but nobody there. He turned to move on, but a nagging doubt told him he'd not looked hard enough. Another door, in the side of the room, was closed.

Striding across the room, crunching glass underfoot, he kicked the door and it swung open, bouncing off the wall. He held it with his hand, squinting into the dark. There, shivering and cowering, curled up in the corner, lay Fru.

"She's here." Into his microphone.

She whimpered as he strode across to her. Dried blood caked her hands, arms and dress. Bruises and scratches marred her skin. "Oh, God!" This time he wasn't here to discuss whether she'd come along, he simply swept her up in his arms and strode back to the corridor.

Now he had to find the quickest route out. The longer it took, the more danger to Fru, who wore no more than a flimsy, torn dress and soft shoes. He ran along the corridor with Fru in his arms, his rifle awkwardly clutched in his hand in case he needed it. Brett appeared at a corner ahead. He waved an acknowledgement and indicated the route he'd just come from. Then he ran off in a different direction, gun aimed ahead.

Dominic ran into the corridor Brett had just left. At the far end, a staircase led up to a door with daylight showing through the edges. He reached the bottom of the stairs. The door burst open and Craig Drake, clutching a handgun, stumbled through it. He held his left hand across his chest, over his bloodstained shirt. As Drake ran down the stairs, Dominic recognised the automatic handgun Brett had shown him. Evil in the palm of your hand.

Dominic turned slightly, pointed his gun at Drake, and fired a short burst. Drake kept coming and raised his gun. Dominic fired again. This time he hit Drake's left arm. It slowed him down, but he raised his gun again.

Stumbling, Dominic lost his chance to fire first. He ducked behind the corner and ran back down the corridor. As bullets strafed the wall beside him, plaster and brick dust stung his face. He was starting to tire now. Fru wasn't heavy, but she was still a weight to carry while running. He had to get somewhere safe to regroup. To think how to tackle Drake.

He made a sudden turn into a room with an open door and slammed it shut. He fumbled to find a way to lock it. A reader device on the wall wouldn't respond to his com-pak.

The sound of Drake's footsteps echoed in the hallway, close to the door. He called for backup. Looking around, Dominic searched for some way to escape, but there were no other doors or windows. Just a bare room with boxes stacked against the back wall.

He raised his rifle and turned to point it at the door. As the door opened, he fired. Drake had been smart, though. He'd kicked the door open and stood aside.

Dominic shot another burst of fire and dropped to the floor. He put Fru down gently, then crouched between her and the door and switched his rifle to continuous fire. When Drake rushed into the room, he swept a burst of fire from left to right. It went above Dominic and Fru, tearing plaster from the walls.

Taking aim, Dominic fired back. He hit Drake's shoulder, but it didn't stop his progress. Dominic rolled away from Fru so Drake would aim at him rather than Fru.

Drake fired wildly, clearly in pain from his injuries.

Aiming more carefully, Dominic fired a long burst into Craig. Craig slumped to the floor, landing at Dominic's feet. Panting, Dominic kept his gun pointed at Drake, holding it with shaking hands until he was sure Drake was dead.

He took a step backwards as Drake's blood crept across the floor. Here was the man who had tried to take the one thing Dominic held most precious. Lying on the floor, unmoving, lifeless, his fearsome, intimidating gaze no more than a memory. His power gone.

Dominic picked up Fru and went to the door. Turning towards the stairs, he spotted one of Drake's men at the opposite end of the corridor. Dominic ran towards the stairs. Aiming a short burst of fire behind him, he missed his target.

Dominic's arm muscles burned with Fru's weight. Shifting her, he staggered up the stairs towards the door. He kicked it open and turned in time to see the man arrive at the bottom of the stairs. Dominic had the advantage. With a quick burst of fire, he cut the man down. He ran out into the cold. Fru sobbed, but she didn't struggle.

He ran straight for the road, passing four grey-uniformed men. One of them stopped and spoke into a com-pak.

After crossing the road, Dominic strode up the slope into the trees and shrubbery where they'd hidden earlier. He wouldn't be able to stay here long, but he needed to check whether Fru was seriously hurt.

He stopped in a spot surrounded by shrubs. Kneeling, he laid her down on the grass. She shivered and stared at him, terror in her eyes. Realising he still had his mask on, he pulled it off. The look on her face changed to surprise. She threw her arms around him and sobbed uncontrollably. He held her tight, stroking her hair, reassuring her.

He was interrupted by the sound of footsteps hurrying through the shrubbery towards them. Dominic started, let go of Fru, and grabbed his rifle. Standing, he swung it around towards the sound.

Five men in grey uniforms stepped out of the shrubs, their guns levelled at his head.

"Drop it." One of them barked.

Dominic unclipped his rifle and dropped it. He raised his hands. "What do you want?"

Their guns didn't waver. None of them wore body armour, but one of them had extra markings on his uniform. He appeared to be their leader.

"We'll take her to the pekays. She's not yours to take."

Dominic's heart raced, and his legs felt ready to collapse.

The grey-uniformed men closed in on him. Two of them shouldered their guns and lifted Fru to her feet.

"What do you want with her? Why the hell are you doing this?" Dominic asked.

The leader spoke. "Her duty is to the state. Not to you." He spat at Dominic's feet. "You make me sick." He bent to pick up Dominic's gun, holding eye contact with him.

"Can't we –"

Brett's voice cut in from behind a tree. "Put down your weapons. You're outnumbered."

The leader hesitated, then swung his gun around towards the voice. A burst of automatic fire sliced through his chest. Without firing a shot, he fell to the ground. The other four dropped their guns and put up their hands.

Dominic grabbed his gun and aimed it. "Your knives too, and com-paks."

They carefully unbuckled their knives and com-paks and dropped them to the ground.

"Now walk away with your arms in the air. Don't look back or you'll die. Go."

They disappeared into the trees. After a brief moment, Brett rushed to Dominic. Beads of sweat ran down his face. His eyes darted around, watching the trees while he picked up the weapons and com-paks.

Dominic stared. "Outnumbered! You were alone?"

"Help me with these." Then he looked at Fru. "Can you walk?"

Her voice was weak. "I think so."

Brett spoke into his com-pak. "Caution. Greys are hostile. Get the gear from the rendezvous point." Then he turned to Dominic and Fru. "Come on." Brett strode into the trees,

Fru held onto Dominic's arm while he carried his load of guns, knives, and com-paks, following Brett. After about a hundred yards, Brett stopped, put down his load and took off his body armour. Dominic did the same. They left it all in a pile with their weapons. Dominic wiped the blood from Fru's cuts, and they tried to make themselves as inconspicuous as possible.

Brett looked at Francesca's bloodstained dress and shook his head. "There'll be a swarm of pekays here soon. Come on." He led them through the trees.

They went in the opposite direction from the House of Fun, deeper into the wooded area. They walked for five minutes until they reached the top of a rise. About two hundred yards down the other side, Dominic saw another road where a car waited, ready for their journey to freedom.

Brett sat in the front. Dominic climbed into the back and put his arm around Fru, holding her close, stroking her tangled hair. The doors shut and they both talked at once. Brett cut them short.

"Listen. We're not safe yet. As far as possible, we mustn't be seen. You need to face into the car. Don't look out of the windows. When we get there, follow me casually. Don't attract any attention, but we need to get indoors quickly. For obvious reasons I can't stop the car right outside the house, but it's not exposed. There are plenty of trees, and the nearest houses don't overlook our walk."

They skirted around to the East side of Midfield. Houses were few and far between, separated by trees and fields. This was the lush countryside in which some of the wealthier Midfield residents lived. Brett stopped in a secluded lay-by near a junction where they left the car. They walked around the corner and about a hundred yards along a quiet lane. There, Brett turned into the front path of a large house, and Dominic and Fru followed him.

When they reached the front door, a man opened it, and they went in. Safe, ready for their new ID chips. Ready for their new lives.

62

5:30 pm

Brett came in with them. He introduced them to Zak, who was an imposing character, tall, broad, and muscular. His lined face suggested that he was in his late fifties or sixties, and his long grey hair was tied back in a ponytail.

"He'll give you new ID chips tomorrow," said Brett. "Everything's ready."

He exchanged some quiet words with Zak. Then in turn, he gave Dominic and Fru a hug.

"Take care, guys." Putting his hand on Dominic's shoulder, Brett's eyes glistened. "You know what to do, man." To Fru he said, "There's a com-pak in your room. Don't use it until you've got your new chips."

Dominic's heart jumped. There was no room for carelessness now. He tapped in the security code to release his com-pak and took it from his wrist. He wanted to ask Brett a question, but was afraid to hear the answer.

"Were the others okay? No-one was hurt were they?"

"No. None of our guys were hurt. They're all safe."

Dominic breathed a sigh of relief. "Tell them thanks, won't you? What they did – what you did – it means a lot. Everything."

Brett smiled. "Good luck." Then he walked out, shutting the

front door behind him.

Zak beckoned. "Come."

They followed him into a dining room where the table was laid with cold meats, pies, pasties and plenty of salad. A full carafe of wine and two glasses stood by their place settings.

"Enjoy your meal," said Zak. "You'll find a living room, bathroom and bedroom through that way." He indicated a door on the far side of the room. "There's a medicine cabinet in the bathroom. And if you need anything," – he glanced at Fru's bloody dress – "just come to the entrance hall and call for me. I'll hear you."

They thanked him, and he left the room, shutting the door behind him. Fru said she wasn't hungry, so they took the wine carafe and glasses through the far door. They found a comfortable living room with deep, cream coloured carpets, soft sofas and heavy curtains. An Axis stood facing one of the sofas.

Dominic tended to Fru's wounds, and once the practicalities of settling in were taken care of, they found themselves alone together for the first time since they were both sixteen years old.

"So, er…how does it feel to be free?"

"Well…I don't know really. I suppose it's a bit early to tell."

Silence descended. After a few moments, Fru spoke.

"I'm glad it wasn't true. You know, the stuff about that woman. Those pictures."

Dominic tried to keep his voice level. "No. It wasn't true. Drake lied."

"I can't get them out of my mind," she said. "I kept looking at them, over and over, trying to convince myself it wasn't true. You doing those things. Being with her like that."

This was awful. What if she wouldn't be convinced? If she didn't believe him?

She shook her head. "I wasn't sure whether to believe you. I thought, well, you'd been living like a monk for a long time. Maybe you didn't want to go on like that. I thought it might be true."

Dominic sighed. How could he reply to that? If she still didn't trust him, if he couldn't convince her he was telling the truth, what kind of future would they have?

She carried on talking. "I'm sorry I didn't believe you." Her eyes were moist. She put her head on his chest. "I'm so, so sorry."

He stroked her hair. She believed him. It felt as though he'd been holding his breath for days, and now, finally, he could breathe again. He understood why she'd had doubts, but now he knew they would be happy, confident, secure.

He reached for the Axis controller and set it to play soft jazz. Taking her hand, he stood and pulled her up from the seat, close to him. They stepped to the music. Slowly she relaxed, so when the second song played they were holding each other close, dancing and turning, feeling each other's warmth.

"This is better," said Dominic.

Fru sighed. "I love you."

He couldn't ever remember feeling this way before. The joy, deep in his heart, ran to his very fingertips as he caressed her hair. "I feel so lucky," he said. "For four years I've not known whether this dream would ever come true, and now, here we are."

"Kiss me," she said, gazing into his eyes. "Don't ever stop kissing me."

"Hey." Dominic stirred at Fru's gentle touch on his shoulder. He was lying on the sofa with his head on her lap where he'd fallen asleep.

"We should watch the news," she persisted. He roused slowly and rubbed his eyes.

Fru picked up the Axis controller and called up the newscast. "Zak's very kind to leave us alone all evening," she said.

"Yes. Yes, I suppose he is. This is his living room, after all. At least, it's one of them."

Fru set the volume for the news and sat back.

The events of earlier in the afternoon were the main headline. "Midfield is rapidly becoming the violence capital of the south with this, the third major incident in the space of one week. This time Mr. Craig Drake, sometimes known as Baron Drake, has been killed in what is believed to be an attack by a rival gang in the criminal underworld. The peacekeepers arrived as the smoke cleared." The newsreader paused and looked at the camera. "Once again, they say they have little idea what happened other than that it was a well-orchestrated attack, and it was carried out with military precision. None of the attackers has been found or identified. Several of Mr. Drake's employees have been killed or injured, and twenty-five customers of Mr. Drake's House of Fun have been taken to the hospital suffering from aftereffects of knock-out smoke."

The camera switched to an outside broadcast view showing the House of Fun surrounded by emergency vehicles and their crews.

"On searching the property in the aftermath of the attack, the police discovered what they referred to as a bomb-making factory in the basement. Among the materials recovered were two disruptor bombs of the type long since banned by international convention. The entire neighbourhood has been evacuated, and bomb disposal experts are still working to ensure the safety of the devices. A woman, understood to be a close confidante of Mr. Drake, was arrested at the scene. She was questioned by police and subsequently released."

The camera switched back to the presenter. "The police say they don't currently have any leads, but they have started a full investigation." The interview with the officer leading the investigation was short and uninformative.

"He doesn't look very keen to find out who did it," said Dominic. "Maybe Drake has trodden on too many toes. I bet most police are pleased to see him gone."

"I suppose whatever they find out, it'll only lead them to Drake, so the investigation would dead end there."

"I never thought of that," said Dominic. "They have nothing to connect this with you or the atelier. Maybe we're safer than we thought. Once we have new IDs, we'll move to some town a long way away. I'll get a job. We'll have a new life. It'll be pretty hard to find us."

"I'm worried that I'll never see mum and dad again."

"I've thought of that. There's a way we can see them. We'll meet them in a prearranged place a long way from either them or us. The place and time are all set up with Brett, and he'll tell your mum and dad. Then each time we see them, we set up the next meeting. It's how other bolters do it. It's a proven method. Works well."

Fru sat up straight, her eyes wide.

"I think it just hit me. I hadn't really thought about what it means to have a new ID. I suppose I thought of it as just an ID chip. Something to make a com-pak work. A way of talking to people and doing shopping, but it's so much more than that. It's who I am. It'll be like I'm a different person, won't it? We'll really be free."

Dominic smiled. "We'll find out our new names tomorrow. It'll be strange not being Dominic Fadden. I'll always think of you as Fru even though I'll have to call you something else."

Fru laughed. He loved her laugh. He'd missed it. Her eyes lit up, sparkled. Her laugh, her smile, so beautiful to see. "Maybe you will be Cuthbert," she joked, "or Marcus."

"I like the idea of Marcus." He sat up straight. "Maybe I'll be Marcus Tribble. Then you can be Esmerelda Tribble or maybe Matilda."

"Hmm." She leaned across and kissed his cheek. "Maybe we should wait to find out. I'm sure we'll be disappointed after setting such high expectations."

Dominic laughed. "I'll stick to calling you *Hon*."

"And I'll stick to *Darling*."

Fru's expression clouded. She cast her eyes down to her lap. "I've had two babies, and I don't even know them. I wonder what their names are."

"I've wondered about that. We don't even know where they live. I suppose there might be a way to find out, but it'd be dangerous. Too dangerous. Anyway, maybe it's best not to know."

"Maybe."

Dominic put his arm around her and pulled her close. "My father has promised he will treat me with the new fertility cure."

Fru pulled free of his arm and sat up straight. "We'll be able to have a baby of our own?"

Dominic smiled. "He offered a few days ago. You know the free stay was nothing to do with me, don't you?"

"I know. Hannah tried to tell me what you'd said, but I didn't know what to believe. I don't have any doubts now."

They sat, cradled in each other's arms. The soft music played and his thoughts raced. They'd start by picking a town. They'd go there and rent somewhere to live, then start their new life.

This was it. A real new beginning. One with hope. A future with Fru.

She stirred. "You remember that sketch you did for me? The one of the little house with the sign showing the house name?"

"Yes."

"Well, I am. I'm over the moon."

Thank you for reading

AN ACCIDENT OF BIRTH

by Tony Benson

If you have enjoyed this book, please tell your
friends and consider posting a review.

Find Tony Benson online:
http://www.tonybenson.org

About The Author

Tony Benson lives in Kent, England with his wife Margo and two cats. He grew up in a Kent village, and had a successful career in engineering before leaving corporate life to make stringed musical instruments, augmenting this work with technical writing. An Accident Of Birth is Tony's first novel.

www.ingramcontent.com/pod-product-compliance
Lightning Source LLC
Chambersburg PA
CBHW032148190626
46814CB00005BA/1893